Alligator Gold

Other Cracker Westerns:

Mack Ruff

Alligator Gold

A Cracker Western
by
Janet Post

Pineapple Press, Inc.
Sarasota, Florida

Inquiries should be addressed to:

Pineapple Press, Inc.
P.O. Box 3889
Sarasota, Florida 34230

www.pineapplepress.com

Library of Congress Cataloging-in-Publication Data

Post, Janet
  Alligator gold / by Janet Post. — 1st ed.
       p. cm. — (A cracker western)
  ISBN 978-1-56164-446-9 (hb : alk. paper) — ISBN 978-1-56164-447-6
(pb : alk. paper)
  1. United States—History—Civil War, 1861-1865—Fiction. 2.
Veterans—Florida—Fiction.   I. Title.
  PS3616.O8384A79 2009
  813'.6—dc22

                                        2008046291

First Edition
Hb 10 9 8 7 6 5 4 3 2 1
Pb 10 9 8 7 6 5 4 3 2 1

Printed in the United States of America

Prologue

"TELL ME WHERE IT'S HID," Jake Barber demanded.

Caleb Hawkins felt Barber's scraggly beard brush the side of his face.

"I swear on my mother's grave, I'll dig it up and give it all to your kid," Barber said. "You're done for."

"Your ma ain't dead, Barber," Hawkins said, his voice a raspy whisper. He knew he was a goner. Suffering from an acute attack of malaria, he lay on the floor of a tent in Pointe Lookout Union Prison somewhere in Maryland. Weak from the ravages of the disease and starvation, he knew he didn't have much longer to live. The endless spring rains of 1864 coupled with the bad air off the marshes of the Chesapeake Bay, meager rations, and poor sanitation had Confederate soldiers dying like flies in the overcrowded camp. It looked to Hawk as though soon he'd be just another body in the nearby cemetery.

Hawk and Barber had known each other for a long time. They both had grown up as cow hunters in central

Florida. The Barber ranch was close to the ocean while Hawk's father and mother had settled a little farther west.

Hawk's father had avoided trouble during the last Seminole War with the aid of friends among the Seminole Indians. With their help, he'd made a small fortune in gold doubloons rounding up Florida scrub cows and selling them to Cuba.

Barber's filthy hand clawed at the neck of Hawk's ragged homespun shirt. "I see'd what you got hanging round your neck with that gator tooth. Is that the key to the treasure?"

Barber gripped the tooth in two fingers. It was four inches long, yellowed, and curved. The tip was twisted and white. His fingers inched toward the key and Hawk pushed him away. He was weak, so weak.

Hawk's father never cared about spending the gold he brought home from Tampa after selling the cows each year. When Hawk's father was a young man, he thought he'd like to be a preacher. It turned out, though, that while he liked God a lot, there were too many things about organized religion he didn't like. He moved to Florida with his wife in 1832 and settled near the St. Johns River. All he cared about was working the cattle, the long days on the plains, and his small family. The gold he saved was stored in three chests Hawk hid away before he set out on his last cattle drive.

Most of the folks who lived on the neighboring farms and ranches knew about old David Hawkins' gold, including the Barbers. Now fate had landed Hawk in the same tent as Jake "the Snake" Barber, the youngest son of a prolific family, both of them prisoners of the Union Army.

Hawk pushed Barber's grasping hand farther away with

the little strength he had. His arms felt like jelly. He couldn't have lifted a spoon to feed himself even if there were something to eat. Malaria had him in its clutches and the fever was running high. He kept drifting in and out of reality. Half the time he thought he was out riding his marsh tacky under the clear blue Florida sky hunting for cows, his leopard dogs baying at the horse's heels—then he'd wake shivering to find the cold tent roof over his head and the colder ground beneath his thin pallet.

Barber had a one-track mind. He shook Hawk roughly. "Tell me where it's hid, Hawkins. I'll give it to your boy. I swear on my mother's grave."

Maybe he should toss the man a crumb. It couldn't hurt. Even if Snake were to try to find the gold, he wouldn't, not where Hawk had hidden it. Unless you'd actually been there before and seen where Hawk hid the treasure, finding the secret of his hiding place would be impossible.

He'd written a letter to Travis detailing how to find the treasure and entrusted it to Joseph, Jimmy Jumper's son. Joseph had escaped the Yankees, but the odds of him making it across war-torn Georgia were slim. But as long as Jimmy Jumper still lived on the D-Wing, there was still someone who knew Hawk's secret. Barber didn't know it, but he was beating a dead horse. Hawk had covered all the angles.

He and Barber had known each other forever, and what Hawk knew about the man was all bad. They'd never been friends, and sometimes they'd been enemies. Barber was known as a rustler and a horse thief. Hawk suspected Barber of stealing his cows and of altering the Hawkins D-Wing brand and ear notches.

But even with good directions, Barber would never find

the gold. So what difference did it make if he gave Barber a hint? It would surely get the man out of his face.

And if Barber did figure out where to look, the three-legged monster gator that guarded Hawk's hiding place would keep it safe. What harm was there in giving the greedy bastard a clue? Then Barber would go away and leave him alone. Alone, so he could slide into his visions, where he was warm and happy. Slide into death. It would be so easy, and Hawk knew it wasn't that far away.

He looked into Barber's face, hideously scarred by a recent saber cut from eyebrow to chin. "I hid Pappy's gold in the blue spring."

Barber's little blue eyes lit up as he leaned forward eagerly, ready to demand details. When the tent flap flew open, he turned, with a snarl on his face, to see who was entering.

"Is that Caleb Hawkins?" a tall Union sergeant asked, pointing to Hawk. He lifted his blue cap and smoothed red hair away from his brow. Hawk groaned and tried to rise, but fell back.

The sergeant glared at Jake. "Well, is it Hawkins?"

Snake Barber relaxed his grip on Hawk's collar. He looked up at the soldier and finally nodded.

The sergeant stuck his head outside the tent and beckoned to two enlisted men. They slipped into the tent, which was packed from one damp, mildewed gray wall to the other with Confederate soldiers, and eased their way through a maze of legs to Hawk's corner. The first Yankee soldier picked Hawk up by his shoulders and the other grabbed his boots. "The provost marshal needs a blacksmith. We were told Caleb Hawkins is our man. Is that correct?"

"I don't know about smithing, but he's the best damned horseshoer you'll ever find," Barber growled. "Where you taking him? I mean, he's my friend and all. And he's real sick."

The sergeant looked at Hawk. "Malaria?"

Barber nodded. "I guess so."

"Major's surgeon will fix him up. He's got quinine."

Barber clambered to his feet as if to stop them. Before he could do or say anything, they were gone with Hawk, the key, and most of Hawk's secret still unspoken.

1

CALEB HAWKINS SMILED FOR THE FIRST TIME in three years—three long years. He was home. Back in Florida, where he'd spent his entire life, except for those two years and two months he'd been in the custody of the Union Army.

He'd never wanted to fight for the Confederacy, but he'd felt an obligation to help feed the army. In the fall of '63, he'd been captured by a scouting party of Blue Bellies while delivering a herd of beef cattle to Brunswick, Georgia. The Rebels had hoped to get the beeves to the besieged troops at Ft. Sumter. Hawk knew the meat would never get that far. The Rebel army was starving. Everybody knew it.

Hawk trotted along on Beau, his high-bred, bay thoroughbred stud, feeling the animal's power, barely contained, beneath him. Major Brady, provost marshal of Pointe Lookout Prison Camp, had given Beau to him as a reward for service when the war ended and the camp had closed.

Brady raised race horses and Hawk had shoed them for the last months he'd spent inside the walls of Pointe

Lookout. Brady swore it was the excellent care Hawk lavished on those horses and his expertise with nippers, a rasp, and hot metal that won Brady so much money.

Now that the war was over, Hawk couldn't wait to get back to his farm on the St. Johns River, see his son, and resume the life the Civil War had so rudely interrupted.

The July sun heated the crown of his floppy hat and warmed his back. He could smell last night's rain shower steaming from the grass and scrub. His clothes were little more than rags, but he wore a brand-new pair of boots presented to him by Brady just before he'd left Maryland. The McClelland saddle he sat in was a gift as well.

After leaving Alligator early that morning, Hawk had headed southeast toward Pilatka and the ferry crossing. Once he got there, he'd turn south toward Volusia Landing and home. The trail he followed wound through oak forests, scrub oaks, pines, palmetto thickets, and stretches of Florida prairie. He kept a sharp eye out for scrub cows, rattlesnakes, deer, possum, coons, or bear—anything he could shoot and stick in his mouth. He was hungry.

He hadn't eaten a decent meal since hitting the long road from Maryland. The South was a war-ravaged land. Most of the folks left behind after four years of fighting were weary, wary, and hungry. Bands of soldiers returning home, deserters, and the homeless scavenged as well. The result was a land barren of game, domestic livestock, fodder, and food.

The sun was hovering over the western horizon when Hawk spotted a wagon. It was the first sign of humanity he'd seen since leaving Alligator. The wagon, piled high with valises, crates, and trunks, was parked under a tree. A tall woman with a long, blonde braid down her back was examining the right front hoof of the skinniest mule he'd ever laid eyes on. No more than a bag of bones covered in reddish fur, the big mule made no objection when the lady hoisted its foot and peered intently at the bottom. Undoubtedly the animal was too tuckered out to protest.

Hawk's stud nickered softly when he spotted the mule. Startled, the woman dropped the mule's foot and stood up. Supporting her back with one hand, she shaded her eyes against the setting sun to look at him. A boy, almost as thin as the mule, appeared from behind the wagon and stood beside her, holding a shotgun as big as he was.

Doffing his hat, Hawk pulled Beau to a stop. "Howdy, ma'am," he said, smiling. Her eyes were huge and she appeared terrified. Hawk could now see she was in the family way.

The skinny boy raised the shotgun and pointed it at Hawk. It shook. "Don't come no closer, mister," the boy said. "I'll use this here gun."

"I don't mean you no harm." Hawk spoke in a soothing voice, the same one he'd use to gentle a crazy horse. "You look like you need some help. Is your mule limping?"

"It's okay, Sam," the woman said to the boy, laying a hand on the barrel of the shotgun. "You go on and check the fire."

She turned her gaze on Hawk and he felt his heart flutter. She had intensely blue eyes set under arched brows. Her face was arresting in its beauty, with high cheekbones and a soft mouth. Her rounded belly only lent her an increased air of vulnerability. He shook his head. Such thoughts were ridiculous, he told himself, and only engendered by a long period of abstinence.

"The mule turned up lame about a mile back," she said in a voice rich with a Georgian accent. "I don't think he can pull the wagon any farther."

"I'm going to tie Beau to this tree and look at your mule. If that's okay by you," Hawk said. "I'm a horseshoer. Maybe I can help."

As he tied Beau to the tree, he kept up a continuous flow of small talk. "You folks headed for Pilatka? I'm on my way home from the war. I plan to ferry across the river there."

He stepped closer to the skeletal mule, moving quietly. He ran a hand over the mule's rump and up his side until he reached his head. The mule barely opened his eyes. When he picked up the animal's foot, he saw its hoof was worn slap off. These people had come a long way and the poor old mule had hauled that wagon as far as he could without a set of shoes. He picked up each of the mule's feet and saw the back ones had some foot left. The mule could probably make it on them with a trimming.

"Your mule's gonna need some shoes on these front feet of his. He's not going much farther without 'em."

"Oh, no," the woman said. "The poor creature has worked so hard for us with no complaints. We need him to get us to Pilatka. My husband's sister, Rachel Carver, and her husband, Edward, live there."

"Well now, we'll see what we can do to get this mule back on the road. My name's Caleb Hawkins," Hawk introduced himself, "but everybody calls me Hawk. I have some spare shoes in my bags. I might be able to make a couple fit."

The woman's face flushed. "I can't afford to pay you, Mr. Hawkins. I can fix you a hot meal, but I have no money."

"I don't need money to help a lady and her boy in a bad

situation. Any man worth his salt would help out here if he could. And a good supper sounds just like something I've been wanting for a long time."

She smiled for the first time, though Hawk noticed it was only her lips smiling. Her eyes stared straight into his without even the hint of a smile. "I'm Mrs. Madelaine Wilkes and this is my son, Sam. I'll fix that supper while you work on poor John mule."

Hawk walked to Beau, unbuckled the girth, and pulled his saddle off. He set it at the base of a big tree on top of the saddle blankets, then tied Beau to a low hanging branch. Beau stretched his neck out and snagged a long strand of gray tree moss. Hawk left him chewing the moss contentedly.

After removing his packs and saddlebags from the saddle, Hawk dug around in one for horseshoes. He found several racing shoes he'd made for Brady's thoroughbreds in Maryland. They should fit the mule's feet. He took several over to size and found two that would hang over in the back but that he thought he could get on. Without an anvil or a forge, shaping them to fit was out of the question.

Hawk took off his gun belt and fastened on a pair of leather chaps. He found his hoof knife, a small leather pouch full of horseshoe nails, as well as his rasp, nippers, and shoeing hammer. They were all well-oiled and wrapped carefully in a square of leather tied with several leather thongs. He stepped close to the mule and laid his equipment out on the square of leather. Spitting on a whetstone, he sharpened the hoof knife, then tucked it into the pocket of his chaps. He ran his hand down the mule's left front leg, picked up the hoof, bent over, and tucked it between his knees.

The mule stood quietly napping while Hawk worked.

He pared the mule's sole with the hoof knife and filed it flat with his rasp. The shoe had to be nailed onto the hoof carefully. Hawk did it fast. He'd shoed many horses. When he was finished with both hooves, he stood back to check the fit, sniffing aroma-laden air. Something wonderful was cooking over at the woman's campfire. His stomach growled.

As he was repacking his bags, the woman's boy came and squatted down next to Hawk to examine his tools. He had slender, delicate hands with the nails chewed to the beds. The boy seemed shy, just like his mother. But times were hard and the lessons learned over the last years harder.

Sam picked up the nippers and turned them over in his hands. "What do these do, mister?"

Hawk took the nippers and showed the boy how they worked. They had foot-long handles, were made of shiny steel, and looked like large pliers, with a flat edge for cutting. "These are sharp for cutting horse hooves. Some horses have pretty tough feet."

"Where is your home?" Sam asked.

"Oh, I live about one hundred miles from here near the river," Hawk said. "We find cattle out in the hammocks and the prairie and sell them."

"Was your family safe during the war?"

Hawk looked at him and thought he detected a deep sadness in the child's eyes. He looked closer and made a startling discovery. Sam could not possibly be a boy. Or if he was, he was the prettiest boy ever born; badly cropped hair and boys' clothes could not hide the child's fine complexion, rosebud lips, delicate nose, and long, sooty eyelashes. "I only have a son," Hawk said. "I hope he's safe. I haven't been home in a very long while."

Sam looked surprised. "Then who's looking after him?"

"Jimmy Jumper takes care of Travis. Him and his wife, Judy Bill, live on my ranch and look after things for me when I'm gone. Jimmy's son, Joseph, was with me on the cattle drive to Georgia. That was when I got captured by Yankees and taken off to prison. They thought I was a spy," Hawk finished.

"What kind of name is Jumper?"

Hawk finished packing his bags and stood up. "It's a Seminole name. My pappy had Seminoles helping him on his ranch since before I was born."

"Seminole Indians? I thought Indians were bad."

"They're friendly," Hawk said. "At least they always have been to my family. We help them and they help us. My wife was part Seminole."

"Where's she at?"

"She passed away, son. All I have left is my boy."

Madelaine Wilkes's daughter looked sad. "I'm sorry," she said. "Did your wife die because of the war?"

"No, she died having a baby, a little girl. It was all my fault," Hawk said. "I shouldn't have let her work so hard."

"Did the baby die, too?"

"Yes," Hawk said sadly. "They both died."

"Did you cry? If my mama died, I'd surely cry."

"No, son, I haven't cried since I was a young 'un. My pappy beat that inclination out of me a long time before I was your age."

No, crying was not something Hawk did. He'd started to cry when his ma died and Pappy had given him the whooping of his life. Pappy hadn't cried, he'd just gone off into the woods and stayed there for two days. When he came back, he never brought up Ma again. It was like she'd never existed as far as he was concerned.

"That sure is a pretty horse, mister," Sam said as Hawk wiped Beau off with a piece of sacking and gave him a handful of corn. "He's a big 'un."

"Yes, he's big. I think I'll breed him to my smaller marsh tackies and get me a horse my legs don't hang to the ground on."

"What's a marsh tacky?"

Madelaine Wilkes walked up and put her hand on Sam's shoulder. "Don't bother the man anymore, Sam. You ask too many questions. Go gather some wood for the fire, sugar. I'm almost out." She looked into Hawk's face. "I hope Sam wasn't bothering you. I know he can be a pest with those questions of his. He's always sticking his nose into everything."

"He wasn't bothering me, Mrs. Wilkes. I haven't spoken to a child in a long time. I miss my own son."

Madelaine went back to her cooking and Hawk hung his Colt Army-model pistol by a cord on his saddle. He kept the Bowie knife in a sheath tied with a leather thong at his waist.

He'd been lucky. Brady had given him a revolver, a carbine, and some ammunition, along with the knife, for the long journey home. He'd said no man should go unprotected or without a way to kill, cut up, and clean game for food. And Brady had insisted Hawk take the tools of his trade as well, so along his route he had done some hoof trimming to earn a little cash and food. Where there were horses, there would always be the need for a shoer. A horse was only as good as his feet.

Leaving Beau tied to the tree, he entered the small clearing where Madelaine Wilkes had chosen to build a cookfire. Hawk found a fallen log nearby and dragged it closer to the fire. He checked it out for vermin before plunking his butt down. You could never be too careful; Florida had more than its share of serpents, alligators, scorpions, and venomous spiders.

Stew bubbled in a kettle hung over the cookfire. A shallow Dutch oven sat on the coals along with a smaller, covered, cast-iron pot. Madelaine Wilkes handed him a fine china dish decorated with delicate rosebuds. Hawk looked it over and realized she must have brought everything she owned in that wagon. No wonder it was piled so high and no wonder the mule was half dead from dragging the thing.

She ladled stew onto the pretty plate and added a scoop of something orange. Hawk sniffed appreciatively as he accepted a chunk of cornbread and a spoon from Sam.

"It's nothing but turtle stew and sweet potato casserole," she said. "Sam found the big tortoise just walking down the road. I knew him for an old gentleman, but I thanked the Lord for His gift, and though a little chewy, the turtle is quite delicious."

Hawk tasted his first bite and almost groaned. It wasn't just good, it was incredible. "What's in this stew besides gopher turtle?" he asked around a large mouthful.

"Sam and I found an abandoned garden in the slave quarters of a burned-out plantation near Moultrie," she said. "It was like finding a treasure. We dug up some turnips, carrots, and sweet potatoes and even found some wild mustards and collards. An old corn crib had burned to the ground nearby and when we dug through the ashes, we were able to salvage a bag of corn for poor John mule. Though to look at him, you'd think he'd never eaten a scrap of food in his life."

Hawk took a bite out of the orange stuff and realized he was in the presence of a woman who knew her way around a kitchen, or in this case, a campfire. The soft sweet potatoes melted in his mouth. And the cornbread was better than any he'd ever tasted. "How old is that mule?"

Madelaine spoke softly in her creamy accent. It sounded so good, Hawk had trouble following what she was saying. He just liked listening to her voice. "I believe John is well over twenty. He belonged to Henry, my old houseboy. After the bands of deserters stole or killed every animal on my farm, John was the only one left. And when the Yankees came, they didn't want him either. I guess he's so skinny and old that they thought he was too tough to eat and too weak to pull a wagon. But John is strong and too ornery to die."

Hawk hated to ruin the pleasant mood around the campfire with questions about this woman's life, but he was curious. He could understand why she had turned her daughter into a boy—a lovely girl like that would be prey for every low-down deserter and outlaw on the road. But where was the father of Madelaine Wilkes's child? And why had she left her home to travel through such dangerous territory by herself?

When he'd cleaned his plate, he leaned back against a tree. "Do you mind if I smoke?"

She shook her head. "No, please do. I have to clean up anyway."

Hawk was immediately overcome with guilt. He leaped to his feet. "Is there anything I can do?" He hated to see her working in her condition. He'd always blamed himself for

Katie's death. He should have sheltered her more and kept her from working so hard.

"There's very little to do and Sam helps me," she said. "But I do thank you for your kind offer."

While she and the daughter worked clearing plates and cookery, wiping them off and packing the remaining food into the wagon, he took out an old corncob pipe and filled it with tobacco. It was the one commodity he'd managed to buy along the road. "So, why did you leave your farm?" he asked.

She stood up and smoothed the folds of a tattered gingham apron over her rounded belly. "All of the members of my family were killed or died in the war. I couldn't keep our farm. I had no slaves left to work it and a band of Yankee and Confederate deserters had moved into the house. Between the deserters taking everything they wanted and destroying what they didn't, it was a miracle the house still stood. There are so many terrible memories there, memories of things I must learn to forget. I decided to take Sam and go where war has not destroyed the land and corrupted the people. I want Sam to live somewhere safe."

"Is that why you're headed for Pilatka?" Hawk puffed on the pipe and ran a hand through his dark hair. She was so pretty. Suddenly he longed for a bath, a shave, and some decent clothes.

"Yes, my husband's sister lives in East Pilatka. I believe we have to cross the river to get there."

"Uh, if you don't mind my asking," Hawk cleared his throat, "what happened to Mr. Wilkes?"

Color stained her cheeks. Oh no, Hawk thought. I've gone and put my foot in it now.

She turned away so Hawk could not see her face. "He

16

died at Shiloh fighting under General Beauregard," she said.

Hawk barely managed to mask his surprise. "I'm so sorry for your terrible loss, ma'am," he said. Shiloh was fought in April of '62. So who was the father of Mrs. Wilkes's baby?

"Oh, I know what you're thinking, Mr. Hawkins," she said, her voice hard. Straightening her back, she held her head high. "You want to know who the father of my unborn child is. Well, I was assaulted." Her shoulders suddenly slumped and her voice cracked. "I was assaulted over and over again by a depraved deserter who inhabited my house without my permission. He said his name was Jake, but his men only called him Snake, and he had a hideous scar across his face. The deserters took over my house and my life, cruelly murdered all of my people, and took anything they wanted."

Madelaine's fine lips drew back in a snarl. Her eyes narrowed as she said, "One day I will find him and kill him."

2

MADELAINE WATCHED CALEB HAWKINS fashion a set of hobbles out of several strips of leather and attach them to John mule's front legs. "Your mule needs to graze at night, Mrs. Wilkes," he said. "That's one of the reasons he's so thin. That and he's old as Moses."

"I did not know that," she said. "Have I been starving the poor old thing out of ignorance? I guess I thought the corn was enough."

She couldn't stop looking at the man. He had such an interesting face. He wasn't exactly handsome, but his eyes were large, brown, and so warm, especially when he gazed at her. His cheeks were hollow and covered with several days' growth of dark beard. His hips were lean, his legs long, and his stomach flat. He was tall, with wide shoulders and heavily muscled arms. The corded sinews of his neck extended into a broad chest. He must have developed that physique working with metal and horses. Under his hat was a wealth of dark brown hair.

Madelaine felt herself blushing. Never had she looked

at a man so closely. What if he noticed? He would think her fast and forward. She shook off the unfamiliar attraction. Behind his warm brown eyes and under his strong chest, he was after all, just another man.

Madelaine had had a lot of bad experiences with men, starting when she was just a child. Her father had been stern and cold. He'd beaten her when he felt she needed it. The beatings had always been extremely severe, leaving bruises and welts. She thought she was escaping his brutality when she married at seventeen. Unfortunately, her husband had been of the same inclination. The beatings, though less severe, were always followed by disgusting, painful visits to the marriage bed. Beneath the skin, men were all the same.

Sarah slipped up beside her and slid her hand into Madelaine's. "He seems like a nice man," she whispered.

"Hush," Madelaine said. "It's impolite to discuss people behind their backs."

Hawk finished working on the hobbles and stepped back to allow John mule to follow his horse into the nearby grass. John seemed to understand the hobbles and was soon cropping grass beside his elegant companion.

"I think we'll be going to bed now," she said to Hawk. "Thank you for all you've done for us."

He made a small bow and said, "It was nothing. I did what any man would do for a woman in need. I'm just lucky I had the skills necessary to render you aid."

Madelaine knew differently, but didn't say so. The men of her acquaintance had never been of assistance to her or wished to be. They had all been shallow, self-centered users who viewed women as little more than slaves to their various needs.

She and Sarah unrolled their sleeping pallets under the wagon and prepared for a night's rest. She carefully unbraided her long hair, brushed it, and then braided it again while Sarah watched. A pang of remorse hit her. Poor Sarah's hair was so short. Before the deserters had arrived at her home, Sarah's hair had been long and the color of corn silk. Then Sarah had become Sam and the hair had been cropped.

But even with short hair and dressed in boys' clothing, Madelaine had hidden Sarah in the root cellar the entire time those horrible men occupied Twelve Oaks. They were so low and so perverted that a pretty boy would no doubt have faired just as ill as a pretty girl. She hadn't even fought them or complained about their mistreatment. She'd needed to be able to move about freely. Keeping Sarah safe had been her only consideration. Even if she died in the effort, Sarah would never endure what she had, never.

Some hours later, Madelaine woke to the sound of a gunshot. She sat up so suddenly she banged her head on the wagon axle. Sarah bolted to a sitting position beside her and Maddy quickly reached over to place a hand across the girl's mouth. Fear clawed at her insides and hot bile burned in her throat. She had to fight the urge to take Sarah and start running.

Sarah nodded her understanding and Madelaine let go. Maddy rolled over and rested on one elbow, protecting the mound of her belly. It was pitch black, without even a glimmer of moon or stars to light the surrounding prairie and scrub. An owl hooted and Maddy held her breath. She smelled pine tar in the clear night air and the earthy scent of the soil beneath their pallets.

Two more shots rang out and Madelaine clenched her

hands into fists. Please, Lord, let us get to dear Rachel's house safely, she prayed. We'll be safe once we are with her and her husband.

A shadowy figure emerged from the gloom. Maddy stiffened momentarily, then sighed with relief. It was Mr. Hawkins. As gracefully as a woman eight months pregnant could, she scrambled out from under the wagon, wrapping an old paisley shawl tightly around herself.

Hawk was carrying an enormous pistol in his right hand and dragging a man along by his shirt with his left hand. He did this with ease, even though Maddy could clearly see that the bulky figure was no lightweight.

"What's happening, Mr. Hawkins? Who's shooting?" Maddy asked in a voice that sounded strange to her own ears.

"This man was trying to rustle Beau and your mule. When I tried to stop him, he fired on me. I shot at him, and I think I've killed him," Mr. Hawkins said as he crammed the big pistol into his belt. "I saw another one in the bushes and I got off a shot at him before he disappeared."

"It's a miracle that you woke up," Maddy said. Her heart sank at the thought of losing John, old and cantankerous as he was. Without the mule, there was no way they would make it to Pilatka. They'd have to abandon the wagon and all their possessions. It was just too terrible to think on.

"I wasn't asleep, ma'am," Hawk said. "I was keeping watch. Out here in the wilds, all kinds of deserters, outlaws, and ruffians abound, as you now see."

"But, Mr. Hawkins, when do you sleep?" she asked, genuinely surprised.

"I would have caught a nap after you and the boy woke up. I don't need much sleep, and I can rest while I ride. It's better to lose a little shut-eye than wind up dead or afoot, which in these parts is just about as good as dead."

"You should have asked me to share the watch with you," she said. "I would gladly have done so."

He chuckled. "I don't think so, ma'am. No offense, but in your condition, you need your rest."

She turned her attention to the dead man. "What do we do with him?"

"He's not alone," Hawk said. "I saw at least one more. Outlaws usually travel in small bands. I'll take care of his body after I gather up your mule and Beau. I think my stud is what attracted them, and I'm truly sorry."

She held the shawl over her belly with one hand and reached out, brushing his arm with the tips of her fingers. "Don't be sorry, Mr. Hawkins. All I can think is, what would have happened to me and Sam if they had come upon us while we were alone?"

Hawk disappeared into the gloom and came back minutes later leading his big stud horse. John mule, relieved of his hobbles, was right behind Hawk's horse. After tying both animals to the wagon, Hawk went to his saddle where it leaned against the twisting roots of a large turkey oak and yanked his rifle out of the attached scabbard.

He motioned to Maddy to get behind the wagon just as a shot rang out from the blackness and thudded into the tree. Frozen, Maddy clearly heard the *thunk* as the bullet buried itself in the thick bark of the oak. Two more shots followed and Hawk dove behind the wagon, grabbing Maddy's arm and dragging her with him.

"I thought as much," he said. "There's more of them. They must want Beau."

"Why would they want your horse, Mr. Hawkins?" Maddy gasped, breathless from fear and the sudden leap to safety.

"Call me Hawk, will you? Beau is a very valuable animal. His bloodlines are the best and he can outrun any horse in Florida, maybe any horse in this country. They probably think they can sell him. And maybe they're hungry. They might want to eat your mule."

Hawk cocked the rifle and fired a shot into the darkness. He pulled the big pistol out of his belt and handed it to Maddy. "Here. Don't fire it until you see someone to shoot at." He turned to Sarah and said, "Use that scattergun of yours, son."

Another shot rang out and Hawk quickly cocked his rifle and fired back. Maddy easily made out the muzzle flash of the distant gun in the darkness, as did Hawk, apparently. His next well-aimed shot drew a scream from one of their assailants.

"How many are out there?" Maddy asked. She held the big pistol in front of her with both hands, while Sarah had the shotgun resting on the side rails of the wagon.

"Two less than there were," Hawk said.

The man Maddy had thought was dead began to moan. "He's alive," she said to Hawk.

He dropped to his belly and inched his way to the injured outlaw. Hawk grabbed the man by the collar and Maddy could see the outlaw was older; his whiskers were gray and his lanky hair was thin and revealed a bald spot. She couldn't see how badly he was hurt. The sandy Florida soil beneath him was absorbing any blood and it was too dark to see the nature and extent of his wounds.

"How many men are out there?" Hawk hissed into the man's face as he hoisted him by the lapels of a dark duster and shook him.

The man groaned. "Tell me how many men are with you," Hawk demanded. "Or I'll finish you off right now."

Another shot rang out from the camp's perimeter. Hawk dropped lower and shook the man harder.

"There were six of us," the outlaw gasped. "You shot one, so that leaves four out there, but one's only a boy."

Hawk dropped the man into the sand and scrambled behind the wagon. "I'm going after them," he said to Maddy. "Take the carbine and answer their fire."

Shocked, Maddy grabbed his arm. "You can't go out there—they'll kill you."

He grinned. "They can't kill what they can't see."

He grabbed charcoal out of the fire pit, blackened his face, and took the big Bowie knife out of its sheath.

"Remember to return fire when they shoot at you," he said. Armed with his Colt and the knife, he slipped into the darkness.

Maddy and Sarah huddled behind the wagon. Far to the east, the horizon began to glow dull red as the sun inched closer to a new dawning. Fear, her constant companion for most of the last four years, received a fresh load of fuel and burned hot in her stomach. She strained her eyes watching for Mr. Hawkins as she and Sarah waited.

The silence was frightening. The injured man had ceased moaning or moving. Was it un-Christian-like to hope he succumbed to his injuries? The big stallion and John propped themselves up on three legs, cocked a hip, and dozed.

A sudden scream rang out and ended in a horrible gurgle. Maddy had to resist the urge to scream, too. The scream was followed by a volley of shots. The stud and John mule plunged and pulled back, stretching their tethers to the limit as two riders burst into view. Sarah loosed one of the barrels of the shotgun, blowing the bigger rider clean off his horse even as the force of it knocked her to the ground. The blasted outlaw tumbled conveniently on top of the one shot earlier and lay still.

"I got him, Mama," Sarah whispered.

"Bless you, my darling," Maddy said. "And you've piled them up so neatly as well."

Sarah giggled and Maddy was conscious of a feeling of remorse over the way her poor daughter had been raised. But she consoled herself with the thought that Sarah had never had to endure assaults on her person or experience the helplessness and humiliation of being trapped in a relationship that tortured the body and smothered the soul. Sarah could shoot the shotgun and a pistol with some accuracy and had shown her courage in more than one dreadful situation. She knew to do what she was told with no complaints. This one accomplishment alone had probably saved her life. Perhaps she would grow up and look back on these years with understanding.

A figure materialized in the gloom of early dawn. After a moment of concern, Maddy saw it was Hawk walking towards them, leading three horses. As he approached the wagon, the fat, injured man lying beneath the outlaw Sarah had blasted into eternity groaned and struggled to rid himself of his dead fellow.

Hawk tied the three horses to a nearby oak tree by looping each set of reins over a low-hanging branch. He bent over and shoved the dead body off the groaning outlaw and helped him to sit.

In the early-dawn light, Maddy saw blood from a wound high on the outlaw's shoulder had covered the sleeve of his black duster and dripped down the front of his filthy home-spun shirt. His belly burst through the shirt in two places where buttons were missing and hung over the top of a pair of pants so dirty their original color was impossible to determine. The bottoms of his pants were stuffed into a pair of boots, the leather old and sagging over the soles. The left boot had a hole in the toe and Maddy could see he wore no socks.

Hawk helped the outlaw move to the wagon, where he sat down with his back to the rear wheel. "Thank ye kindly," he said in a wheezy baritone.

"Are they all gone?" Maddy asked.

"I killed two out there just now, and Sam got one. There was the one I took care of earlier. I saw no sign of him, and I think the boy escaped too. According to this guy," he pointed to the man sitting against the wagon wheel, "that should be the lot."

He began rifling through the saddlebags of the three horses. He pulled out a small sack of coins, handed it to Maddy, then gathered a staggering pile of firearms, weapons, and ammunition. He took a long whip off one saddle and unwound it. He cracked it a couple of times and smiled. "It's been a long time since I had a whip in my hands, and this is a fine one."

After coiling it carefully, he placed it with his own saddle. Then he untied the cinches of a bulky saddle with a four-inch horn and a deep seat, snatched it off a stout bay horse, and tossed it next to his own gear. "I will be glad to get back into a big, comfortable saddle," he said. "The Army can have all the McClelland saddles it wants."

"Should we be taking these men's possessions?" Maddy felt weird about benefiting from their deaths.

"They were planning to kill you . . . or worse, and steal everything we had," Mr. Hawkins said. "And I don't think they're going to be needing any of this stuff anytime soon."

He turned to the fat man. "Who are you?"

"The name is Roscoe Beale," he said. "I'm very pleased to make your acquaintance. Exactly what do you plan to do with me?"

"Well, Mr. Beale, as far as I'm concerned you're free to go. You can have that sorry roan gelding tied to yonder tree and any of this stuff that's yours," Mr. Hawkins said. "But first, I am hoping you'll answer a few questions, like who are these men you were riding with and what did they want with us?"

"Three were deserters, and I think two of them were brothers. I met them at a drinking establishment in Moultrie," Beale said. "I was planning to travel with them as far as Pilatka and catch the riverboat to Jacksonville."

"That's a pretty roundabout way to get to Jacksonville," Hawkins said.

"Well, they planned to . . . I mean, I'd hoped . . ." Beale hesitated.

"Oh, I get it," Mr. Hawkins said. "They planned to steal and rob their way to Pilatka and you hoped to enjoy some of the spoils."

"I'm truly sorry," Beale said. "I've fallen on hard times,

and I thought I saw a way to improve my situation. I know it was wrong."

"Why in the world did they take you on?" Hawk asked. "No offense intended, but you don't seem like the outlaw type or of much use to this bunch."

"I understand perfectly," Beale said, "and I'm not offended. I can cook, and I have certain skills with explosives they thought they might use."

"You still haven't said why they attacked this woman and her boy."

Beale ran his hand over his head, touching a big red welt on his forehead with the tips of his fingers. "It wasn't the woman or the kid they was after. They coveted your fine horse."

Maddy listened for a few minutes as the two men talked, then decided to cook some breakfast. She had no taste for the stew but thought the cornbread and sweet potatoes would be good.

As she was stoking up the fire, Hawk brought her a greasy burlap sack. "There's a slab of bacon in this." He handed the sack to her and another leather bag. She opened the second bag and found salt in a twist of brown paper, as well as lard, flour, and plenty of dried pink beans.

"I'll get rid of the bodies while you're cooking," he said.

"Are you going to bury them?"

"Don't have time for it. There's a sinkhole in that hammock across the trail. I'm going to drag them over there and dump them. Buzzards got to eat, too."

Maddy stared hard at Hawk. One minute he was kind, considerate, and civilized, and the next he would shock her with the most primitive behavior. He had killed those men without a moment's hesitation. And she had to admit, she was glad. She'd learned the hard way what hesitation could cost. She rubbed her belly. If she had opened fire on those deserters the minute they stepped on her land . . . well, not doing so was something for which she had berated herself every day of the last year.

When breakfast was ready, Mr. Hawkins took Mr. Beale a plate. The fat man ate like he was starving, shoving food into his mouth and spilling crumbs and grease onto his shirt. When he was finished eating, he wiped his mouth with the tail of his shirt, stood up, and rubbed his belly. He'd found his wide-brimmed floppy hat in the dirt close to the camp. It must have fallen off when Hawk dragged him to the wagon. He swept it off as he bowed low to Madelaine. "The meal was delicious. I thank you, ma'am, for your courtesy and compassion. I will remember you and Mr. Hawkins well if ever we meet again." He then turned to Hawk. "Sir, if you ever have need of my services, please feel free to call upon me. I am deeply in your debt."

Mr. Beale then hauled his portly self onto the back of the rickety roan.

As they watched him ride into the rising sun, Hawk began brushing his horse. "It's time I saddled up and was on my way," he said. "That big bay seems kind of gentle. You might want to hitch him to the wagon and give poor John a rest."

He was going to ride off and leave them? Suddenly Maddy felt like she'd known Hawk forever and couldn't conceive of traveling without his protection. She walked to the wagon, sat down beside Sarah on the tailgate, loosed her hair from its long braid, and began brushing it. "We need Mr.

Hawkins, Sarah. He's planning to ride off to Pilatka without us. What should I do?"

Sarah looked at her as though she were an imbecile. "Ask him to go with us, Mama. I think he likes you."

Maddy smiled. Children saw things so clearly. Adults seemed to cloud everything with fear and anxiety colored with a little panic. Maybe all she had to do was ask.

3

"WELL, SHORTY," Snake Barber said as he propped his feet up on a chair, leaned back, and spit tobacco juice into a can on the floor, "where is she?"

Shorty McCue was only sixteen, and he was scared right down to his worn, slopped-over boots. Snake could see the fear dripping out of him in the sweat beading across his cheeks and forehead.

"We found her, Mr. Snake, just south of Alligator. She's got all her stuff packed on a wagon pulled by a skinny old mule. And she's got a boy with her."

"Did you see her? What does she look like now? Is she still pretty?"

"I, ah, I don't know, Mr. Snake. Some of the other guys saw her. They said it was her. But I never did lay eyes on her."

"Well, if you found her, why isn't she here? And where the hell are my men?" Snake had seen Shorty ride in alone, his horse covered with sweat. He knew something bad had gone down. He should have known better than to send idiots to do a man's job. If you wanted something done right, you had to do it yourself. But he hadn't really believed they'd find her in the first place.

In Jacksonville, in the arms of a whore, he'd had a blinding realization. He'd realized Maddy was the one—the one woman he could not live without. There was something about her quiet ways and beauty that made him feel at home. But when he'd gone back to get her, he'd found the house full of Yankees and her gone. So he'd left some men to hunt for her trail and track her down while he rode off for Volusia to find the Hawkins family's gold.

But one thing bothered him. Why would Madelaine have a kid with her? She'd never had a brat with her on the farm in Georgia. He shrugged. Oh, well, maybe it was just some orphan she picked up along the way. She was too ten-derhearted.

"When we caught up to her, she was with some drifter I never see'd before," Shorty said. "He was hell, man. He shot up the lot of us. I was the only one got away. He kilt Brother John. And the kid blasted Texas Murphy right out of the sad-dle with a scattergun. I rode out of there as fast as my horse could tote me." Shorty paused. "I'm lucky to be alive, Mr. Snake."

Snake leaped to his feet, smashing his chair into a wall with one quick swipe of his hand. Uncontrollable fury filled him. His face felt like it flamed red. *She was with a man?* "So you think you're lucky to be alive?" Snake snarled, his voice shaking with anger. "What did this saddle tramp traveling with my woman look like?"

Shorty seemed to think this over. He clawed at the thicket of straw-colored hair on top of his head and then scratched his crotch. Snake wondered if stimulation in either place would activate his brain and help the moron remember something useful.

"He had this jam-up horse, Mr. Snake. I mean, that stud was a rare piece of blood and bone. Looked fast, real fast. We was gonna take him too."

"I ain't interested in the man's horse," Snake snarled. "Tell me what he looked like."

"He looked strong, real strong. He had brown hair and was kind of tall. He sure did have him some muscles, I tell you what. Big arms. They bulged all over him. His chest swelled out of his old blue shirt, and when he fired his gun, I could see in the muzzle flash he had a key hanging on a cord around his neck with a big old tooth. Looked kind of like a gator tooth, but I never know'd a gator big enough to have teeth like that." Shorty's voice trailed off as he finished this short speech.

The man Shorty described hit a raw nerve in Snake. He only knew one person to wear a gator tooth with a key around his neck, and that person also had huge muscles from shoeing horses. But how could Hawk have met up with Madelaine? Could God actually be that cruel, to put the one woman in the world Snake felt something for into the hands of his worst enemy? Did the man who had always had everything Snake could never have—land, money, position in the community, a loving family, and lots and lots of cows—now possess the only woman for whom Snake Barber had ever felt the slightest bit of affection?

If Shorty weren't the only person alive who could identify the man traveling with Maddy, Snake would have killed him right then and there. He had no need for the loser or any of the men that had failed him. Rage filled him, impotent rage made worse by needing to stifle the urge to murder Shorty. He clenched his fists and swallowed hard. *No*. He needed him. It seemed Shorty's short life would be prolonged for at least a few more days while Snake pondered this new development.

It looked like Hawkins was on his way back to Volusia to reclaim his home and family. That could present a problem. Snake and his men were currently ensconced in Hawk's home while they searched for the gold doubloons hidden somewhere on the property.

Hawk's kid and the ranch hands had disappeared before they got there. Snake had two men out looking for them right now. He would need the kid to force the location of the gold out of Hawkins if they couldn't find it themselves. Snake rubbed his hands together at the thought of all that gold. He'd be so rich he could move up North and live like a king. He'd kind of liked it up there. Nobody knew him and he could start fresh, leave Volusia and his rotten family that had disowned him behind. He'd take darling Maddy with him. She'd probably be just as happy as he would to leave the South behind.

But first he had to find the gold. Hawk had told him it was in the spring. The only one Snake found close to the house was a big one, with a deep boil. Water rushed out of the spring from a depth of what had to be fifty feet or so with incredible force, boiling the water on the surface.

The depth of the spring wasn't the problem. Searching through the caves and shelves in the underwater cavern would not be a problem. He had plenty of people that could swim like fish. No, the problem, as he had just discovered early that morning, was gators. The banks of the spring were loaded with the damn things, and some were as big as four-teen feet long. They slept wall to wall on the banks, basking in the sun after surely having feasted on the abundance of fish found up and down the length of the spring all the way to the river. In the water, some floated like dead logs, watch-ing through half-opened eyes. The blue spring, as Hawk had called it, burst from the ground about a half a mile from the river and ran deep all the way to the St. Johns.

If the gold was in the spring, as Snake was beginning to doubt, getting to it was going to be troublesome. Snake shook his head and got out of his chair. How could Hawk have hid-den anything in that spring? The gators had been there since time began. Snake strode out of the dining area in the house, through an open door, and into the dogtrot.

Hawk's house consisted of two sections with an open dogtrot in the center. Porches surrounded the house and a walkway from the porches ran to the cookhouse out back. It was large and comfortable.

Crossing the dogtrot, Snake went into his personal bed-room. All his men had to share rooms with each other or sleep on the floor, but he had his own room. It had a com-fortable bed with a patchwork quilt and rag rugs on the floor. There was a mirror on the wall in his bedroom. Snake found it and admired himself. He tried not to focus on the scar as he smoothed the big drooping black mustache with two fin-gers and then the strip of beard that traveled down his chin from the bottom of his lip. Making a face in the mirror, Snake decided he might need to shave soon. He liked to keep a neat face. Twisting the ends of his mustache, he grabbed his flat-crowned leather hat off the coat rack and walked onto the porch.

Snake pulled a twist of tobacco out of the pocket of his greasy pants and cut off a chunk with his knife. Stuffing a big wad in his cheek, he looked around for Skeeter, his right-hand man.

Skeeter Jerkins was breaking a mule in the corral next to one of Hawk's barns. He had the big animal chained to one of the support posts of the barn and was beating it with the end of the chain. The mule plunged and twisted to get away from the chain, and Skeeter kept on whipping. The mule would be pulling logs and plowing fields by tomorrow. Skeeter's ways were crude, but they worked.

When he and his men first took over the ranch, they'd found the barn full of lame, sick, and injured animals. Snake smiled as he remembered finding them. The boys had gotten a little rough, and eventually killed all of them. Some they'd eaten, like the little buck with the broken leg. What sorry, weak idiot would try to save animals that were only put on the earth to eat anyway?

"Hey, Skeeter, that big som bitch giving you trouble?" Snake walked to the corral fence. It was made of split rails stacked five feet high.

"Hell, no, I'm just explaining the facts of life to this here mule. He's the mule and I'm the boss—that's the main fact he's a-learning." Skeeter laughed a high-pitched laugh that mostly came out of his nose. Snake thought it ironic that Skeeter's laugh sounded a lot like the braying of a jackass or a mule.

"Think if we toss the mule in the water, it'll keep the gators occupied long enough for us to search the spring for Hawk's gold?" Snake said.

Skeeter bleated out another braying laugh, then said,

"Nah! Too many gators. They'd have him picked clean before you could skin a cat."

Snake and Skeeter had been friends since they were little shavers hardly big enough to ride a horse. Skeeter's family had driven a wagon to Florida from Texas and gotten work on the Barber farm.

Before the Jerkins family came, Pa had a schoolmaster working the ranch. Sometimes he'd give the many Barber children lessons in reading and writing and speaking good English. Snake actually enjoyed the book learning. But the schoolmaster drifted on and the Jerkins arrived with Skeeter. Snake's book lessons stopped, and he and Skeeter took to learning lots of different things.

Snake's parents were involved in a feud with another ranching family, the Mizells. Snake's pa didn't have time for his youngest son. Pa hardly noticed him when he was around and never missed him when he wasn't. Snake and Skeeter were always in some kind of trouble. The punishment for getting caught was severe, so early in life Snake learned to avoid it at all costs. By the time they were in their teens, the two of them were very close.

Snake was the tenth child out of his poor mamma, Emma, and not her last. Snake's pa, Henry, spent all of his time with his two eldest sons planning how to cheat the Mizells out of land and cows. Far as he knew, the feud with the Mizells was still up and running, and not likely to end in either his pa's or his brothers' lifetimes.

Snake had left home when he was only fourteen, taking Skeeter along. They'd robbed houses, farms, travelers, stores, and saloons and rustled cows and horses. It was a lawless time and there was no one who could stop them.

They spent their days rustling and their nights in saloons and fancy houses. When the Civil War started, Snake and Skeeter decided to travel north into Georgia and join up. They'd thought it would be a lot of fun to kill some Yankees.

But military life hadn't suited either of them. All that marching and saying "Yes, sir" and saluting got old fast. And after Snake got into a fight with an officer who sliced his face open with a military saber, they'd deserted. They'd found themselves in Virginia, and unfamiliar territory. It hadn't taken them long to get picked up by Yankees and tossed into prison.

At the Yankee prison camp in Maryland, he'd met up with his old buddy Hawk. It had been like a ripe plum falling off the tree into his hands. Hawk had been sick. Snake had just about wormed the whole secret of the gold out of him when the damn Yankees took him out of the tent. Hawk must have gotten better since then, because it looked like he was headed home. And that would sure complicate things.

Travis Hawkins peered through the palmetto thicket at his home and barn. Ever since this band of scum, deserters, and outlaws had moved into the D-Wing, he'd had a red film over his eyes and a knot of rage balled up in his chest. He could see one of the men who had helped kill his patients, the sick animals he'd been caring for in the barn. Taking care of sick and injured birds and wild animals was something Travis had been doing since he was just a little boy when Pa had given him a baby bird that'd fallen out of its nest.

Travis had hidden and watched some of the slaughter of his poor animals. It was like an awful nightmare. He wanted to murder every one of those men slowly. He wanted them to suffer. He clenched his fists, digging his nails into his palms. His rage had grown until it filled his whole body and he had to fight every minute to keep quiet and maintain his calm. Their time would come, he vowed silently, their time would come.

Jimmy Jumper had been warned of the approaching band of outlaws by his cousin Joe Tiger. Joe and several other Seminoles had been slipping around on a hunting expedition. Most of the Seminoles were living in the southern part of Florida where they had taken refuge in the Great Swamp after the last Indian war. Seminoles were not welcome in the settlements. They avoided contact with all white people except his family. Travis's mother had been half Seminole, raised in the camp of Billy Bowlegs himself.

After Joe had warned Jimmy and then headed out again, Travis, Judy Bill, and the two hands had moved into the original cabin built by Grandpa and Grandma when they first settled on the land. It was small but well hidden, overgrown with vines, seedling oaks, and pines and palmetto. Taking great care not to disturb the concealing foliage, the small group had taken up residence in the cabin. They'd brought the dogs and the marsh tackies with them. Travis drew some small comfort from that. If they'd left the dogs behind, the outlaws would probably have killed them too.

Peering now through the concealing bushes, Travis saw a skinny, short man with long whiskers and thin, straggly hair trying to break one of Pa's mules. The mule was a four-year-old, big and strong and wild. Jimmy wouldn't touch a mule, and John R. and Gabby, Pa's two hands, had been too busy, so the mule was still wild. But it didn't look like the skinny little man would have much trouble breaking him. He was plumb full of mean, a lot meaner than the poor mule.

Travis crept silently out of the clump of palmettos. He knew six feet away from him a fat diamondback rattler was basking in the sun. He wouldn't bother it and it wouldn't bother him. He got along with all critters, it seemed, except men. But animals did not kill for pleasure or fun, only for food. They were honest in their intentions and men were not.

He heard the call of a red-tailed hawk high overhead and looked up. Sky Diver was a big female Travis kept for hunting. Suddenly, Travis smiled. He'd been struck with a devilish idea. He whistled a high-pitched screech and Sky Diver slowly flew in a circle, turned, and then dove toward him.

Travis broke off a tree branch with a fork in it and snapped off the forking limbs so they were only two-inches long. Still smiling, he slipped behind the rattler and stabbed the fork over its neck at the base of its skull. Pinned, the rattler thrashed, his rattles making a dry shaking sound. Travis carefully picked the snake up behind its head with his right hand, and held it while it coiled its body around his arm.

The hawk landed on Travis's extended left arm. Eyeing the snake with interest, she cocked her head to one side, her eyes bright, and opened her beak. "This ain't for you to eat, girl," Travis said. "I'm gonna need you to make a delivery."

Dropping the rattler's head, Travis held the snake by its rattles. The snake was only five feet long with six buttons, a mere baby compared to some of the monsters Travis had seen on the prairie. Travis held it as far away from his body as he could, and offered the tail to the hawk. Diver grabbed it and took off. The bird circled with the snake hanging from her strong beak. Travis whistled again and pointed to the corral. It was as though the hawk could read his mind. Diver soared over the outlaw and the mule. When Travis whistled again, she dropped the snake.

The rattler fell slowly, twisting and turning through the air to land on the haunches of the harassed mule. The outlaw was in the middle of hitching the mule to a six-foot section of log with heavy trace chains. The terrified mule kicked his heels high over his head. The snake shot into the air once more and landed across the chains, less than a foot from the outlaw. The man saw the snake, swore loudly, and jumped back.

Travis doubled up and clapped his hand over his mouth to hide the loud guffaw of laughter that threatened to erupt. The mule tore over the fence, half jumping, half climbing. With the chains slapping behind it, the mule shot past Travis's hiding place.

When the mule had exploded out of the corral, the snake had flown into the air for the last time. Flicked off the chain, the rattler landed right on the outlaw's chest. He yelled "Damn!" and slapped at the rattler. When it slid to the ground, the man took off in the opposite direction from the mule. High overhead, the hawk screeched. Travis answered her with a whistle. Time to go home before he was discovered.

Animals always did what Travis asked of them. He never tried to control them. They did what he asked because they knew him and trusted him. Trust was the key in dealing with all creatures, man and animals. Relationships were all about trust. Boy, didn't he know that.

Travis stepped along with a swing in his stride. He'd struck back for himself and his family. It had been a small thing, but it was a step. They still had to reclaim their home. How could Jimmy and Joseph just hide and do nothing? But what did he know? He was just a kid, and it wasn't his place to ask. He knew the Indians didn't like messing with white folk, though. That had to be the reason. No doubt they would have run away already if it weren't for him.

Moving as quietly as a panther, he found his small horse, Light Foot, waiting where he'd left him. Leaping easily onto the horse's bare back, Travis headed home. When he rode into the grassy clearing near the cabin, Jimmy Jumper appeared from behind a thick oak and grabbed Light Foot's reins.

"We have been worrying about you, Travis," Jimmy said. "Have you been back to the house again?"

Travis slid from the horse's back. "They're trying to break one of Pa's mules," he said. "And they've been spending a lot of time down in the big spring. Another one rode in a little while ago. He'd been riding pretty hard. His horse was just about done in."

"We must hope they find what they want and leave soon," Jimmy said.

"Maybe they plan to use our house as a headquarters for raiding the neighbors and robbing folks and stealing cows," Travis said. "What do they want with our place?"

"Who knows what white men do or why they do it?" Jimmy said. "If they are searching in the big spring, they may be looking for your Grandpappy's gold. They'll never find it there. But you listen to me, Travis. I know dangerous men when I see them. Stay away from the house. You test your spirit guides by risking so much. One day your father will come home and all will be right again."

"My pa is dead," Travis said. "I heard the war is over. If he's still alive, where is he? He's been gone for over three years, and no word in all that time. Accept the truth, Jimmy. Pa ain't coming back."

4 ☀

"WOULD YOU CONSIDER RIDING to Pilatka with us, Mr. Hawkins?" Madelaine Wilkes asked.

Hawk could see desperation and fear in her wide-opened blue eyes. He almost groaned. But he should have known it would come to this. To her, he must seem like a godsend.

"I haven't seen my family in three years, ma'am. I can travel much faster alone." He didn't want the burden of this woman and her child. He felt an increasing urgency to get home as each day passed. It gnawed at his innards. He wanted to see Travis, the homestead, Jimmy, and Judy Bill. He needed to know they were safe. And ever since Mrs. Wilkes had told him the father of her child was named Snake and had a scar on his face, he'd been tossing around an absurd idea: What if Jake the Snake Barber was the father of this woman's unborn child? It seemed impossible. Barber had been safely locked up in Pointe Lookout Prison when last he saw him.

But things changed—prisoners were released, and some

escaped. If Barber were on the loose, he could have gone back to Volusia Landing. He could have gone out to Hawk's ranch and tried to find the money. His son and the Jumper family might be in danger or in terrible trouble, and if Snake and his men were there looking for the gold, it was his fault. He'd been so sick when he gave Snake those clues. What had he been thinking? He had to get back as fast as possible.

Mrs. Wilkes moved in closer. She smelled clean, like laundry that had aired in the sun all day, with a hint of roses. Her hair was loose around her shoulders and hung to her thighs. It mesmerized him. It had been a very long time since he'd seen a woman's hair unbound. She pressed something into his hand. He looked down and saw the bag of coins he'd taken from the outlaws. "Please, keep this bag of money and help me and my daughter on our journey to Pilatka."

"How'd you know I knew Sam was a girl?" Somehow she'd realized he knew her secret.

"You don't treat her as I imagine you would treat a young man. I wasn't sure you knew, but I've been observing you, and I know you are not a fool. Sarah's hair may be short, but she still looks like a girl. I feel we must trust you with her secret because we need you, Hawk. Please don't turn your back on us now."

Hawk's gut churned. He wanted to saddle up and ride Beau as fast as the big horse could carry him. He could be in Pilatka in two days. With them, it would take four or more. He sighed. It would only add a couple of extra days to the trip. He'd been gone so long already, what harm could two more days possibly do?

"I'll travel with you on one condition," he finally said. "You got to pack up right now and get on the road straightaway. We'll travel as fast as we can, pushing the horses. The days will be long, and we won't have many breaks. It'll be hard, and you're gonna get real tired, real fast. Are you sure you can do it?"

Madelaine surprised him by bursting into tears. She grabbed his hand. "Thank you, kind sir. You have eased my mind and my heart of the terrible fear of continuing down this dangerous road alone."

Hawk could see the buildings of Pilatka through the gloom of a rapidly approaching dusk. The sun was a red ball shining through the tops of a line of oak trees far to the west. The air shimmered with the heat of the long summer day, and his shirt was wet and plastered to his body.

When he clucked to the tired bay horse, the animal lifted his head and plodded a little faster. Maddy was slumped on the bench seat next to him with her head resting on his shoulder and one arm draped across his lap. A damp tendril of hair was glued to her forehead.

Somewhere along the forced march of the past four days, all formalities had been dropped. He was now Hawk and she was Maddy. Sarah sat on a pile of crates and trunks in the back of the wagon with her feet dangling over the edge. Beau and a small, chestnut-red gelding Hawk thought might have Cracker blood were tied to the wagon. John mule was tied behind the red horse.

Pilatka had been a big town before the war. Folks from up north had ridden steamboats down the St. Johns to vacation on the river in the sunny Florida weather. The war had changed all that, though, and now the town appeared to be virtually deserted. Hawk had heard the Yankees were occupying it during the last year of the war. Residents living in Pilatka for years had vacated the town.

Hawk's shoulders hunched as he looked at one boarded-up building after another, and he felt his spine begin to tingle, never a good sign. He passed a local bar with a large sign on the front declaring it to be the Bone Orchard Saloon. It was the one bright spot of activity in town, which was kind of ominous. Lights blazed inside from oil lamps and candle-filled chandeliers. Happy music from a piano echoed through the empty streets. Saddled horses tied up at the rail switched their tails and cocked an ear in the direction of the wagon. He watched as a cow hunter rode his marsh tacky right through the door of the saloon, dogs trailing behind.

He gazed with longing at the lighted windows. A drink would go down right smooth. That was just another thing he hadn't tasted in a long time.

When the saloon was only a light shining behind the wagon, he woke Maddy. "When was the last time you heard from your sister-in-law?" he asked.

Rubbing her eyes and sitting up, Maddy quickly placed several inches between herself and Hawk. He had to turn his head so she wouldn't see him smile. She'd been draped all over him for the past five miles. As she smoothed her rumpled dress, she resumed a safe distance. "The last letter I had from Rachel was over a year ago," she said. "They own a large boardinghouse and store off Ferry Road in East Pilatka. They said Sarah and I would be welcome. They have plenty of room and could use our help in their business."

"Well, I hope they're still there," he said. "It looks like

this town has been abandoned."

"I'm sure they're still there," Maddy said. "They've lived in Pilatka since they married in forty-five. Where else would they be? They have a business to take care of, you know."

Hawk shrugged, but her words did nothing to still the uneasy feeling that had crawled into his stomach. As they turned down the main road heading east, Hawk could see the river ahead shining silver beneath the newly risen moon. He pulled the wagon onto a side street next to a hotel. The St. Johns River Rest had its doors open, and there was a beckoning light glowing from the open door and the windows.

Hawk felt under the seat for his saddlebags. He pulled the poke of coins out and handed Maddy a three-dollar gold piece. "Take Sarah into the hotel and get a room for the night. Have a meal and a bath and enjoy sleeping in the comfort of a real bed," he said.

"Won't you be staying here as well?" she asked.

"I'm going to find a place to stable these animals for the night and I'll sleep with the wagon."

"But, Hawk—"

"No, someone has to watch over the wagon. I don't trust it to be here in the morning. Everything you own and my belongings as well are on it, or in my saddlebags. I just got that big Texas saddle, and I don't plan to lose it."

She didn't argue. She was tired, and the lure of a hot bath, food she didn't have to cook, and the soft bed were too much to resist.

In the morning, Maddy and Sarah emerged from the double front doors of the St. Johns River Rest smiling, with freshly washed hair and clean clothes. "I declare, I haven't felt this good in years," Maddy said. "Let us catch the morning ferry. I'm in a great hurry to see my sister-in-law and her husband. I haven't seen them since my wedding, and I haven't had a safe home in such a long time."

Hawk said nothing as he helped Maddy into the wagon. He had a bad feeling about the day but didn't want to ruin her cheerful spirit and hope for a brighter future.

The ferryboat ride took over an hour. The river was wide and shallow. There were few passengers, which Hawk took as a discouraging sign. Pilatka seemed like a ghost town. After passing so many boarded-up houses and businesses, he had feared the ferry might not be running. But activity on the docks showed there was life in the town yet. Two steamboats were tied at the city docks unloading barrels of what looked like molasses, along with a multitude of crates and boxes. One more boat could be seen steaming north toward Jacksonville and the river's mouth.

The St. Johns was unusual in that it flowed north, dropping only thirty feet in the entire three hundred–plus miles of its course. Its headwaters were in a large lake very close to Hawk's land and the town of Enterprise.

Maddy and Sarah could hardly contain their excitement. The long journey from their farm in Marshallville, Georgia, was about to end. The ferry docked and Hawk guided the wagon onto Ferry Road and up the hill on the east side of the river. All he had to do after he deposited Maddy and Sarah at her relatives' house was turn south and head home.

The bay horse trudged up the hill from the dock. A lonely fisherman waved from his spot on the bank where he fished with a cane pole. Sarah waved back. The first house they came to on the left-hand side of the road was a large three-story, rambling affair coated with peeling gray paint. A sign hung over the porch proclaiming it to be Ned's Boarding House and Emporium. Adjacent to the boarding house, and connected by the porch and a wall, was what appeared to have been the emporium part of the business. The door on it was completely boarded up and the glass in the big storefront window lay on the porch in sharp fragments.

"That's the place," Maddy said. "It looks to be in terrible shape. I thought Rachel and Edward were prosperous. Their letters were so cheerful. Rachel talked about the good business they were getting close to the river and the ferry. She said the house was always full of travelers off the riverboats and that the store was busy. They loved Pilatka."

The steps leading up to the wraparound porches were falling down and the windows on the ground floor were covered with boards. Hawk knew what was coming. It was as he had feared. The place was shut down and closed, just as many others were in this town. All that remained was to find out that Maddy's in-laws, Rachel and Edward Carver, had closed up shop and disappeared.

"Stay in the wagon," he told Maddy.

"No," she insisted. "I must see for myself. They may still be living here and only closed the business. It's a fine old house. Why would they abandon it?"

Hawk sighed and helped her down.

Maddy waited on the overgrown strip of front lawn while Hawk climbed the stairs, picking his way across a missing board and over two broken steps. He banged on the door while she paced back and forth through grass a foot high. The door had lumber nailed across it, and the knocker was missing. He could see where it had previously hung. When no one answered, he walked across to the storefront and peered inside the broken window. The shelves were empty and the countertop covered with a thick layer of dust and debris.

"What can you see?" Maddy called.

"Nothing. The store's empty. It's all closed up." Hawk walked around the side of the house on the porch and jumped off at the rear of the building. A cookhouse in the back had burnt to the ground. He knew it for the cookhouse because a wood-burning cookstove with three ovens and an eight-hole top sat in the midst of the ruins. Made of sturdy cast iron, the stove was scorched but salvageable. Hawk wished he could load it up and take it home with him. It even had a water reservoir and a large warmer. His mother had always wanted a cookstove, but she'd died before Pappy could buy her one.

The back steps were intact, so Hawk climbed onto the back porch, cleaned a spot on a window with his elbow, and looked inside. He could see furniture covered with white sheets and rolls of carpet pushed against the walls. The Carvers had vacated the premises, and it looked as though they planned to be away for quite a while.

What was he supposed to do now? What could he say to her? She was so full of hope for herself and her daughter. He knew he was getting ready to destroy all that hope.

When he walked around the house to the front where Maddy waited, she had one hand on her belly and the other on the side of her face. She looked like her last friend had died and maybe that was exactly how she felt. She clearly already knew the house was empty and didn't need Hawk to tell her. Her last hope and prayer for something like a normal life had just fallen apart. When he got closer, he could see tears welling in her blue eyes. He felt panic blossom in his chest. Oh no, anything but tears.

He could remember his mother crying only once. Pappy had just shot Ma's favorite horse. Old Barney was at least thirty and crippled, and winter was coming. Barney had pulled down to skin and bones, but Ma had not wanted to let go of her old friend. She'd sobbed her heart out on Pappy's shoulder. Hawk had been only ten at the time, but his mother's tears, so seldom shed, had burned themselves into his heart. His Pap had told him later that it was the same for him. A woman's tears were a powerful weapon. Pappy had confided that he'd felt like the meanest man in Florida when he'd only been saving the old horse from suffering through another winter.

Hawk wanted to put his arms around her and comfort her. But Maddy was a little prickly about physical contact of any kind and, except when she was sleeping in the wagon, kept a proper and decorous amount of space between them at all times. She had obviously been raised a lady and was doing her best to hang on to the remnants of that upbringing, along with her dignity. So he stood at a distance and felt extremely awkward and uncomfortable. What was he supposed to do now?

Maddy gathered her skirts. "I'm going across the street. The house over there still looks occupied. Perhaps they may know where the Carvers have gone. I can follow them. I can join them wherever they are. Surely they plan to come back to Pilatka and reopen this boardinghouse."

Hawk followed her across the street. Several small houses with picket fences and landscaped yards filled with shrubs and flowers stood on a small bank along the road. Paving stones made walkways out to the street. Most of the yards were overgrown with weeds, the fences falling down and the windows on the houses boarded and shuttered.

Maddy walked toward the only house that appeared occupied and well maintained. She marched through the gate and into the yard. When she knocked on the door, an elderly woman dressed in black with a white apron answered. She had a lacy white cap that covered her gray hair tied under her chin with a ribbon. The cap had slipped and was slightly askew.

"Please, dear lady," Maddy asked. "My name is Madelaine Wilkes and I'm here looking for my sister-in-law, Rachel Carver. Do you know where the Carvers have gone? You see, they sent for me and my child to come and stay with them."

The old lady followed Maddy's pointing finger. "Oh, them boarding house folks. When we heard the Yankees were coming to Pilatka, they was one of the first to move out. I think Mr. Cornelius down at the shipping dock told me they went to Jacksonville." She paused and looked thoughtful. "Or maybe he said it was St. Augustine. I can't rightly recollect, but it was one of them places."

"Does anyone around here know exactly where they went?" Maddy asked.

"I can't say. I'm the only one left on this block. It's just me and Samuel, my houseboy. The place went crazy when we heard them damn Yankees were moving into town. They'd been up and down the river for months in those gunboats of theirs. Folks were out of their minds thinking they were going to come in here and kill everybody. I figured they'd leave me alone. I'm just an old lady and I ain't got nothing they'd want anyway."

Maddy thanked her and tottered back to the wagon. She sat down on the grass, clearly shocked. "What am I to do? I can't stay here and I haven't two pennies to rub together. I don't know anyone . . . and just look at me. I can't even take care of myself, much less Sarah."

Hawk made the only decision he could. He'd put himself in the position of her guardian, and now he was fairly caught. He wasn't a gentleman. He wasn't educated or of a religious nature, but even he knew abandoning a pregnant woman and a beautiful thirteen-year-old girl in this place would be a criminal act. Besides the old lady they had just met, the only folks he had seen in abundance were the cowhands and roughnecks at the bar last night.

He sat down next to her. She was twisting a handkerchief in her hands. She'd dab at the tears on her face and then twist some more. The small square of white lace and cotton was almost tied in a knot.

"Why don't you come on home with me," he finally said. Once the words were out, he felt a lot better. He knew he was doing the right thing, it just changed his circumstances so much. He'd taken on a pregnant woman and her child, and that was a huge responsibility. "After you have the baby and get to feeling more like yourself, you can come back here and see if the Carvers have returned, or maybe open up the boarding house and stay there . . . or something."

"I really couldn't impose on you like that, Mr. Hawkins," she said, squaring her shoulders and thrusting out her chin.

Oh, no, now he was Mr. Hawkins again.

"It wouldn't be an imposition. I have a little extra room in my house. You can cook for me and Travis, and Sarah can help clean and do chores with the horses and livestock."

Where would he put them? Hawk had no idea. The house was small. He guessed Jimmy and his wife would have to stay in the one-room cabin his father had built when they first settled the land. It was a mile from the main house and deep in the woods. No one had lived there for five or six years. He hoped the Jumpers would understand.

"The entire situation would be just too improper," Maddy said. "An unmarried man and an unmarried woman living together like that? What would your neighbors say? No, no, it just won't do, Mr. Hawkins. There's no way I could behave in that fashion, as I must set an example for Sarah. Life has been very difficult for her for over a year. I must think of Sarah."

"You need to stop worrying and getting yourself all upset," Hawk said in a soothing tone. "It's not good for your unborn child or for Sarah. And if you're thinking about the girl, what in the world are you going to do to take care of her here? There's really no other options, Miss Maddy. Believe me, I've been wracking my brains for a solution. The only smart thing you can do is come home with me."

She looked as though she were about to fall apart or go into hysterics. He felt totally at a loss. He glanced around to see if there were any gawkers. Thank God the folks riding the ferry had already mounted the hill and were out of sight. Maddy's face was the color of chalk, with two bright red spots on her cheeks, and she kept wringing that poor hanky.

He reverted to speaking to her like she was a young horse he was trying to gentle. "Miss Maddy, stop tying that hanky into knots." He firmly took it from her and held her hands. She looked at the grass under her stained dress, but didn't snatch her hands away from him. "We have no neighbors. The nearest we got are over twenty miles away. If anyone does question your presence, I'll tell them you're my housekeeper, there to take care of me and my boy. I really should have hired one for Travis years ago. I just never found the right person."

He couldn't tell her Travis was an angry, unhappy young man. His son had been thirteen when Hawk left with the cattle drive and mad as a hornet because he couldn't go. He could ride better than any hand Hawk had ever hired, shoot the eye out of a snake at fifty feet, and track an Indian across flat rocks in a drought.

His boy loved all animals and would not kill unless they needed the meat. The barn was always filled with injured creatures he'd brought home to care for. After his mother passed, Travis seemed to care only for those animals and nothing for people. It was as though he had no love or trust to give anyone. As a result, the boy had become opinionated and judgmental, quick to anger and slow to let that anger go.

And then there was Judy Bill, Jimmy Jumper's wife. Judy Bill would not take kindly to having another woman—and a white, unmarried one at that—taking over her house and her kitchen. Judy Bill's views on morality were extremely straight-laced and inflexible. What would she say about Maddy bearing a child out of wedlock?

Things would not be easy for any of them if Maddy came to live on the D-Wing. But they would all get used to it quickly, and she would be a big help with taking care of the house. There was no denying her skills in the kitchen.

Maddy looked up at him, her eyes damp with unshed tears. For a minute, he felt a shock of recognition.

Momentarily, he'd felt as though he'd known her for years. Then she sighed and closed her eyes. When she opened them she said, "I'll come to your home with you, but only because of Sarah. I must keep her safe. We've been through so much already, and she doesn't deserve being subjected to any further danger. All I want is a safe home for Sarah."

5

"Is THIS STILL THE LAKE, or is it the river?" Maddy asked Hawk as they turned the wagon along yet another large body of water. "It feels like we've been going around this lake forever."

Hawk noticed her voice had an edge to it. Her complexion was pale again, with those two bright spots of color high on her cheeks. She was wearing a large sunbonnet to shade her face from the hot sun, but tiny curls of damp hair clung to her face. Since Pilatka she'd been very quiet, and now Hawk feared her pregnancy was starting to wear on her. Each day she seemed more drained and tired, yet she would not admit it.

"We're still going around Lake George. It's big. Are you feeling okay?"

"I feel exactly the same as I did the last time you asked me that question," she said.

"And how would that be?"

Hawk didn't expect her to answer and she didn't. He shaded his eyes and looked to the west. The sun flamed big and red just above the tree line. It was hot, and thunder rumbled ominously overhead.

"I think we need to find a place to camp for the night," he said. "It looks like a storm is brewing, and it's almost dark."

A mosquito buzzed his neck and he swatted it. Desire to get home burned in him. He knew if he climbed on Beau right now and rode all night, he could be home by tomorrow evening. The trip from Pilatka should have taken three, maybe four days, and here they were pushing a week on the road. He closed his eyes and sighed. But he was stuck taking care of Maddy and Sarah, and he couldn't leave them now.

Hawk guided the wagon out of a low spot in the trail and onto a hammock, looking for a sheltered place to camp. Lightning sparked in the sky to the east and thunder followed. A clump of pines on a nearby hill looked good. At the base of the hill on the far side of the hammock, the lake glistened beneath threatening skies. Hawk clucked to the tired bay Madelaine had named Spirit. Spirit, as big a slug as was ever born, had yet to live up to his name.

He found a grassy spot under the pines and pulled Spirit to a halt just as fat raindrops began pelting them. Hawk grabbed his slicker from under the seat and slid into it. "You two get under the wagon until it stops," he ordered.

Maddy flopped heavily to the ground under the wagon, but Sarah stood looking at him. "I want to help," she said.

Rummaging in the wagon, he found a slicker he'd taken from one of the outlaws. He handed it to her. "Put this on and gather some wood."

Sarah slid into it and made a face. "Oh my, this thing stinks."

Hawk tried not to laugh. "I bet it does." Not only was

the raincoat smelly, it hung down past her ankles and dragged the ground.

The sound of a galloping horse drew their attention as the rain began to slow. Hawk reached under the seat of the wagon and pulled out his rifle. In the distance he made out the figure of a lone rider on a skinny roan horse. The chunky rider was slapping along on the back of his horse in a punishing manner, punishing for himself and for the poor animal. When the rider got closer, Hawk recognized him. It was Roscoe Beale. Now what in the world could he want?

"It's that fat outlaw," Sarah said, "the one you wounded."

"I see that. Go find some wood while I see to these horses."

The brief squall passed and Beale slowed his pace. Hawk unhitched Spirit, set up a picket line from one pine tree to another, and tied the horses to it. He unsaddled Beau and the red gelding and stacked the tack close to an oak tree, covering the saddles with saddle blankets.

When the rain stopped completely, Maddy came out from under the wagon and began rifling through her pots and pans and the boxes of food. She walked to the fire Hawk was urging to life carrying a pot of beans she'd been soaking all day, and saw the rider.

"That's Mr. Beale," she said to Hawk. "What could he want? I thought he was going to Jacksonville."

"I don't know what he wants," Hawk said. "But I think we're fixing to find out."

"Hello the camp!" Beale called out.

Hawk waved in answer. Beale was breathing hard and soaking wet, even though he wore a black duster that covered him from his thick neck to his worn boots. The roan was breathing hard too. Hawk momentarily felt guilty for giving the man the horse. Between Roscoe Beale and all the tack, the roan had to be carrying three hundred and fifty pounds.

Beale rode into the pines and stopped his horse. "Do you mind if I dismount?" he asked politely.

"Surely, Mr. Beale," Hawk said. "Come rest yourself. You look plumb tuckered out."

"Thankee kindly," Beale said as he floundered to the ground. He landed hard and grunted, and it took him a minute to straighten up. He kicked out one leg and groaned. "My knees are killing me," he said. "I'm getting too old to be bouncing all over the territory."

Beale tied his horse to the picket line and loosened the cinch.

"You might want to walk him," Hawk said. "At least until he cools off."

"Couldn't do it, my man," Beale said. "I'm afraid I couldn't walk two feet right now. It's my knees and my back. I've got the rheumatism in my joints, you know; makes them hurt something fierce."

Beale fumbled through his roomy saddlebags and pulled out a bottle. He popped the cork, guzzled some of the brown liquid, then wiped his mouth on the duster's sleeve. "That's the dandy," he said. "That'll fix me up all right and tight."

He offered the bottle to Hawk, and Hawk was tempted. What harm could one little shot of whiskey do? He took the bottle from Beale, wiped the lip off with his sleeve, tilted it, and let some of the fiery alcohol slide down his throat. "Thanks," he gasped, feeling the liquid burn all the way to his stomach. It had been a long time since he'd tasted whiskey, and this stuff was raw. He handed the bottle back to Beale, who took another pull on it before recorking it and putting it back in the pouch.

"Sam," Hawk called to Sarah. "Take Mr. Beale's horse and walk him."

Sarah's eyes grew round with fear. "Please, Mr. Hawk. He'll step all over me and he'll hurt me."

Well, Hawk thought, you learn something new every day. It had never occurred to him to ask for Sarah's help with the horses before, so he'd never learned she was scared of them. Hawk untied the roan's reins and handed them to her. "He's real tired, Sam. Just walk him down to that clump of palmetto and bring him back. Stay on his left, and don't let go of him."

She took the reins gingerly and started off. The roan didn't have the energy to do anything but try to snatch a mouthful of grass as they walked. Hawk went to check on the fire. Maddy had the beans bubbling and was creating something with cornmeal. He'd shot two wild turkeys that morning. One was hanging in the back of the wagon, while the other one was cooking in the Dutch oven. He could smell it.

Worried about how Sarah was doing walking the roan, he stood in the pines and searched for her at the edge of the hammock. She had rounded the palmettos and was on her way back, looking a little more comfortable and relaxed. The roan horse was reaching for a weed, and she was tugging on the reins with a determined look on her face.

Mr. Beale had collapsed on a big chunk of ancient lime rock and was rubbing his knees. "I thought you were headed for Jacksonville, Beale," Hawk said. "What changed your mind?"

Beale looked up at him, still rubbing his aching joints. "I had to catch up with you, Hawkins. After what you done for me, I couldn't let you ride into a trap."

❖ ❖ ❖

"You know I hate to do this to you, Rosie," Travis Hawkins said to the black and white skunk tucked under one arm. "But I need to get them out of the house, and this seems like the only way I can be sure they're all outside."

Travis could see the house in the late-evening gloom. The sun had already set, and Travis knew there would be no moon. The outlaws had two men on watch. One sat by the barn, and one stood leaning against a support on the back porch.

Earlier, fifteen of them had ridden out with their leader, leaving his home in the hands of a handful of outlaws. If he was ever going to get in there and get the letter, now was the time.

The scumbag by the barn was tall with red hair. He was ugly as sin and it looked to Travis like he was a deserter. Travis could tell by the remnants of Confederate gray he wore. The deserter seemed to think he was a big bad gunman. He kept drawing his pistol over and over again, practicing. Travis had to admit he looked pretty darn fast.

The other moron on watch was a deserter too, but he looked to be wearing yellow Union breeches and a Confederate coat. No telling what army he'd belonged to and left. He had a thick black beard and no shirt under his gray jacket, and he was even uglier than the other guy. His chest was covered with black hair thick as fur on a bear. He was chewing a huge wad of tobacco. His cheek bulged and he spit constantly. Both men were wide awake and alert.

Travis grabbed the basket with four of Rosie's grown kits in it and slid on his belly toward the house. The house sat

high, built on top of an old shell mound, and the log foundation had the house over a foot off the ground. There were no
shrubs or bushes in the front yard, and the backyard was dirt,
swept clean. A big oak tree shaded the house in the back, and
thick woods grew just behind the oak. The well was back
there, along with a smokehouse and a springhouse. Travis
crept through the woods behind the house. He could see he
had twenty feet of swept yard to cross to make it to the porch.

The outlaw on the porch spit again, hitched up his sus-
penders, and moseyed down the back steps. After looking
around the yard, peering under a washtub by lifting it with
the barrel of his rifle, opening and shutting the doors of the
smokehouse and springhouse, and checking the trees border-
ing the yard, he headed down the path to the outhouse.
Travis smiled.

Slipping quietly to the porch, Travis ducked under it
and crawled under the house, pushing the basket ahead of
him. When he got to a spot under his bedroom, he reached
up and found the rope handle to a trapdoor. He'd been sneaking out of his room through a trapdoor he'd cut into the floor
since he was ten. Pa didn't even know about it. Travis had
covered it with a rag rug Judy Bill had made for him.

When he pushed on the door, a crack of light gleamed
from inside the house through the rag rug. He pushed it up a
little more, peeked inside, and closed it in a hurry. The place
was crawling with outlaws. He'd seen at least seven, counting
the ones outside. He was afraid Rosie would be sacrificed, and
he hesitated. Killing or even allowing the killing of any critter except for food was strictly against his personal code. But
if the outlaws found Pa's last letter, they would know how to
get to the gold.

Pa had written to him the night the Yankees had captured him. He'd told Travis exactly where Grandpa's gold was hidden and how to get to it. The letter had arrived two years ago, brought to the house by Joseph, Jimmy's son. Joseph had been on Pa's last cattle drive. He'd been captured with Pa. Joseph told them the Yankees hadn't watched him so close because he was an Indian. They weren't interested in holding Indians, or so the Yankees had told Joseph. He'd managed to escape and make it home with Pa's letter.

The outlaws had been sniffing around the spring. They must be looking for the gold, so Rosie would have to take her chances. If they found Pa's letter, they would know right where to go.

He stroked the black and white striped head and slid Rosie into the lighted room. He quickly stuffed all four kits in after her. The kits were less tame, and Travis breathed a sigh of relief when they didn't spray him.

The result of Rosie and the kits' insertion was quick and extreme. Apparently, the outlaws had been drinking. Furniture crashed and the front and back doors flew open. Outlaws ran into the dogtrot, fell off the porch, and yelled cuss words a mile a minute. Travis could hear Rosie and the kits scratching their way across the wood floors. Then gunfire erupted, and Travis cringed.

But this was his chance. He slipped into his bedroom, found the hole in the cotton cover of his moss-stuffed mattress, and pulled out Pa's letter. Rosie waddled over to him, clearly confused. Travis scooped her up along with three of the kits. He couldn't find number four. After tossing them under the house, he tucked the letter into his pocket and peered through the bedroom door. Kit number four was waving his tail like a flag. That was a sign of things to come. One of those bad men was taking aim with a big pistol.

The gun weaved back and forth in the outlaw's drunken hands as the man tried to get a bead on the kit. But before he could get off his shot, the kit turned around and sprayed him. The outlaw fired and the shot went wild.

Travis wrinkled his nose. He'd forgotten just how awful skunk spray could be. He darted in and scooped up the kit while the poor guy was scrubbing at his eyes, and then dove through the trap, slamming it shut behind him.

Travis tossed all the skunks into the basket and then scrambled around under the house, dragging the basket behind him as he checked out the situation. He saw most of the activity centered in the front yard and the dogtrot, and the outhouse door was still shut. Leaving the skunks behind now that they were safe, Travis crawled out from under the house and scampered across the swept backyard and into the woods. He climbed a tree in the woods behind the house. It was well covered in thick bushes, moss, and vines. Satisfied that his mission had been accomplished, he settled in the crook of a large branch and watched. Drunken outlaws poked under the house, behind the outhouse, and at the edge of the woods with their pistols and rifles drawn, still cussing. Travis smothered a laugh. *What goobers, thrown into a panic by a few little skunks.*

It was dark. The moon was a thin sliver in the sky and the stars were covered by a hazy layer of clouds left over from the evening storm. There was no light to help the confused men. One or two had lanterns; the rest were just about blind, searching only with light cast from the open doors of the cabin. The hunt quickly ended, as it was a half-hearted attempt anyway. The bad men didn't really want to find the skunks. Released from the basket, Rosie and her kits made their escape into the dark woods.

Travis patted the pocket with the letter. Pa's secret was safe. The letter was important to him, since it was the last time he'd heard from Pa. Joseph had come back and told them Pa had been taken prisoner by the Yankees. So many things could have happened to his father and they had no way of knowing. He and the Jumpers had no idea how to find out where Pa was, how to contact him, or how to find out what had happened to him. Pa could even be dead. He must be dead, or he would have come home by now.

Travis remembered the last time he'd seen his Pa. He'd been mad because Pa wouldn't take him on the cattle drive. It wasn't fair as he'd helped round up the cows, helping out with the branding and castrating right along with Pa, Joseph, and Jimmy Jumper. Pa should have taken him on the drive. Then he would know where his father was and he wouldn't be here alone now just waiting and not knowing.

As things were, it felt like he and the Jumpers could end up waiting forever. And the Jumpers wouldn't do anything about these outlaws living in their home. They were afraid. Indians were hunted and killed in these parts. The only thing the Jumpers were considering was leaving. Now that the war was over and Pa hadn't come home, they had started to talk about going south to live with the tribes in the Great Swamp.

Travis knew he would be welcomed by the Indians. That wasn't the problem. But if they all left, no one would be here if Pa did come home. The outlaws would take over and run the D-Wing and the Hawkins' ranch would be no more. Travis clenched his fists. He would not leave and he would not allow that to happen. If the Jumpers decided to leave, he wasn't going. He was staying. He would fight for the family and for his birthright.

6

"WHAT KIND OF TRAP?" Hawk demanded. "What are you talking about, Beale?" Hawk grabbed the roan from Sarah and quickly tied him to a tree. The horse had stopped blowing, and the bands of sweat were drying in the cooler breeze after the brief storm.

"Go help your mother, Sam," Hawk ordered, sending the girl away so she couldn't overhear what Beale had to say. What could the man be talking about? What trap?

"Snake Barber has taken over your home," Beale said simply. "He's waiting for you with over twenty men. He's the one sent me and the boys after you."

Hawk felt like he'd been hit with a hammer. His chest was tight and he couldn't catch his breath. Beale had just told him the one thing he'd most feared hearing. Anger replaced the moment of shock, rage so sudden and so intense it made his head feel like it was going to explode. He grabbed his face with the tips of his fingers and squeezed. Snake Barber was in his home? Oh God, then where was Travis? What about the Jumpers?

Hawk grabbed Beale by his lapels and jerked the heavy man to his feet. He put one strong hand around the outlaw's thick neck and squeezed. "You better start from the beginning and explain everything to me right now," he snarled, inches from Beale's quivering jowls. "You were in on this with Barber. I ought to kill you right now."

He let Beale go. The large man flopped onto his rock with a wheeze as all the air left him. He rubbed his throat and looked up at Hawk. "No, Hawkins, it's like I said. Barber moved his men into your house. I had nothing to do with it, I was just there. Barber's got them all looking for something and he won't tell any of us what."

"Why did they attack us the other night?" Hawk asked. "Did he know I was there? Was he looking for me?"

Beale shook his head, still rubbing his throat. "No, no, he wasn't after you. It's the woman he wants. He's in love with Mrs. Wilkes, and he wants her back."

Hawk's head spun. His entire world felt upside down. It was as though everything he had always known and trusted to be true had been proven false. His home was under attack.

Damn, he remembered feeling he needed to get home when they were back in the woods south of Alligator. But it was a good thing he'd stuck with Madelaine. Suddenly she'd become his ace in the hole. He'd hate to have to use her as a bargaining chip, but when it came down to dust, Travis and the D-Wing were everything.

His mind churned over the many possibilities Beale's information had created. If Barber wanted Madelaine, then Snake had to be the father of her unborn child. Snake was the man who had taken over her home and forced himself on her. And the big question in Hawk's mind was, did Snake know Madelaine was expecting?

"What about Travis? Where is my son?"

Beale cringed. Hawk had stepped closer, hovering like he was ready to grab Beale again. Hawk saw the man's fear and stepped away. "I won't hurt you," he said. "Just tell me about Travis."

"When we took over the house, no one was there. It was empty. It looked like whoever had been there had left, run off in a hurry. The cookstove out back was still warm. There was hot water on it for washing, and dirty plates were stacked in a tub on the floor. I don't know where your boy is. We never found him."

Hawk needed to think. He couldn't understand how all this had come about. "Start over and tell me how all this happened, right from the beginning."

"I don't know what all went on in Georgia. It was like I said, I met them in a saloon and they told me they were planning a job with a big payoff. None of the men seemed to know what the payoff was. They just said it was really big, so I asked if they needed a man good with explosives, and they signed me on."

Beale's face was the color of wet flour. He was dripping with sweat and smelled like fear. Hawk knew the smell well from his prison camp days. The stink of fear never left any of them at Pointe Lookout. It suddenly occurred to Hawk that the man was doing him a favor by coming here and telling him all of this, and he had done it voluntarily to pay back Hawk's good deed.

He could barely handle the emotions rushing through him. He was terrified for Travis, mad as hell, and confused. It wasn't a good blend.

"Hey, man, I'm sorry I jumped on you, it's just that I'm a little worried about my boy and my home. Please go on."

Color eased back into Beale's face. He mopped his dripping chin and cheeks with a soiled handkerchief dug out of the pocket of his duster. "I made friends with one of the guys. He was a deserter from the Union Army, down here from Pennsylvania somewhere. His name was Lester Suggs, but they called him Red. He told me the boys moved into an old plantation called Twelve Oaks while the war was still being fought. There were twenty or so of them when they moved in. He said some of them left and some more joined. It was a fine place for them to hide out because there was plenty to eat, fair hunting in the area, the house was grand, and they even had three women slaves. Most of them had never had it so good.

"Old Red said the lady that owned the plantation was real pretty, and Barber spent a lot of time with her. When the Yankees started getting close, the men left, but before they left, they killed 'most everything on the place and took all the food with them. Red told me Snake couldn't kill the pretty lady, so he left her there to make it on her own."

Hawk leaned closer. "And then what?"

"Well, that was when they were headed for Jacksonville and I met up with them. Barber decided he couldn't live without the pretty woman and sent some of the men back to get her. I rode to your ranch with them and then Barber told me to find his boys and see what they were doing. I found them getting ready to jump your camp. And that's all I know, Hawkins. I've told you everything."

Hawk paced back and forth. Madelaine must have supper ready because he could smell the turkey. His mind churned, turning the possibilities over and over. He knew without a doubt all of them were in terrible danger. What Beale had told him made that much plain, and Hawk knew Snake wouldn't leave it alone. If he really was after Madelaine, he would come for her again. And if the kid who had escaped the other night had made it safely back to the D-Wing, Snake Barber must know or at least suspect that his woman was with Hawk.

He could feel himself slipping into his warrior role. That's what Jimmy Jumper had always called it, Warrior Hawk. Without thinking about it, he would shut all of his emotions away in a dark place where they would not interfere in any of his decisions. He was immersed in the danger, wrapping it around him, probing every possibility, making plans and discarding them.

The first conclusion he immediately came to was that tonight would be the most dangerous night. He calculated time needed for the boy to get back to the ranch and for another, bigger party of raiders to make it to their position. The moon was only a sliver tonight, and it would be extra dark because of the cloud cover. The hair stood up on the back of his neck. He could feel them out there. Snake Barber was coming.

"Don't get comfortable," he snapped to Beale. "I got a feeling we're going to have company tonight. We need to move Madelaine and Sam to safety."

Beale's eyes flew open inside their nests of fat. "What are you trying to tell me, Hawk?"

"I'm saying, if they're coming, it'll be tonight."

"But how do you know? How can you be so sure?"

Hawk shook his head. "Don't ask, 'cause I don't know. I

just know if they're coming, then tonight's the night. I can feel it in here and here." He pointed to his gut and his chest. "And one thing I'm flat sure of, if Snake Barber knows Madelaine and I are together on this road, he'll come to us. He ain't gonna wait for us to come to him. He's not a patient man."

"You can say that again," Beale said.

Taking long, purposeful strides, Hawk went straight to Madelaine. There was no point in keeping this from her. She had to know the danger and what was happening. He worried about the effect it could have on her. Would she be able to handle the additional stress? Life kept dealing her one nasty blow after another.

And what was Maddy going to think when she heard Snake Barber was tied to him as well as to her? The coincidence was incredible. She might not want to come home with him. Her fear of Barber was very real. The potential danger she faced from Barber was just as real.

With Barber's men camped out in Hawk's house, it might put her in even more danger to take her anywhere near the D-Wing. He hardly knew what to do. She would have to know and make the decision herself.

Madelaine looked up when she heard Hawk approaching. She saw right away that something was bothering him, something was wrong. His face was made of steel. His jawline was hard, his mouth thin and set, and his eyes narrowed and black. She stood up, cradling her aching back with one hand. "What's wrong now?"

While he explained the situation, Madelaine stared at him. Every word he said filled her with more and more dread. Just the thought that Snake Barber wanted her back was enough to send her screaming, but Barber was in possession of Hawk's home. Somehow, their fates and their lives seemed to be tangled together, tightly woven into a ball of craziness with Snake Barber at the center.

"Why does Snake want your ranch, Hawk?" She asked when he had finished. "What is he after?"

"He wants the gold my father saved over years of selling cattle to Cuba," Hawk told her. "But all the gold in Cuba is worth nothing to me without my son. I know in my heart Barber will be here tonight. Everything is right for it and I can feel him coming."

Maddy looked into his eyes. She saw determination and strength of purpose, but couldn't understand how he knew Barber was coming here or why he figured it would be tonight. She didn't want it to be tonight or any night. She wanted to just blank it out and not think about it at all. She was so tired, and just thinking about Barber anywhere close by sent waves of fatigue washing over her. She felt ready to drop into a swoon.

"This is all so crazy, Hawk, I hardly know what to say. What should I do? I hate walking into a trap, which we will be if we go directly to your home. Barber scares me. He scares me so badly, I can't think straight. Why are you so sure he's coming here? Please, I can't handle too much more. It's all too much, really too much."

"I know it sounds crazy, but I really believe Barber's headed here and headed here tonight. It's my firm belief that we're not going to have to wait to deal with him until we get home. If I'm right, he's probably on his horse with his men coming here now. I know the man, he's no dummy and he has no patience. If he thinks you're here with me on the road home, he'll be coming after us."

Madelaine could feel the bottom dropping out of her stomach. Snake Barber headed here. How many times had she imagined Barber catching her and dragging her off to live as a slave with him again? And what would Snake do if he knew she was carrying his child?

Madelaine put the back of her hand to her forehead. Suddenly dizzy, she glanced around for a place to sit. Her fragile world was crashing down around her. And what about poor Sarah, what would happen to her?

Hawk must have seen her waiver. His strong arm wrapped around her back, giving her support. "I'm sorry to have to tell you all this, Maddy, as I do know and understand some of what you've been through."

She shrugged off his arm and stood up straight. She could handle this. She'd lived through worse and didn't need his sympathy. "You do not know what I have been through," she said through lips stiffened with fear and indignation. "Please do not ever say that again. No one knows what I lived through." She straightened her back and smoothed her dress over her belly. "Now, tell me what we should do, for if Snake Barber is truly on his way here, I wish to do all I can to make ready."

"Now that's the Maddy I know," Hawk said.

Maddy felt like boxing his ears. Just once, she wished she could be permitted the luxury of collapsing in a fit of hysterics. Just once she wished she could let someone else carry her burdens. But she had to be strong, strong for Sarah and the new baby. "Tell me what I need to do to help," she said.

"Well, if the food's ready, let's eat," Hawk said. "Then we're going to have to do some desperate things you're probably not going to like. But with some preparation and determination, we'll get out of this. You'll see."

She narrowed her eyes and glared at him. Things she didn't like. What on earth could he mean? Half the things she did every day she not only didn't like, she actually hated. Like bouncing down a rutted trail eight and a half months pregnant, for example, or sleeping on the ground with only a thin pallet beneath her. It was hard enough to get comfortable toting a baby around in your belly. She hadn't had a decent night's sleep since she'd left Twelve Oaks. Whatever Hawk came up with, it couldn't be much worse, could it?

After supper, Maddy and Sarah packed a few important necessities into knapsacks. Leading Beau, with the bay horse Spirit and John mule tied behind, Hawk led them into the lake. Madelaine suddenly realized there were worse things than sleeping on the ground, much worse things. She was terrified.

"I know there are alligators in this water," she hissed to him as they waded in up to their knees. "And what about snakes?"

"We'll be fine," Hawk said. "I've been dealing with gators all my life. Just don't dawdle."

Madelaine snorted. *Just don't dawdle.* She weighed a million pounds and her wet dress was adding to the drag. Was he expecting her to get up and run like a gazelle? Sarah took hold of her hand as they plowed through water now up to her waist—or what used to be her waist.

Beale slogged along behind them. Both Hawk and

Beale had rifles ready. Madelaine fell into a hole. Water rushed into her nose. She snorted and floundered, but Hawk was there. He dropped Beau's lead rope and lifted her by her elbow. "You all right?"

"I'm perfect," she said, slapping at the swarm of mosquitoes around her head.

"It's only a little farther to the island. Keep your chin up."

He retrieved Beau's lead line and immediately cocked and fired the rifle. The water erupted in a flurry of movement, causing the horses and the mule to plunge and snort. Madelaine could hear something large thrashing in the water. She heard more thrashing and grunting, and Madelaine was sure Hawk had shot a gator that was now being devoured by its mates.

"It's gators, ain't it, Ma?" Sarah said. "Mr. Hawk just shot a gator and the others are eating it."

"Just keep walking, Sam," Maddy said.

The water quickly grew shallower. Maddy dragged her wet skirts onto dry land and shook them out. She wished she had just taken them off and waded over in her shift. Who cared what Beale or Hawk thought anyway? Cabbage-head palms and one gnarled oak grew on the island, along with palmettos and grass. The soil was mostly sand and crushed shells. She knew this because she could feel it crunching beneath her feet. A long time ago this had probably been an Indian camp.

It was now pitch-dark and Maddy could barely see the ground. Hawk took a lantern from John mule's pack and lit it, but the faint gleam it cast illuminated little. He then led them to the center of the island, which was a small hill with the clump of palms and the one twisted oak growing out of it.

After hobbling the horses, he helped Maddy spread a blanket on the island's highest point at the base of the oak tree. "Sit down here and wait until one of us comes to get you—Beale and I have to go back. And Maddy, whatever you do, don't leave this island. Gators hunt at night."

Madelaine gasped. "You knew that and you led us out here? Are they going to come up here after us?"

"I told you I knew what I was doing. You can see them by the red of their eyes. They only drop below the surface of the water right before they attack. If one comes up on the island, use Sam's scattergun and shoot it in the belly. The others will fall on it and eat it." He handed the shotgun to her and turned around to leave.

"Don't leave us here, Hawk, please. I'm afraid of the alligators."

"Don't worry so much, Maddy. If the gators get too close, climb the oak tree. It has lots of low branches."

"I'm so comforted," Madelaine snapped.

"Listen, Maddy, I don't want to leave you and Sam, but I have to. How else are we gonna deal with Snake Barber? I have to go. I have to take him on and defeat him. Then he won't bother us ever again. Now don't you be worrying yourself, it's bad for that baby. You know I wouldn't leave you out here if I didn't think you'd be fine. You and Sam are a lot safer out here, especially with what I have planned."

Are we? Madelaine thought as she watched Beale and Hawk enter the water and wade back to the camp. What would happen to her and Sam if Hawk was killed by Barber? She shook her head to clear the terrible vision. He had to win and he had to kill Snake. Tears rolled down her cheeks.

Hawk was her only hope—and right now he was wading through gator-infested water.

She tried to arrange her bulk more comfortably—if only killing Snake did not involve her sitting here on this island surrounded by alligators and swarms of mosquitoes.

Settling onto the ground, she took stock of her situation, what was here and what she was responsible for. Hawk's big stud, her new wagon horse, and John mule all cropped the thin grass on top of the mound of sand Hawk had euphemistically labeled an island. The horses were restless. Small wonder, since they were all sitting ducks in the middle of this lake. They had two packs filled with some water, a few biscuits, and dried meat, along with blankets and mosquito netting.

Hawk had left the little red Cracker horse back on dry land along with Beale's roan and all her possessions. Everything she owned was on that wagon. Not to mention that she and Sarah would likely be sucked dry of blood by mosquitoes before morning, if the gators didn't eat them first.

"Here, Mama." Sarah handed her a mosquito net she'd taken out of her knapsack. "Mr. Hawk said we have to make a tent out of this with some sticks. If we let it touch our skin, the mosquitoes will just bite us through the netting."

Sarah felt her way to the gnarled oak and snapped off several dead branches. She came back and stuck four in the ground, then draped the mosquito netting over them.

"See, Mama, with this little tent over us we'll be just dandy."

The two of them huddled together on the blanket under their little mosquito net tent, and they waited. The night was warm, with thin clouds drifting across a sliver of moon. Maddy could smell the lake. It smelled of vegetation, fish, and dampness, with a hint of something floral. She and Sarah watched the far shore where Hawk had a fire blazing away, shedding enough light for Maddy to see him and Beale moving about, preparing something. She hoped it was the nastiest surprise Jake the Snake Barber had ever had. She hoped it killed him.

7

"So, Beale, what's in your saddlebags?" Hawk said. "You got any of those explosives you said you were so good with stashed in them saddlebags?"

"I don't have nothing fancy like nitroglycerine, though I have worked with it," Beale said. "But I think I have everything you'll need." He opened his bulky saddlebags and began pulling out oilcloth bundles tied with string. He opened one and Hawk smiled. Beale revealed several pouches of black powder, some cylinders, each with what looked like a long string attached, and some blasting caps—all the makings of several nice explosives.

"I've been playing around with chemicals, saltpeter, and gunpowder most of my life," Beale explained. "My father came here from England, where it was his job to make fireworks displays for the queen. It's fascinating stuff, really."

"I can imagine," Hawk said, picking up a long string of red paper tubes with tiny wads of tissue paper sticking out of each tube. "What are these?"

"Those are Chinese firecrackers," Beale said, smiling.

"Lots of noise, but no destruction. Here, see these? They're called ground rats." He handed Hawk a hard paper tube that was similar but was open at one end. "Light this little fellow and throw it on the ground and it spins around shooting flames out this end over here."

"This is all we need right here, Beale," Hawk said. "I sure am glad you're on my side. Oh boy, I'm gonna have me some fun."

Beale smiled. "Let's get to it, then. What ya got in mind?"

After they set what Hawk thought was enough traps for Barber and his men and he felt confident that his plan would work, he told Beale to leave. "Get on your horse and go somewhere safe, Beale," he said. "You've done all you can for me and Madelaine. Get out of here and save yourself."

Beale looked confused. "I had planned to stay and help," he said. "I do like blowing things up, you know. I was looking forward to the excitement."

Hawk put his arm on the large man's shoulders. "It's going to be dangerous, Beale, a lot more dangerous than I would wish you to be exposed to. You really helped me here, old man," he said kindly. "And you've helped Madelaine. There's nothing you can do now but get in my way, and I don't want you to get killed. This is my fight and I know what I'm doing. I like working alone. It's what I do best."

"You just have to fire your pistol into each of those ground charges to ignite them," Beale said as he climbed up on the big limestone rock to ease his way into the saddle. "The one under this rock has a three-minute fuse. When you light it, you better be running."

"Thanks for everything, Roscoe," Hawk said as they

shook hands. "I'm in your debt."

"Quite the contrary, my lad," Beale said as he spurred the staggering roan forward. "We're even."

Hawk walked to Madelaine's wagonload of belongings and started lifting boxes and trunks, looking for anything useful. "What in the world is she planning to do with all this rope?" Hawk muttered to himself. There were several large coils of fine hemp rope under a heavy brass-bound trunk. He pulled it out and fingered the twisted hemp, which was over one inch in diameter.

Hawk had always liked messing around with rope. He'd been known to use it when working cattle and breaking horses like those Texas cowboys did. He still worked with dogs and his whip, but sometimes you just had to rope a cow or a bad horse. He'd made himself a lariat rope by braiding rawhide cut from two entire cowhides. He would start cutting the rawhide for the rope on the outside of the skin and continue around the edge of it in an unbroken strip. The hemp rope was different, but just as strong.

Maddy had many other interesting things hidden deep in the wagon. He found a new ax, two shovels, coils of slick wire, several tanned deer hides, and a cow hide. He briefly wondered what was in the crates and trunks, but didn't have the time to look. The wagon was a veritable treasure trove.

He puttered around stringing some of Maddy's wire and hanging ropes from the pine trees. It was something he'd done as a boy, swinging from one tree to another and swinging off ropes into the big spring. His father had laughed at him, but now it seemed his old game might come in handy. When he was finished, he grabbed a satchel filled with surprises for Snake and shinnied up a tall pine, where he lodged himself firmly in the crook of a thick branch to wait.

If Snake was going to attack tonight, he would not do it in the dark. He wouldn't even be able to find this camp in the dark. Which was why Hawk had built a huge fire. He wanted Snake to find him.

The camp was only accessible from the north or northeast. The south side of the hammock was lowland filled with brambles, palmetto, weeds, vines, and scrub trees that formed an impenetrable, snake-filled thicket. It faded into wetland that was probably full of snakes as well. On the west side, the lake wrapped around the hammock, blocking any access from that direction. No, Snake would have to come at him from the north.

Hawk figured dawn or first light for the attack, because that's when he would do it. Snake's men needed to be able to see each other to coordinate their movements, otherwise they could end up shooting each other. Hawk laughed to himself as he shifted his position in the tree. It would be funny if they started shooting at each other in the dark and would sure save him some trouble. When it was about two hours till first light, Hawk settled himself in the tree and tried to rest.

As Snake rode out of the D-Wing, a red-tailed hawk flew over his head and screeched. He wasn't superstitious, but it seemed like a bad omen. He spurred his horse into a lope and took off toward Pilatka. The fresh animal bucked once, then settled into a steady pace.

He had thought this out good, and if he was calculating

right, Hawk would have crossed the river in Pilatka and turned south. Snake had counted days and figured in time for dragging a wagonload, a woman, and a kid. By his estimate, Hawk should be getting close to Lake George right now.

Things were quickly turning sour at the D-Wing. The whiskey barrel was empty, and the men were getting restless. They wanted to know what the big score was and when they were gonna find it. Snake had no answers, and he didn't want to tell them what they were after. Those men were all the scum of the earth, and every one of them would kill his own mother for a three-dollar gold piece.

He needed to turn the tide and get things moving in his favor somehow. If he could capture Hawk and make him talk, they could grab the gold and get out of there. Keeping Hawk's ranch was not part of his plan. He had no intention of staying in Florida. No, he wanted to go up North, somewhere like New York City where it was more civilized, where he felt he would find men like himself with more discerning tastes and interests than these cow-hunting fools in Florida.

He'd seen some of the fine things to be had in the North, and he knew it was different up there. There were cities there with lots of opportunities for a man with his skills. No more working in the heat, sweating and swatting flies and gnats. He fancied himself all dressed up in a swallowtail suit with a silk tie and hanky, living high on the hog in a big brick house with servants waiting on him hand and foot. Now that was the life.

Maybe he could use Madelaine as a bargaining chip to get Hawk to talk; maybe Hawk was sweet on her. Hawk's kid was sure out of the picture, as his men couldn't find hide nor hair of the brat. Travis Hawkins had disappeared like smoke into a night sky. Snake shrugged. He wasn't giving up. He knew that money existed and there had to be a way to get to it.

He rode on silently, his men straggling behind him. Many were already starting to complain. He swore to himself. If he didn't need them, he'd shoot them all right now.

Skeeter rode up beside him, and the two men trotted out ahead of the rest. "The men don't think this trip is worth a nickel whore," Skeeter said. "They want to turn around and go back. There's two that just want to keep riding and head north. They're sick of all this waiting around."

"You think I don't know that?" Snake jerked his horse's reins hard, causing the animal to drop his head and plunge.

"Don't be jobbin' that *caballo* in the mouth," Skeeter said. "He'll buck your ass off. He needs a lot more riding than we been a doing lately."

"You think I don't know that?" Snake snapped, and jerked the reins again. His horse crow-hopped a few steps and lashed out at Skeeter's mare with a hind foot. Snake easily brought the gelding under control by stabbing the animal in the sides with his spurs and spinning the horse in a tight circle. "If he don't straighten up, I'll tie him to a tree, choke him with a log chain, throw him on his side, cover him with a tarp, and leave him there in the noonday sun."

"Well, he don't deserve it," Skeeter said. "He's a good horse. You're the one riding like an idjit. You got the worst hands of any cow hunter I ever knowed."

"Do you think the men will hang on long enough for us to find Hawk's gold?" Snake said, ignoring Skeeter's cutting remark. He tolerated Skeeter's insolence because they'd been close friends since childhood. All the men understood this relationship and respected Skeeter.

"Hard to say." Skeeter filled his jaw with a huge chunk of tobacco. " 'Pends on how long it takes. I'd say they're all in need of a little action. They either need to kill something or get laid."

"Maybe I should let them go to Enterprise for a Friday night of fun," Snake said.

"That might could work, Snake. But I don't know if they'd come back when you needed 'em."

"If I can just capture Hawk tonight and get Maddy back, things will change," Snake said. "And hell, if we do run into Hawk, there'll be action enough for all of them. He won't give up without a fight, a big fight."

The day wore on. The horses slowed their pace and had to be pushed. It was hot, and the mosquitoes and yellowhead flies made it twice as miserable. When the sun began setting over the trees to the west, Snake stopped. Storm clouds rolled over the treetops. They took shelter under their slickers as a cloudburst drenched them.

After the rain, Snake let the men break for several hours. They sat sullenly on the ground and ate cold meat and bread out of their saddlebags. With their bellies full, they rolled cigarettes, chewed, or napped. Two hours after dark, Snake got them moving again. Grumbling under their breaths, the men climbed back on the horses and the group moved on.

With the moon a mere sliver and the stars obscured by a thin layer of clouds, the going got rough and slow. It was dark and the horses were tired, but Snake kept pushing them. About two hours before dawn, Snake spotted a huge fire blazing in a clump of old pine trees on top of a hammock.

"What kind of dumbass would build a fire that big?"

Skeeter asked as Snake lifted his hand and stopped the men.

"Either a stupid woman trying to get rid of mosquitoes or someone setting a trap," Snake answered. He hoped it was a stupid woman. A stupid woman named Madelaine.

The fire on the hill slowly died, and as dawn grew closer, Snake could feel the excitement and anxiety building in his chest. He knew that had to be Maddy up there. He wanted her so bad it was a burning in his belly. The wanting had been a fire he hadn't been able to quench for the last eight months, and it was making him crazy. He wanted to rush up the hill to that hammock and claim her right now. To hell with being careful.

The men slept rolled in their blankets with their heads resting on saddles while the hobbled horses grazed. Snake hadn't been able to close his eyes. He walked the perimeter of the hammock and discovered there was only one way to approach it. The big lake bordered the hammock on the west, and the southern approach was a mass of bramble bushes, palmettos, Spanish Bayonet, small trees, and—no doubt—snakes. It would take a man with a machete a week just to cut a path to the top of the hammock. And he'd make enough noise doing it to wake the dead. No, his only approach was from the north. There was plenty of cover on the north slope of the hammock from scrub oaks, small palms, and clumps of broom grass. He moved in closer. He just had to see.

While the men were asleep, he slipped from one clump of cover to another until he got close enough to see a big wagon and a horse tied to a tree. The wagon was piled high with boxes and trunks that looked like mostly women's things. No man would tote around a yellow carpet bag with embroidered roses on it. But what really clinched it for Snake was the horse. He recognized one of the tethered horses as Texas Murphy's little red Cracker gelding. This was the right camp and Maddy was here somewhere, probably with Hawk.

He wanted to get closer. He wanted to rush in and steal Maddy away. He could make out several large lumps near the dying fire that looked like sleeping folks wrapped in blankets. He didn't see anyone on watch, but if Hawk was in charge of this party, there was sure to be at least one man on watch, and that man would be Caleb Hawkins.

The far eastern horizon showed the first fingers of light when he began waking the men. Skeeter rolled over and slowly climbed out of his blanket. "I hope this is the right camp, boss. I'd sure hate to attack a bunch of strangers for no reason."

"Oh, it is," Snake said with satisfaction. "I saw Murphy's horse tied to a tree and a wagon filled with women's crap. I know she's here. She's gotta be."

Skeeter hauled himself to his feet and stretched. "I wish you'd ferget about that dang woman. She's poison, I'm telling you, she's poison."

Snake frowned at Skeeter. "Watch your blasted mouth when you talk about my woman. Don't even talk 'bout her at all. You don't know the first thing about love. You don't know what it feels like when a woman gets under your skin and you can't get her out of your head. You ain't never been in love."

Skeeter nodded. "Yeah, you're right about that, boss. And I'll tell you something—I don't ever want to be in love. It looks like a dang uncomfortable condition to me from watching you. Well, if it's the right camp, I guess we better get up and get this show rolling."

The men were slow getting up. They grumbled at first, but came around when Snake told them he knew this was the right camp. There were fifteen of them. That should be enough men to take out one man, one woman, and a kid. Snake forgot about the blazing fire. He forgot all he knew about Hawk. In his haste to get Maddy back, he forgot about the red-tailed hawk flying overhead as they'd pulled out of the D-Wing in the early-morning light. He forgot about everything but Maddy Wilkes.

Travis was tired, but happy. He'd decided to follow the out-laws after he had the letter safely in his possession. The letter had weighed heavily on his mind. It contained the last words he'd had from his father, and it might be the last time he ever did hear from Pa. But holding on to the letter represented too much risk. It imparted knowledge best kept secret. So Travis had burned it, sad to see it go up in flames but happy to know his father's secret was safe.

It took hard riding to catch up to the fifteen outlaws, but his marsh tacky Light Foot was fast and game. Barely over fourteen hands, Light Foot could run from sunup to sundown without breaking a sweat. Bred for the climate out of Spanish stock left in Florida hundreds of years ago, marsh tackies were as tough as nails, agile, and the perfect horse for cow hunting on the palmetto plains.

When the leader of the group had stopped and made camp for the night, Travis had seen the fire on the hill. He knew for a fact that if the camp on the hammock were his dad's, there would be no bonfire. But for some reason, the outlaws were lying low and camping out of sight of the hammock. There must be something up there or someone they wanted.

Travis felt the disappointment sink in. He'd been sure they were coming for Pa. But something on that hammock had the outlaws' attention. If they were interested, then he was interested. After dismounting, he kept Light Foot saddled but dropped his reins and let the little horse graze. Then he took his rifle out of the scabbard and crawled on his hands and knees up close to the sleeping bad guys.

Snake was clearly upset. He paced back and forth until finally, close to dawn, he left the camp, skulking around the base of the hammock. Travis followed.

He watched Snake slip from cover and approach the camp. He saw the man look over the wagon and the red Cracker horse tied to a tree. He saw him stand in plain sight and stare at the dying fire. Then he came back down the hill. Travis shrugged his shoulders. What the heck? He might as well check it out a little better than that.

As he crawled on his belly closer to the fire, Travis noticed several small mounds of dirt that had recently been piled up. He saw a long string running out from beneath a large limestone rock. He ducked beneath a thin wire stretched tightly between two trees, looked around, and saw several more lines between other trees. Memories stirred deep inside his mind. He'd seen his father set traps like this before. The whole hammock was littered with traps. When he looked up, he saw ropes dangling from tall pine trees and he smiled. He could have laughed and danced a jig. Pa was here.

8 🌾

HAWK WOKE FROM A DOZE high in his tree and saw Jake the Snake Barber standing near and staring at the dying fire. He only saw the man's silhouette, but easily recognized the flat-crowned leather hat favored by Barber. When most men were wearing large hats with a wide, floppy brim, Snake always wore one with a stiff brim and low crown.

So it was true. His jaw tightened as he ground his teeth and clenched his fists. Hawk hadn't really doubted Beale's story, but seeing Barber standing in the small clearing set his anger ablaze.

He leaned forward, straddling the limb of the pine tree, and sniffed the wind like a wolf. He fancied he could smell the rank outlaw. Ice filled his heart. This man had moved into his home and threatened his family. He was cruel and evil and about to die.

Barber stood fully exposed for a moment, and Hawk knew he was probably looking at the bundles of blankets he'd laid close to the fire. Snake just standing there silhouetted against the flames was a tempting target. Exposed like that, Hawk could shoot him easily. But then he would still have Barber's men to deal with, and shooting Snake would give his position away. He needed them all dead or running scared.

Barber must be a fool to think Hawk would build a giant fire out here on the Florida prairie and then go to sleep like a greenhorn. But if Beale was right, Barber was in love. And maybe Snake didn't really know for sure he was here with Maddy. Maybe he'd an idea, but no proof. A man in love could make some stupid mistakes, and it looked to Hawk like Barber was making his.

When Barber disappeared back down the northern slope of the hammock, Hawk got ready to descend the tree, and then he stopped. Another figure, taller than Barber but slender and infinitely more careful, crept into the camp. It looked like a young man or perhaps a slightly built adult Indian.

Hawk watched closely. There was something familiar about the way this new intruder moved, the care he took to remain out of sight, his manner of crouching and hiding, and the set of his head. There was no way he was with Barber. He'd stayed hidden until Snake was gone. Hawk had trouble following this new guy. He was good, damn good.

Hawk slipped out of the tree by sliding quietly down one of his ropes. He dropped to the ground in his stocking feet, leaving his boots in the tree. A flicker of movement over by Maddy's wagon caught his attention. Racing noise-lessly, he pulled out his Bowie knife. He saw the figure in front of him looking at the red Cracker horse and moved into position behind him. Just as he was about to grab the stranger from behind, the figure whirled around and faced him.

"Hey, Pa, where you been? We missed you."

Hawk froze, his knife in his hand. It was Travis, but he had grown. He was as tall as Hawk, only slighter, slim as a reed. For a moment, he didn't know what to do. Twenty visions raced through his head. Travis mad at him for leaving him behind, Travis as a baby in his mother's arms, Travis in front of him right now smiling his crooked grin and looking so like his mother with raven's-wing black hair and ice-blue eyes. Love for his son overwhelmed him and he grabbed Travis in a choking hug. "Son, I'm so glad to see you."

"We thought you was dead, Pa. Jimmy and Judy Bill both said you was never coming home."

Hawk released the boy and stood back. "Well, they were wrong. I'd never abandon my family. No matter what, I was coming home. I sure am glad to see you, son, but you need to explain to me why you're here. Where's Jimmy and Joseph? How'd you get away from them? Don't you understand that Snake Barber is getting ready to attack this camp?"

Travis grinned wider. "Dang it, Pa, I knew you'd make it home if you could, but the war's been over and still you didn't show up. We knew from Joseph you'd been taken prisoner. But heck, we thought you'd be home long before now." Travis's eyes held his father's.

"Shoot, Pa, I had a feeling these old boys were coming to find you. They been holed up in our house for weeks looking through everything. I thought maybe I'd just foller along and see what they was up to. Jimmy and Joseph don't have no say about where I go anymore. I'm a grown man. I come and go as I please."

Hawk's chest filled with pride. His son was almost a

man. He'd discarded his childhood and was maturing into a resourceful person. "We don't have much time, Travis. I've got traps set all over the place, with explosives and wires. Barber should be coming up the front of this hammock any minute. Do you know how many men he has with him?"

"There's fifteen, counting him. Tell me what to do, Pa. I want to help."

Hawk had planned this as a solo operation. How could he fit Travis in? "You'll be in danger if you stay here, son. I'm the only one who knows where all the traps are."

"Don't send me away, Pa, please."

Travis stared hard at Hawk with his head canted to the side, one eyebrow raised. The boy looked him right in the eye, and Hawk remembered seeing that same look in Katie's eyes. He'd called it her evil eye. "We're in a lot of danger here, son, but I see you've grown up. I can use your help." He paused. He hated to put Travis in danger, but he remembered being sixteen. It was such a tough age—not a man, yet not a child, with the recklessness of youth a fire in the blood. "Hide your horse in the brambles back behind the hammock, then take your rifle and get up that big pine over there. Don't shoot until I tell you to and do not leave the tree. Can you do that?"

"Course I can," Travis said, and shot him another crooked grin.

"You didn't bring that crazy red-tailed hawk of yours with you, or any of the dogs, a trained coon, squirrel, or some other wild, crazy critter?"

"Nah, I left Diver home. She's nesting. I didn't want the dogs with me. And Barber's men killed most of my critters," Travis said as he shinnied up the big pine.

Hawk thought of the time that red-tail of Travis's had attacked him over a dead rabbit and torn a chunk out of his hand. He felt his son's sadness over the loss of the animals he'd taken care of in his barn, the sick ones and the ones he had spent hours teaching tricks. He knew what they'd meant to Travis. It was just more pain Barber had to answer for.

Hawk climbed back into his tree as the sun was lighting the eastern sky. Mist flowed over the ground as the first rays of sunlight heated the rain-damp grass. He couldn't help but smile. Travis was here with him right now. They were both in danger, but he felt good, very good.

It wasn't long before a flash of light caught Hawk's attention. He whistled to Travis and pointed. It was the first of Snake's men. The outlaw was a hundred and fifty feet away, sneaking out from behind a palmetto clump. The morning sun was glinting off the barrel of the outlaw's rifle.

Travis whistled back and sighted down the barrel of his rifle. Hawk held up his hand, clearly telling Travis to hold.

A minute later, Hawk spotted another one within the camp's perimeter. He whistled to Travis again, then aimed at one of the clumps of dirt covering Beale's explosives and fired. Just like Beale said it would, the little bomb exploded. Hawk gave a Rebel yell and immediately detonated another one. Then he lit the fuse on a string of firecrackers and tossed them into the dry pine needles under the tree. Pandemonium reigned on the hammock.

Outlaws stood up, leaving their cover. Hawk thought he saw at least eight. They started firing at anything and everything. Travis, a first-rate shot, began picking them off from his perch. Hawk exploded two more bombs and tossed two of those crazy rat things into the mess. He saw five outlaws go down and several more ran back down the hill as fast as they could hoof it.

A bullet whined past Hawk and smacked into the trunk of the pine where he was roosting. Hawk spotted Snake's flat-crowned hat and sent a bullet in his direction. Snake dropped to the ground.

Five mounted riders came charging up the hill, heading for Hawk's tree. The lead horse was ridden by a man Hawk recognized as Skeeter Jerkins, Snake's right-hand man. Jerkins was a crazy man on a horse. It was said Skeeter could make a mustang walk and talk.

Jerkins must have seen the wire strung between the two trees. He pulled up sharply and spun his horse on its hocks. Three of the men behind him weren't so lucky. They hit the wire, stretched tight and neck-high to a horse, at a full run. Two of the horses went down, dumping their riders at the base of Travis's tree. The other horse hit the wire so hard, the thin gauge steel cut into his jugular vein before snapping. Blood sprayed everywhere. Hawk shot the injured horse in the head and then shot his rider as he fell.

Two more riders raced up the hill. As Travis picked off one of the downed riders, Hawk dropped another string of firecrackers in the middle of the group of horses.

Smoke from the firecrackers and bombs filled the clearing. A small fire had started in the pine needles, burning its way down the north face of the hammock and adding more smoke to the confusion. The fire began to set off all Hawk's bombs. One after another, explosions rocked the hammock.

Hawk swung from one tree to the next using his ropes, looking for Snake and trying to see what was happening. He thought he spotted Barber by Maddy's wagon. Sliding down one of his ropes, he landed lightly behind one of the outlaws. The man had his gun drawn and was crouched low, trying to make his way out of the clearing through the smoke and back down the hammock. Hawk slid up behind him and grabbed him by the throat, shoving his Bowie knife into the man's side up to the hilt. The outlaw grunted and slid to the ground, and Hawk cleaned his blade on the grass.

With the smoke from the fires hanging low to the ground, Hawk couldn't see anything down here. Every now and then a shot would ring out. A terrified horse barreled toward him out of the smoke and Hawk dove to the right, barely avoiding getting run down. There was no way to keep track of how many he and Travis had killed or wounded. He had no idea how many were left or where Snake was.

Frustration and anger filled Snake Barber to the boiling point. One of his men pushed past him in the thick smoke and almost knocked him down, running away, running down the hill to safety. Snake shot him dead in the back. Cowards. They were all yellow-bellied crying babies. There wasn't a decent set of balls among the bunch.

Snake had figured out Hawk was up a tree. He climbed on the wagon and looked up into the trees. He spotted Hawk perched high in a pine and loosed a shot at him. Smoke billowed as Hawk tossed another string of those infernal noisemakers among the horses. Snake dove under the wagon as two horses plunged and bolted toward him, crashing into the wagon. One climbed up on the back of the wagon and slithered off the other side. They both tore down the side of the hammock. This was crazy.

The entire operation was a disaster. Maddy wasn't here. The only thing waiting for him on this hammock was Hawk and Death, and Death was busy collecting black souls and sending them straight to hell.

He left the cover of the wagon and walked into the smoke. What did it matter if he died? Who would care anyway? But if he was going to die, Hawkins was going with him. Damn if he'd let the man have his woman and all that money too.

Skeeter, struggling to control his horse, emerged from the smoke. Snake grabbed his reins and pulled the animal to a stop. "How many men are left?" He had to yell over the commotion of screaming men and horses, explosives, shooting, and firecrackers.

Skeeter leaned low. "Can't tell, boss. I seen seven down, probably dead, don't know for sure. Some done run off. I think I'm the only one left on horseback."

"Where's Hawk?"

"I seen some crazy man swinging around in the trees like a gosh-darn ape. He was shooting at everything off his hip while he was a-swinging. Durndest sight I ever see'd. That him?"

Snake nodded. "Yeah, that'd be him. Where'd he go?"

Another explosive blew behind Skeeter's horse. The animal reared, almost going over backward. Skeeter brought him down. "He was headed toward that big chunk of limestone over yonder."

More smoke billowed from the fire on the slope of the hammock. Snake coughed. "Is that it over there?" He pointed toward the base of the tallest pine.

"Think so, boss."

"Find me a horse. I'm going after him."

"Right," Skeeter said. Spurring his frantic mount forward, Skeeter shot down the side of the hammock and into the smoke.

Snake dropped to his belly and began crawling toward the pine Skeeter had pointed out. He ran into the dead body of Lige Tremblat. Blood still trickled out of a knife wound in his side. Snake hesitated for minute. Lige was a hell of a man. He wouldn't have run. Snake crawled over poor dead Lige and kept going until he finally made it to the big rock.

It was old limestone, white and gray, crumbly, and covered with shells from long ago. Someone had probably pulled it out of a sinkhole nearby or maybe a spring. It could have been brought there in a flood. The rock had several small ledges and rose six feet in the air at its tallest point. Flames from the fire licked toward its base.

No longer afraid of dying, and angry and frustrated to the breaking point, Snake felt like he had nothing to lose. His men were scattered, many dead, and his only way off this hammock was blocked by a brush fire. If he wanted to win this war, he had to kill Hawk. To do that, he had to find him. Snake climbed onto the rock.

He could see over the smoke from his vantage point, and what he saw sent the blood flooding into his head. Hawk was no more than thirty feet away with his back turned to Snake. He was talking to a tall kid Snake had never seen before.

Snake could see they were both armed. He cocked his rifle and took aim. This was going to be easy. He had them both right where he wanted them. He'd take them prisoner and maybe he could use the kid to force Hawk into telling him where he'd hidden the gold. Then he'd get rid of them both.

"I've got you in my sights, Hawkins," Snake yelled over the noise of the crackling flames being driven onto the hammock by a rising wind.

Hawk spun on his heels.

"Both of you, drop them repeaters and put your hands high where I can see 'em." Snake waggled his rifle.

Hawk opened his hand and let the carbine slide to the ground. The kid looked at Hawk kind of funny. Snake noticed the strong resemblance and figured the kid had to be Hawk's son. For a minute, Barber thought he was going to have to shoot the kid. The boy finally opened his hands and dropped his rifle.

"Take off that Bowie knife and let it drop," Snake ordered, standing tall on the rock. Relief and exultation flooded through him. He'd won. He'd won after all. Forget all screaming red-tailed hawks. He had Hawk and his kid right where he wanted them.

At that moment, Snake's world exploded in noise and flames. He threw up his hands and screamed as the rock shattered beneath him in a monstrous explosion. The huge chunk of limestone blew into a million pieces and Snake was launched skyward along with thousands of rock shards. Snake's world went dark and silent.

9

"TRAVIS, SON, ARE YOU ALL RIGHT?" Hawk had felt the explosion before he saw Snake Barber fly into the air. It had started as a deep vibration, followed by the noise and the blast of shattered limestone and hot air. The second he'd realized the rock was going up, he'd thrown Travis to the ground and fallen on top of him, Beale's parting words echoing in his head: "You better be running."

But even knowing the danger, he'd had to look. And he'd seen Snake lit up like a candle, flying high into the early morning sky.

He pulled himself to a kneeling position. Travis was still lying facedown in the dirt. The boy started groaning and slowly rolled onto his back.

"What hit me?"

"It was me, son. I felt the rock blowing, threw you on the ground, and jumped on you."

"Why'd the rock blow?" Travis asked as he propped himself on one elbow and wiped mud, leaf mold, and sand out of his face.

"It must have been the brush fire. It caught that long fuse afire and blew the rock. Beale said he put a pile of gunpowder under it."

"Who?"

Hawk gradually made it to a standing position. His back stung from hundreds of tiny cuts. Chunks of the rock must be imbedded in his flesh. It hurt. "I'll tell you about him later. I think I've got half the dang rock stuck in my back."

Travis grabbed Hawk's hand and pulled himself to his feet. "Let me look."

Travis examined Hawk's back carefully. He had the gentle touch of a doctor. "Yeah, I'm gonna have to pull some of this stuff out, Pa. You're bleeding."

"It can wait," Hawk brushed him aside. "I want to see what happened to Snake Barber."

The two of them picked their way through the devastation. Chunks of the rock, some as big as cannonballs, lay everywhere, and all that was left was a small crater where the rock had once sat whole. The tree that had been next to it was a smoking stump, the top of it gone. Hawk looked around to see if he could spot it, but all he saw were wood chips, pine needles, and smoldering limbs. "Beale sure knew what he was doing. He told me to take off running when I lit that fuse."

They searched the hammock. There were two dead horses and seven dead outlaws, but no Snake. Everything was covered with rock dust and tree debris.

Hawk saw something hanging high in a pine tree branch "Travis, is that Barber's hat?"

Travis looked up, shielding his eyes from the glare of morning sunlight with his hand. "Yeah, Pa, it sure 'nuff looks like it."

"I don't see him anywhere," Hawk said. "But he's gotta be dead. He couldn't have survived that blast—I saw him heading skyward with his pants on fire. But I'd feel a lot better if we could find his body."

Travis nodded. "It sure would be nice to know he was dead. Hey, Pa, I think one of these outlaws is still alive."

Travis was kneeling over one of Snake's men, trapped beneath a dead horse. All you could see was the man's head. As Hawk drew closer, he thought he recognized him. "I think that's the boy that got away the first time they attacked us."

Travis looked up. "You mean you been attacked twice by Barber?"

"Yeah, he attacked us just south of Alligator over a week ago."

Travis cocked one eyebrow. "Us? You mean that 'Beale'?"

"No, but I'll tell you all about that later too," Hawk said, thinking, *Oh, damn, I need to go get Madelaine.* He looked out at the island. It was still wrapped in early morning fog. He couldn't see anything.

The hindquarters of the dead horse practically covered the boy. Hawk grabbed the dead horse's tail and pulled. Between them, Hawk and Travis managed to pull and shove the horse off him.

The kid groaned. "Where does it hurt?" Travis asked, as he half-lifted the boy into a sitting position.

The kid's hat lay a few feet away in the pine needles carpeting the hammock floor. He had a lot of straw-colored hair, freckles, and a pug nose. He couldn't be more than fifteen or sixteen. The boy felt around on his head, then felt his body and grinned. He had an infectious smile. It exposed big horse teeth with a gap between the two square front ones. "To tell the truth, mister, don't hurt much anywhere. What happened?"

"A big rock exploded. Do you remember that?" Hawk asked.

The kid shook his head. "Nope, don't remember no big explosions, just lots of little ones."

"Well, this horse must have fallen on you and knocked you out," Hawk said. "Were you riding it?"

"I guess maybe I was," the kid said. "Thanks for helping me, mister. My name's Shorty, Shorty McCue."

"My name's Caleb Hawkins, but everybody calls me Hawk. This is my son, Travis. Can you stand up?"

Shorty grabbed his hat and with Travis's help, slowly climbed to his feet. He slapped the tan, wide-brimmed felt hat on his knee to remove a layer of rock dust, and stuck it on his head. Suddenly, he got a really spooked look on his face. He ducked his head and shoulders and glanced around, eyes wide. "Where's my boss?" he said. "I don't think I'm supposed to be a-talking to you folks."

"I think your boss done got blowed all over the countryside," Travis said. "He was standing on that big rock yonder, the one that ain't there no more. I wouldn't be worrying none, least not 'bout him anyways."

Relief plainly washed over Shorty. He grinned, showing off those big teeth. Hawk grinned back. You just couldn't help yourself. But no matter how charming Shorty could be, Hawk knew it could all be a ruse. When he looked into the kid's eyes, he didn't see any mean, but Hawk planned to keep a close eye on the boy until he was sure Shorty McCue could be trusted.

"I don't like speaking ill of the dead, but I'm plumb tickled to hear it," Shorty said. "I think he was planning to shoot me or feed me to the gators. That's what the boys done told me."

"I wouldn't put it past him," Hawk said. "Did he blame you for the loss of his men when ya'll bushwhacked us south of Alligator?"

"Hell, yes, he did. Said it was my fault he didn't have his woman back."

Hawk cussed. "Damnit, I keep forgetting about Madelaine. We have to go get her off the island."

"Who's Madelaine?" Travis asked. Then his face brightened. "Oh, I see. Madelaine must be the person you've been traveling with, the one who owns all that stuff in that there wagon. Well, Pa, I think she got tired of waiting."

Hawk spun on his heels. Maddy was toiling up the hill, holding her soaked dress up above her ankles with both hands.

"Don't worry about rescuing Madelaine," Maddy said as she shook out her dripping skirts. "She's already saved herself."

Madelaine looked tired. Wisps of hair clung to her face, and her long braid dangled limply over one shoulder. Her face was pale with dark circles under her eyes. She walked slowly and heavily with Sarah beside her toting two haversacks and a blanket.

"I'm sorry, Maddy. We just found this young man alive and were tending him. I swear we would have come out to get you in just a minute."

Maddy smiled. "I know. We were watching everything from the island. It was hard to see what was going on through the fog, but we did see the big explosion and after that, it was real quiet. Then Sam spotted you and this young man walking around searching, so I figured it was safe to come back to the camp. You still have to go out there and get the horses." She was breathing heavily. She leaned on Sarah and took off a shoe. Water ran out of it. She took off the other one. "I think these are ruined. Who's the young man, Hawk?"

Hawk smiled proudly. "Travis, meet Madelaine Wilkes and her son, Sam. Travis is my son."

"Pleased to meet you, Travis." Madelaine looked over at Shorty. "Isn't this the boy that escaped when we were attacked the first time?"

Shorty's fair skin turned red and he whipped off his hat. "Sorry 'bout that, ma'am. Weren't none of my idea."

"His name's Shorty," Hawk said. "I guess he'll be riding with us." He turned to Shorty. "Will you ride with us to take back our ranch? With Snake dead, it should be easy to roust the rest of his men. I can promise you work, when we're safely home."

Shorty nodded and stuck his hat back on his head. "I'm ready to ride when you are." He turned his head and looked around. "But I guess I'll be needin' me a horse."

"Is Snake Barber really dead, Hawk?"

Maddy's blue eyes looked so anxious. Hawk wished he could be more reassuring. "I think so, Maddy. Barber was standing on that rock when it exploded. I don't see how he could have survived. We searched for him and we'll search some more, but all we found so far is his hat. Don't worry so, Maddy."

"I can't help but worry. He's a horrible, evil man. Are you sure it's safe for me to be on this hammock alone while you go for the horses? You swear he's not going to jump out from behind a tree and get me and Sam?"

"We'll sweep the hammock and the surrounding area before we go get the horses," Hawk said. "Travis, you take Shorty and check the south and west sides of the hammock. I'll check the east and north sides."

"Okay, Pa, but be careful. That's the way them outlaws come up here."

"Well, I am going to get out of these wet clothes," Maddy said. "Come with me, Sam. Let's go find something dry to put on."

As Maddy made her way to the wagon, Hawk began his sweep of the hammock. Travis and Shorty went in the opposite direction. Hawk turned and watched for a minute. Shorty and Travis were talking up a storm. It seemed as though they were getting to be fast friends. That would be a good thing for Travis. He'd never even met someone his own age before.

Hawk carefully searched the ground as he made his sweep, checking under every clump of grass and in every bush. He found pieces of clothing, a boot, a half-empty pouch of tobacco, tree debris, rock shards, and two unexploded bombs. He thought he may have buried them too deep.

The fire had scorched everything on the north side of the hammock. The ground still smoldered in many places, and down the hill, close to the trail, there were several small fires still burning. Up on the hammock where the pine needles were deep, the fire had blazed. The rain of the previous evening had soaked the ground enough to keep the fires from spreading, at least. They were lucky the wagon was parked on grass. The tailgate and one wheel were slightly singed, but all of Madelaine's possessions were safe.

Shorty and Travis were just completing their own trip around the hammock when he came back. Travis had recovered his little marsh tacky. "There's nothing back there but brambles and vines," Travis said, pointing to the south side of the hammock. "We found a sinkhole. I think there's a tiny cave and a spring at the bottom. We tried to get into it, but it's dark and pretty narrow. There weren't no tracks close by anyway. And down by the lake it's all clear. We pulled all the dead guys into one spot over there."

Hawk followed Travis's pointing finger and saw they had piled the dead outlaws beneath his pine, the one he'd been sitting in when they attacked.

"What should we do, bury them?" Travis asked.

"Yeah, so you two boys will have to dig one heck of a hole," Hawk said. "Let's wade over and get the horses first."

"What about your back, Pa? It needs tending."

"Later," Hawk said. "We got things to do."

Hawk went looking for Madelaine and found her changed into dry clothes and building a new fire where she'd cooked supper the night before. That meal seemed like it had happened years ago. Hawk realized he was starving. "You always think of what we need," Hawk said to her.

"I'm hungry, so I thought you must be famished," she said. "I'll make all you boys a big breakfast. I still have some bacon left."

"We're gonna wade across to the island now and fetch back the horses," he told her.

"Don't be too long, this will be ready fast. And watch out for those gators. We saw a few on our way back; I guess we were lucky they weren't interested in us."

Hawk gathered up Shorty and Travis and the three of them headed for the lake.

"Who the heck is she?" Travis demanded when they were halfway to the island. "She looks to be breedin'."

"Yes, she's in the family way. I ran into her and her boy north of Pilatka," Hawk said, and then unfolded the complete story for Travis, leaving out the truth about Sam. When they climbed out of the water on the island, Hawk sent Shorty off to catch the horses.

Travis seemed stunned by Madelaine's story. "Snake Barber is her baby's father? And you just happened to run into her? Wow, that's a coincidence."

"Don't I just know it? I think Barber really came here to claim her, not just to catch me," Hawk said. "But I'm not sure."

"Why is she traveling with you? Is she gonna live with us?"

"I said she could. She doesn't have anyplace to go, Travis. What would you have me do?"

"Do you like her?" Travis stammered. "I mean, are you gonna be marrying up with her?"

Travis's words stunned Hawk. That's what everyone would think. Maddy'd been right about that. What really shocked him was how he felt when he thought about marrying Maddy. They'd been together for almost two weeks and had evolved a comfortable relationship. She was a good, God-fearing woman, a great cook, had book learning, was a good mother, and she sure was easy on the eyes. When he really got to pondering the thought, it didn't seem like all that bad of an idea. He wondered how she felt.

"I don't know, son," he finally answered. "She is going

to have Snake Barber's child. That's something I'm not sure I'm willing to handle. But we'll have to wait and see what happens. "

Shorty walked up leading the two horses and the mule. John hung back, dragging behind as usual. Travis shut up when Shorty got close, but his eyes told Hawk he was still mulling over Madelaine's story.

As they waded back to shore, Travis told Hawk what had been going on at home.

"How many men are still there?" Hawk asked.

"I don't know, Pa. There were seven or eight when I left. They come and go. Do you think the ones that got away from here went back to our house?"

"Can't say, Trav. We have to assume they did. I think eight survived, though we might have wounded some of them. We're gonna have to come up with a plan before we get there, do some scouting, find out what we're up against."

"Why are they in our house, Pa? What do those outlaws want with our ranch? They been lookin' in the blue spring and searching everywhere. Are they after Grandpa's gold?"

"Yes," Hawk said. "Snake Barber has always known about it, and we were in the prison camp together. While I was sick, I kind of gave him some clues. I imagine that's why he's lookin' in the blue spring. Did you ever get that letter I sent with Joseph?"

"Yup, and I had to break back into the house for it. I forgot and left it there when we run out. It's burned up now. I destroyed it."

Hawk patted Travis on the back. "I knew I could trust you, son."

Travis smiled and threw out his chest.

As Hawk led Beau onto the shore, Travis got his first good look at the big stud horse. "Dang, Pa, that's a heck of a horse. Where'd you get him?"

"He was a gift from the provost marshal at the prison camp. I shoed his race horses, so he gave me one. Maybe we can use old Beau to add some size to the marsh tackies. Even you're getting too tall to ride them."

"Is he fast?" Travis ran his hands over Beau, feeling his legs, looking into his eyes.

"You tell me. I'll let you ride him home. He needs to stretch his legs. He's been walking behind the wagon for days."

Travis was beside himself with excitement. One minute he was a man and the next he was a boy. Hawk remembered being sixteen. It was a crazy time in life.

After eating Maddy's breakfast, the boys buried the outlaws. Maddy took a Bible out of her belongings. It was a well-worn King James in a hand-sewn, stained fabric cover. The book contained many ribbons and slips of paper to mark passages and verses. The men removed their hats as she read from it over the grave. Then Maddy led them in prayer in her soft Georgia accent. She thanked the Lord for her deliverance, for the safety of Hawk and Travis. She thanked the Lord for making Shorty see the light of goodness and change his evil ways. She thanked God for saving them from Snake Barber and asked Him to bless the dead, even though they were bad men.

Hawk and the boys said amen when she was done and donned their hats. "Should we take a day off, Maddy?" Hawk asked. "Do you need to rest?"

She looked up at him, and once again he felt that connection to her. Her blue eyes, shining and so clear, seemed to see right into him. "No, Hawk, let's get out of here and get to your farm. I don't know how much longer I have. My back's been aching and my feet are swelling."

They walked together. Sarah stayed away from the two young men, which Hawk thought was a very wise thing to do. It wouldn't take long for them to discover she was no boy.

When they reached the wagon, Maddy grabbed him by the arm. "Now, you let me put this Bible away and then we're going to pull those rock shards out of your back."

"But, Maddy, Travis was gonna do it. He's practically a doctor."

"I don't care who does it, but you need to get those shards out and those wounds cleaned up."

It took two of them to get Hawk's back cleaned up. He'd missed the brunt of the flying rock and debris by falling down, but he even had splinters of wood imbedded in his flesh. Travis pulled the big pieces of rock and splinters out, and Maddy washed his back with lye soap and water. Then Travis put some pine tar on the wounds. It's what he did to wounded animals all the time, he assured Hawk, who complained through the whole process. When Travis was finished, he patted Hawk on the back and told him that he would be as right as rain in no time.

It wasn't until noon that they were packed and ready to go. Hawk had had to climb the trees and take down all his ropes while the boys took down the wires. When it was time to leave, not one of them was sorry to see the last of the hammock, even though it meant traveling through the heat of the day.

Hawk looked back as he urged Spirit down the trail. He hoped they'd seen the last of Snake Barber.

114

10 ☀

SNAKE BARBER OPENED HIS EYES. Where the
hell was he? The world was silent. He couldn't hear anything. No bugs, no birds—nothing but a ringing in both his
ears. High above him a narrow crack in the earth let in a
shaft of sunlight. He tried to move and white-hot agony shot
through his body. After a few minutes spent trying to recover from the pain, he'd narrowed down that most of it was his
right leg.

It was cool where he was, cool and damp. He lay on wet
sand. When he dug his fingers into the moist sand, pools of
water formed. He tried moving his arms and realized they
worked fine. After feeling around, he discovered a bigger
pool of water next to his head. He scooped some up in his
palm without moving his lower body and drank greedily.
Damn, he was thirsty.

The effort of moving his arms and drinking exhausted
him. He passed out, and when he woke up again, there was
no light coming in through the crack. He was in total darkness and the pain in his leg was worse. No matter how little

115

he tried to move, it still throbbed and caused him incredible agony.

He realized he was in a cave, maybe formed by the spring next to his head. How he'd gotten through the crack, he couldn't remember. His ears still rang and he couldn't hear anything, but he wasn't sure if it was because he was deep in the earth or because his ears were damaged.

For a while, he was afraid to shout, afraid Hawk and his kid would still be up there somewhere trying to find him. But the pain got so bad that soon he was shouting and screaming for help. After a time, he passed into a nightmare-filled sleep.

When he woke for the third time, he was conscious of being able to hear a steady drip. Somewhere in his refuge— or his prison, depending on how you looked at it—water was dripping into the pool. Light beamed steadily in from above. He lifted his head and got up the nerve to look at his injured leg. It was a frightening sight. From the knee down, his leg was mangled, the pants torn off and his boot gone. His foot was black and the ends of bones stuck out of his skin above the ankle. Most of the skin was gone; charred remnants of flesh were all that was left.

His left leg was burned as well, but the boot was still on, though torn in half. His toes stuck out. They were black and the skin was gone. He let his head fall back to the cool sand. He was a goner, done for. He closed his eyes and wondered how long it would take to die.

As the day wore on, the pain grew more intense. Snake dragged his ruined leg, ignoring the agony, into the pool. The cold water slowly numbed the limb. He sighed with relief and dropped into a doze.

He dreamed his mother was calling his name. He could

hear her, though she sounded far away. When he opened his eyes, he realized someone actually was calling his name, but it wasn't his mother. He looked up and saw Skeeter staring through the crack.

"Snake, are you down there?" Skeeter called into the hole.

Snake could only croak in answer. He tried to call out, but his voice was too weak.

"Hello!" Skeeter called. "Is somebody down there?"

Snake tried to call out to Skeeter again, but his voice was gone from yelling and screaming the day before. The frustration and anguish choked him and tears ran down his face. He could see Skeeter, so why couldn't Skeeter see him?

He closed his eyes, and when he opened them, Skeeter was gone.

His one chance to be saved had left with Skeeter. He was doomed to die in this hole. Him, Jake the Snake Barber. He would never ride a horse again, drink whiskey with his buddies, or see his Maddy ever again. And he would never find Hawk's gold. Pain and despair filled him completely. It was hours before he passed out again.

He woke up to the feel of someone's hand on his shoulder. Startled, he opened his eyes. It was Skeeter. Tears started rolling down his cheeks and he let his eyelids shut.

"Boss, I got a rope here I'm gonna slide under your shoulders. You're hurt bad, boss, but I'm gonna try to get you out of here."

Snake opened his eyes and more tears filled them. He couldn't speak, but he lifted his hand and touched Skeeter's arm.

When the rope was under his arms, Skeeter lifted a pint

bottle to Snake's lips. "Drink this, boss. It's whiskey, but it's all I got to numb the pain."

Snake drank. Whiskey ran out of his mouth and down his face, but he didn't care. The sharp liquid burned its way into his stomach. He knew there wasn't enough whiskey on earth to dull the pain of his ruined leg, but he drank anyway. When the bottle was empty, Skeeter let his head fall to the damp sand.

"I got this rope hooked to my horse," Skeeter said. "Getting you out is gonna be tricky. I got nobody here to help me. All them sons o' bitches run off and left me here looking fer ya. I got me a travois rigged up to put you on, then I'm gonna try to get you to a doctor."

Snake nodded. He loved Skeeter, and he wished he could tell him so. Maybe it was the whiskey in his brain, but he felt Skeeter had always stuck by him when no one else did.

Skeeter climbed out of the cave and the next thing Snake knew, the rope under his arms tightened and he was being dragged out of the water. He discovered his voice as he began to scream and scream and scream. It was just a hoarse croak, but inside his head, the screaming went on and on. Finally, blackness claimed him once again and he passed out.

When he woke up, it was night and Skeeter hovered over him. The man's face mirrored his deep concern. "I thought you was gone fer sure, boss. Yer in a real bad way. I was gonna load you in the travois and tote you to a saw bones, but I didn't think you'd make it. Here, drink some of this water."

Snake drank thirstily, guzzling the sweet liquid down his parched throat. As he drank, he realized the pain in his right foot and lower leg was gone. With that agony removed, he could feel intense pain coming from several other places.

He looked around. It was night, and a fire burned low a few feet away. Crouched over the fire was an old Indian woman stirring a pot, and Skeeter sat on a log next to Snake smoking a hand-rolled cigarette. An Indian boy sat cross-legged near the fire roasting a rabbit on a spit. Who were these people and where had they come from?

"More water," he managed to whisper. Skeeter laid the cigarette on the log and got up to lift the water bottle to his lips. When Snake had finished drinking, Skeeter sat back down.

"I'm sorry to have to tell you this, boss, but it's a thing you be needin' to know, and I don't believe in beatin' around the bush," Skeeter said. "Or in wrappin' up bad news in clean linen. Plain speakin', that's my way and it always has been."

Snake closed his eyes. What was the man trying to tell him? His head was swimming. He opened his eyes and glared at Skeeter.

Skeeter nodded. "I can you see you're lookin' daggers at me, so I'll just open my budget and tell you. We had to cut it off. That is the old Injun woman cut it off. It was a good thing you were unconscious. I helped some. Her boy there ain't right in the head, but he can hunt and fish like nobody's business and he keeps us eating."

Snake could see Skeeter's lips moving and hear the words coming out of his mouth, but it took a few minutes for him to comprehend. What had the old woman cut off? And then it dawned on him—his leg. He lifted one hand and felt his right thigh. He could barely lift his arm, he was so weak. At least his thigh was still there. His hand flopped limply and he realized a lot of the pain he was feeling was coming from below his knee. Suddenly, he didn't want to know how much had been cut off. He'd worry later. For right now he was just too tired and weak.

"Indian?" he managed to croak.

"Oh, her? She and the boy were fishing in the lake. They paddled by and I tried to get them to stop and help me, but she wouldn't, so I had to rope the kid. Kept him tied to a tree while she took off yer leg. They ain't scared of me no more. They know I ain't gonna do nothing to 'em. They live on some island in the middle of this lake. She says there's another spring over there somewheres, a real big 'un."

Snake listened to Skeeter's voice. It sounded so good to him. The words ran together and for the first time since he'd been blown up, he fell into a natural sleep.

When he woke again, he was stronger. Skeeter was there to lift his head high enough for him to see what was going on around him and to see his lower body. His leg was gone from right below the knee. The stump was wrapped in something that was plastered in mud. His left foot and lower leg were wrapped up and plastered with mud, too. Weirdly enough, he swore he could feel his right foot, and it hurt.

"Drink some of this," Skeeter said. "I know it smells godawful, but she says you have to. It's some kind of medicine she's been brewing for days, and she's been giving it to you all along. She says it will make you sleep and help with the pain and infection. It's got a lot of tree bark in it and some other plants and roots and stuff she gathered around here."

Snake sniffed at the wooden bowl Skeeter held to his lips. It did smell terrible, but he drank it anyway. Maybe it would kill him. Who cared? He was probably going to die anyway. And if he did live, what would life as a one-legged man be worth? Nothing, that was what.

"Your fever was pretty high last night, boss. The old woman says you might live if it breaks. She's hoping you do live, 'cause she wants to get out of here."

"How'd you find me down there?" Snake asked. His voice was stronger. It still rasped, but he could hear himself.

"Buzzards," Skeeter said. "There was about a hundred of 'em in the trees right around your little hole in the ground. They knew you was down there, but they couldn't get to you. I couldn't see nothing when I looked into the hole, but I decided to jump down there anyway. I'd done searched everywhere else."

"Are all the men gone?"

"Yeah, they skeedaddled and left me looking fer ya. I knew you was too ornery to die, so I kept on hunting."

Snake lifted one hand and let it flop limply back to the pallet beneath him. "Maddy?"

"Them folks left right after they buried all the dead. That boy Shorty went with 'em."

Snake nodded and closed his eyes. They were headed for Hawk's ranch. Hawk would be anxious to get home now that he knew Snake was the one tracking him. No doubt they all thought he was dead and were glad of it.

"Hey, boss, did you know yer woman was in a breedin' way?"

Snake's eyes flew open. He reached up and grabbed Skeeter by the front of his leather vest with one shaking hand. "What?"

"She was as big as a cow, no kiddin'," Skeeter said. "I saw it with my own eyes. She looks ready to hit the straw. I mean, she's bred heavy, boss."

Snake fell back to his pallet. Maddy was having a baby? He mentally calculated the time. He'd left her about seven months ago. If she was that big and that heavy, it had to be his child.

11 🌿

I⟶T WAS HOT AND MADDY'S DRESS clung to her. The large sunbonnet she'd donned for the trip shaded her face, but under it her hair was wet, glued to her scalp. Gnats walked across her face and buzzed in her ears. She brushed them away with the back of her hand for the hundredth time. Overhead, puffy white clouds drifted across a clean blue sky. Far to the east, she could see storm clouds billowing on the horizon for the daily afternoon deluge.

It wasn't just the heat that was making Maddy miserable. Her back ached constantly, and the center of the throbbing pain was low. She reached behind her and absently rubbed it. The baby had not moved all day, which was a good thing since it had dropped so low her belly rested on her knees when she sat. If the tiny creature were to start squirming now, she'd have to stop and pee every five minutes. She put her hands on the edge of the seat and braced herself for yet another bump and jostle.

What a morning they all had experienced. But if Snake Barber was truly dead, she was happy. He scared her and his men terrified her. The memories of the months she had spent sliding around her own home trying to stay out of sight and keep poor Sarah hidden haunted her dreams. The thought that he wanted her back and was looking for her was almost more than she could stand. One of the happiest days of her life had been the day Snake had taken his men and pulled out of Twelve Oaks, leaving her and Sarah alone. But her relief had been short-lived; the Yankees had ridden in two days later, pushing Maddy out of the frying pan and into the fire.

What would have happened if Snake had discovered she was with child before he left Twelve Oaks? She'd been fairly sure of it way before he'd left her farm. She would have died rather than tell him of her fears. He was mean and ruthless, but she knew he would have stayed with her if he'd known, and now, if he was alive and found out, he'd leave no stone unturned to find her and recover her.

Snake Barber was extremely possessive—what was his was his. If he had gone to this much trouble to locate her and get her back, what would he have done then if he'd known she was breeding? She shuddered. It did her and the child no good to dwell upon such evil conjectures. She brushed more gnats off her face and tried to direct her thoughts in another, more pleasant direction.

She spotted Travis riding the big stallion. He and Shorty had their heads together, talking as they rode. Shorty was riding the little red gelding she'd named Copper. Hawk's son was tall like him, but slender. He had jet-black hair and light blue eyes. Hawk's sable-brown locks and dark brown eyes gave him a different look, warmer and more approachable. Travis had his father's strong chin and jawline, but his eyes tilted slightly and were nothing at all like Hawk's.

Hawk's eyes were large and rounder in shape. Travis had an eerie way of looking right into your heart with those eyes of his.

She looked out on the palmetto plain they were crossing and saw Travis galloping wildly on Hawk's big horse. The boy was like a burr, glued tightly to the saddle even when the big horse jumped a fallen tree or a creek.

Maddy stretched and rubbed her distended belly, then changed hands and massaged her lower back. Deep inside, she suddenly felt the beginning of a cramp, which quickly grew into what she recognized as a labor pain. The pain grew in intensity and she breathed deeply. Maybe it would go away. She knew they sometimes did. Maybe it was just all the jolting in the wagon that was making her ache so.

The jarring ride over the rutted trail continued late into the afternoon. Black storm clouds filled the sky, and the occasional rumble of thunder issued from them, along with frightening bolts of lightning. They would have to find shelter from the storm soon. She glanced at Hawk and he nodded. He had seen the sky too.

Maddy was now certain she was in labor. Why did it have to happen out here in the middle of nowhere? She'd so hoped to make it to a town first. Well, that had been her luck lately, bad or terrible, take your pick.

Hawk stopped the wagon under a tree as the wind picked up and blew across Maddy's wet back. It was such a relief to feel the coolness in the rising breeze.

"I think we need to set up camp here and wait out this storm," Hawk said to her. "If it passes over, we can put some more hours in before dark."

Maddy looked up and stared at the approaching blue-black clouds. The sun was gone, blotted out by the descend-ing darkness of the storm. An eerie light surrounded the wagon. After bright sunshine all day, the sudden gloom was strange and disconcerting.

Smiling tightly and trying not to grimace with discom-fort, Maddy stood up. As she did, a rush of fluid covered her stout boots and ran onto the floorboards.

Hawk was reaching under the seat for his tobacco and saw the flood. He looked up at her. "It's your time, isn't it?"

Another pang hit her and she squeaked, "I believe so."

Hawk paled under his tan.

Maddy allowed him to lift her out of the wagon. "Don't worry, Hawk. I'll be fine. I had an easy time with Sarah. This one will no doubt be the same."

"I hope so, Maddy. I sure hope so."

Travis and Shorty rode up when they saw the wagon under the trees. "Why did you stop, Pa?" Travis asked. "Pa, Beau is the fastest horse I've ever ridden. He's like the wind, Pa. I mean it. He practically flies."

"We stopped for the storm, or didn't you two even notice?" Hawk said. "And I believe Maddy's time is on her."

Travis jumped off Beau. "I can help, Pa. I've delivered hundreds of babies—puppies, coon babies, piglets, foals, and lots of calves."

Maddy stared at the boy. Did he really equate her with a sow?

❖   ❖   ❖

Hawk looked thoughtfully at his son. Travis was right. Out of all of them, he undoubtedly had the most experience delivering babies of every kind. After all, birth was birth, wasn't it? Travis had taken an early interest in birthing and always took joy from holding a newborn creature in his arms.

For his own part, Hawk was filled with terror for Maddy. He remembered Katie going into labor so filled with hope at the arrival of another child. Travis had been ten when his mother died. He and Katie had tried for so long to conceive. They'd wanted a large family. When Katie's time came, the three of them stupidly rejoiced. He shook his head. Travis knew the most about the birthing process. He'd certainly allow the boy to help.

There really was no other option anyway. His experience with childbirth had been forever poisoned by Katie's death and the death of their stillborn daughter. His fear threatened to paralyze him. All he could think was, what if Maddy died?

He had faith in Travis. Not only had Travis been healing animals since he was little, learning the Indian healing methods from Jimmy and his wife and using them successfully, but Travis also had some kind of magic touch with sick and ailing creatures. He seemed to know instinctively what to do to make them better, which medicines would and wouldn't work. He'd said it more than once: Travis was almost a doctor, and in some ways, he was better. He had knowledge many doctors didn't possess, knowledge of natural healing methods, herbs, and practices he'd learned from the Indians.

"Get the tarp and set up a tent for Maddy," Hawk told Travis and Shorty. "Put your slickers on, 'cause it's about to pour."

Hawk pulled his own slicker out from under the seat of

the wagon and shrugged it on over his clothes. It was hot and it smelled, but when it rained, there was nothing like it.

Shorty didn't have a slicker, just a huge poncho. He pulled it over his head and Hawk saw it was a large square of tarpaulin with a hole cut in the top for his head. He'd seen lots of them during the war. They weren't pretty, but they worked.

"Put some muscle into fixin' that tent," Hawk said to the two. "It's gonna rain any second. And make sure you tie it down good. The wind's kicking up something fierce."

The two boys set to with a will. Fat raindrops were pelting the top of the canvas when Hawk helped Maddy to the pallet they'd made for her inside.

Sarah hovered close by her mother and Hawk could see pure fright in the girl's eyes. He knew exactly what she was feeling because he was feeling it too. He drew the girl aside to speak to her before she gave it away to Travis and Shorty she was a girl by bursting into hysterics.

"Sam, why don't you go down to that creek and get some water. Take the two big buckets and fill them slap up with as much as you can carry," Hawk ordered gently. It would be best to keep her occupied. She must know if she lost her mother, she would be truly alone and abandoned in life. Her mother was her whole world.

When the storm hit, he and the boys huddled under the wagon. Maddy was in the hastily erected tent, and Sarah was still out there at the nearby creek with her buckets. If she didn't come back soon, someone was going to have to go look for her.

The wind gusted and splattered them with dirt and debris. Hawk prayed the storm would pass quickly, but instead it grew in intensity. The trees around them began to whip in the wind. Limbs cracked and a bolt of lightning struck close by. As they recovered from a flash that dazzled them, another strike hit a tree less than fifty feet away. The top of the tree crashed to the ground so close that its limbs brushed the wagon.

Hawk began to fear for Maddy out there in that tent by herself, and someone was going to have to brave the storm to search for Sarah. Where could that girl be?

The boys had tied the improvised tent down with rope and stakes and even braced it with several stout cedar posts they had cut in the woods. But Hawk didn't think it was strong enough to hang together in this kind of wind.

"Stay here," he yelled to Travis over the crash of the storm. "I'm gonna go get Maddy."

Travis and Shorty huddled together in the small amount of shelter afforded by the wagon. Travis held on to his hat, looked at Hawk, and nodded.

Hawk climbed out from under the wagon and ran to the tent. A wind gust blew leaves and rain into his face. He held his hat to his head as one side of the tent blew up in a sudden gust, tearing the ropes free. The loose ropes flapped wildly, and one of the posts pulled out of the wet ground. Maddy was suddenly completely exposed to the elements.

He grabbed her hand and dragged her to her feet. She tottered unsteadily and he scooped her up and ran for the wagon just as the tent and all the blankets in it flew into the air and swirled away.

"Where's Sam?" Maddy asked when she saw her daughter was not under the wagon with the rest of them.

"She went for water and never came back," Hawk told her.

Maddy's face whitened. Another crack of lightning struck close by and the boom of the following thunder was deafening. What should he do? Sarah must be huddled somewhere for safety and it seemed foolish to send someone out to look for her, but one look at Maddy's terrified face told him he must.

He didn't want to send Travis because of Maddy's condition. He couldn't afford to have Travis gone if Maddy's labor progressed rapidly. Shorty seemed like the obvious choice, but he hated to ask anyone to go out into that maelstrom. He didn't have to ask, though. Shorty scooted forward. "I'll go look for the boy," he said.

Relief washed over Hawk. What a good kid Shorty was. He grabbed the boy's hands. "Thanks."

Shorty ducked out from under the wagon and disappeared into the pouring sheets of rain.

The storm raged as the three of them huddled together. Maddy's crates and boxes began to blow off the wagon as the wind grew stronger. The horses were tied to a nearby picket line. They plunged and neighed in fright as the boxes blew into them, along with tree limbs and leaves. Travis, worried for their safety, ran out and loosed the horses. They ran into the surrounding prairie like the Devil himself was on their heels.

Another lightning strike hit a tree, exploding it like one of Roscoe Beale's bombs. Shorty reappeared, leading Sarah by the hand. The girl was sobbing hysterically and when yet another bolt of lightning cracked close by, Sarah screamed. Shorty and Travis stared at her. Hawk grabbed Sarah and held her and Maddy close. It was a hell of a storm.

Maddy started pushing at Hawk as another punishing gust of wind tore at them.

"Now!" she screamed in his ear. "The baby's coming now!"

"What?" He stared at her. Her face was contorted. She pointed between her legs. He couldn't believe it—she was delivering right now.

The storm raged, and Hawk prayed the wagon wouldn't blow away as he made room for Maddy to lie down. Without even a blanket to lay her on, Travis tore off his shirt and bunched it up under her head. Hawk shot him a grateful look as he took his slicker off and slid it beneath her.

Maddy rucked up her skirts as Shorty and Sarah moved behind her to support her back. Travis and Hawk delivered Maddy's son while the summer storm wrought its fury all around them.

Travis held the baby wrapped in Hawk's shirt. The look in his eyes was tender as he rubbed blood and mucus off the baby's body with a scrap torn from Maddy's skirts. Hawk made Maddy as comfortable as possible under the wagon with the wind and rain hammering around them.

It was hard for Hawk to read Maddy's expression when Travis handed her the tiny boy he'd wrapped in some of her petticoat. She held him close to her body and looked up at Hawk. He realized she was worried. Worried he wouldn't accept her child because it was also Snake Barber's.

"What are you going to name him?" Hawk asked.

"You pick a name," she said. "I'd hoped for a girl, and I was going to name her Emily."

"Let's name him Storm, Pa," Travis said. "He was born in one heck of a storm."

Maddy smiled at Travis. "I like that. We'll call him Storm Travis Wilkes, because Travis did most of the delivering."

Travis's face turned bright red. "I'm real honored, ma'am," he said, and reached out one finger to rub the tiny boy's downy head.

Maddy cradled the boy close, leaned back, and closed her eyes. The storm had abated, and the land smelled washed and fresh. The heat had gone with the storm, leaving behind cooler temperatures and a brief respite from the eternally buzzing flies and gnats.

Travis helped Maddy deliver the afterbirth, and Hawk was impressed by how businesslike the boy was as he scooped the bloody mess up and went off to bury it.

Hawk moved to sit cross-legged next to Maddy's head. They said nothing. The silence felt heavy. Maddy had been a trooper, delivering her child with no fuss in the worst of circumstances. He was filled with admiration for her. Life had dealt her so many hard blows, yet she persevered.

She was holding the baby to her breast, urging the tiny scrap of humanity to suck. For a moment he felt embarrassed to be sitting here with her at this most intimate of moments. But Maddy wasn't embarrassed. She looked up, her blue eyes shining. "He might be Snake Barber's son, but he's mine as well. He won't grow up to be anything like Snake. I'll make sure of that."

"Of course he won't. Not with you as his mother," Hawk said. He felt tenderness in his heart for her and for the boy. "You did good, Maddy. You were incredible."

"I had no choice," she said, looking into his eyes again. "But you and Travis were wonderful too. You should be very proud of him. He has a great heart."

"I am," Hawk said. And he was proud of his son. Travis was a fine boy. He'd grown so much in size and spirit while

Hawk had been away. "I think I'm going to leave him and Shorty here to watch out after you while I ride ahead and reconnoiter. We need to know what's going on back at the D-Wing and what to expect. I'll get the two of them working on a chickee. Travis knows all about making shelters out of palm fronds and poles. His mother was part Indian, you know. We need to make you more comfortable with that baby."

He crawled out from under the wagon. Travis was not going to like staying behind. But Hawk knew he could make good time on Beau, and checking out the situation at home was a one-man job.

The boys had built a fire and were heating a pot of water. "What should I cook?" Travis asked. "I found some grits. I can make fry bread and sofkee. I think I could even find a cabbage head and cook that up."

"I'm sure that'll be fine," Hawk said. "Listen, Travis. I want you to build a chickee for Maddy. She's going to have to stay here until she can travel again. This isn't such a bad campsite. We have a little shelter and the creek's pretty close."

"I'll get right on it. Shorty can help."

"That's fine, son. I'm going to head out in the morning on a reconnaissance mission. I need to know how many men still occupy our home so I can plan how to recapture it."

Travis stared at him, those icy blue eyes cutting right through him. "You want me to stay here, don't you? You're always leaving me behind while you go off."

"It's not like that this time, son. I'd take you with me if I could, you know, because I really need you with me. But you're the only one I can trust to look after Maddy and Sam."

"Uh, Pa, I don't know if you've noticed, but Maddy's

boy Sam ain't no boy. Shorty said when he found the kid by the creek and it was a stormin', he was crying fit to bust. I don't care how he was raised, but boys don't do that, not ever. We done decided, after looking Sam over, well—me and Shorty think he's a gal."

Hawk grinned. No fools, them. "You're right, of course. Sam's name is really Sarah. Maddy was afraid to travel with her all alone. She was afraid someone would hurt Sarah, if you take my meaning."

Travis nodded like he was sixty years old and a sage. "We figured as much. All right, Shorty and I will stay and watch out after the womenfolk. But don't take too much time, or I'll pack the whole camp up and come after you— don't think I won't."

12 🌿

IT TOOK SHORTY AND TRAVIS all evening to get the chickee built. They moved Maddy into the simple hut made of cypress poles with a palm-thatched roof and walls just as the sun was setting. Hawk made Storm a cradle out of one of Maddy's boxes. She had packed and brought some of Sarah's baby blankets with her and had made some simple clothes for the child while she was traveling.

Cleaned up, with the baby swaddled in a clean baby dress and tucked into his makeshift bed, Maddy came out of her chickee with a smile on her face. Relieved of her burden, she walked with a light step. Hawk met her as she headed toward the campfire and took both her hands in his. She looked wonderful.

"Shouldn't you be lying down on a bed?" Hawk asked.

"Pooh on that," Madelaine said, smiling. "I feel like a new woman. I'll lie down later, after I get something to eat. I'm famished."

Travis handed her a plate with boiled palm cabbage and fry bread and a bowl of sofkee with a spoon. She sat down on a log next to Sarah and ate. Hawk couldn't take his eyes off her.

"How are you feelin'?" Travis asked.

"Fine, thanks to you," she said. "Who cooked this? The food is very tasty. I don't believe I've ever eaten this vegetable or grits cooked quite in this way before. What is it called?"

Travis looked at his hands and smiled shyly. "I cooked. My ma taught me how. She was always fussin' in the kitchen, so I'd sit and watch and sometimes help. That's the heart of a cabbage palm cooked over the fire, and the grits are something the Seminoles make called sofkee. All it is is grits with a little dried deer meat in it. My ma put a lot more stuff in it than that, but that's all we had."

"Well, it certainly tastes delicious, especially so, since I didn't have to cook it. And now I know who to ask to help in the kitchen."

Hawk sat down close to the fire and poked it absently with a stick. "The boys know about Sarah," he said.

Her eyebrows lifted. "Shorty too? I suppose they figured it out for themselves."

"I for one am glad," Sarah said. "I'm sick of wearing boys' clothes. I can't even talk for fear of giving myself away. I haven't been able to be a girl for a long time."

"It might be best if you continued to dress as a boy," Hawk said.

"Why? Aren't we almost to your home?"

Hawk patted Sarah on the shoulder. "You'll be a lot more comfortable, and safer."

Sarah hunched her shoulders and looked at Maddy. "Oh, I suppose so. If you think I have to."

"I think it would be best, darling," Maddy said to her.

"We've been through so much, you should understand. You never know what's going to happen next out here in the wild or who you next might meet."

Early the following morning, Hawk saddled Beau and left the camp. He felt reasonably safe leaving them. Snake was dead, and Travis and Shorty should be able to handle things until he returned. He only planned to be gone for two or three days at the most anyway.

The sun rose slowly on the eastern horizon. Hawk was enjoying the freshness of the morning. All around him, he could hear and see birds and small creatures waking up and beginning another day. Beau cantered along easily in huge ground-covering strides. The power of the animal always impressed Hawk. He could feel the strength in Beau's hindquarters through the saddle. He felt almost as though he were nearly home already.

He'd wrapped his whip around the saddle horn, his rifle hung in a scabbard attached to the saddle, and his slicker was tied behind his saddle along with a bedroll. He wore his pistol on a gunbelt. Everything else, he'd left in the camp. He intended to ride hard with little rest and make it to the D-Wing in ten hours.

After a while, he pulled Beau up and made him walk. Then he set the horse in a distance-eating trot headed for his ranch. Several hours before dusk, he was close enough to the D-Wing to slow to a walk again. He knew he was on his own land when he began to notice certain landmarks.

He saw an oak that had been struck by lightning when he was a boy. Downed, the tree had grown a new tree out of the middle of its exposed trunk. He remembered the storm that brought down the tree when he was twelve. It had been the worst storm he'd ever lived through, with the wind blowing hard enough to knock trees down all over their land. The wind had blown the roof off their cabin, and the river had flooded all the way to the mouth of the blue spring.

He crossed a creek that he knew began in a small spring and ran to the river. His house was just a mile away. He decided to turn away from the house and go to the old cabin where he knew Jimmy and Judy Bill were staying. He hoped they were still there.

Travis had told him what had happened when Snake's men first came. He knew they had all escaped to the cabin. Travis had also told him Jimmy wanted to head south to the Seminoles. Hawk hoped they were still here because he needed their help.

When he neared the cabin, he saw definite signs of habitation. Wood had been cut, and he saw signs of both horse and dog presence. The cabin was well hidden in scrub oak and vines. He'd forgotten how long it had been since he'd been there. No one had lived in the cabin for years and the land was swiftly taking it back.

He dismounted slowly, and, leading Beau, advanced toward the cabin. He still hadn't seen anyone. After tying Beau to a low-hanging branch, he walked through the underbrush, clearing away thorny vines, slipping through palmetto and Spanish bayonet, ducking under hanging creeper. He saw the hog plum trees had gone wild. The small orchard was overgrown with new trees, the fruit already gone for the year. Wild grapevines hung from the branches of the trees, tiny clusters of fruit crowding the vines.

The one-room cabin his grandparents had built was buried in the wild growth. When he pushed his way through, he discovered a clever path. Bending low, he approached the house and the front door. He tried to open it, but it was barred, so he knocked.

The barrel of a rifle appeared in the one window at the front of the house and Hawk heard the deep growl of a dog. "Who are you?"

Hawk smiled. He recognized the voice. "Jimmy Jumper, don't you recognize me, old man? It's Hawk."

The door creaked open and a broad, dark face appeared. "Hawk? Is that you, boy? I hardly recognize you with that scruffy beard all over your face."

Jumper came out, propping the rifle up against the door frame. He enveloped Hawk in a massive hug. Jumper was almost as large as Hawk. Hawk slapped Jimmy on the back. "Where's Judy Bill, you old dog?"

"I had to send her away, Hawk. Joseph took her down south to visit her family. There has been much badness here and at the homestead. Many bad men captured the D-Wing and took it for their own. We have been staying here."

"I know, I know."

"I must tell you, Hawk—Travis has disappeared as well. He left four days ago, and I don't know where he is."

"Don't worry, old friend. He found me. All will be well as soon as I clean house of those outlaws."

They moved into the dark cabin. With the vines so heavily overgrown around and even on the house, no light made it through the three windows. A big gray dog with black spots and tan points eyed Hawk suspiciously. Hawk didn't recognize the leopard dog. It must be one of his foundation dog's puppies.

"Who's this fellow?" Hawk asked, cautiously patting the big dog's wide head.

"He's one of Buzzard's pups out of the Abby gyp. His name is Sam. Buzzard went and died about a year ago."

Hawk was sad to hear his old dog was dead. Buzzard had been one of the best cow dogs he'd ever seen. "Where you keeping all the dogs?"

"We only got Sam here and two gyps, Sadie and Sally. The rest are gone, run off or killed. The other two gyps went with Joseph down to the villages."

"How are you hiding the horses? I can't believe the outlaws haven't found them."

"First off, we put the herd in the corrals back in the sinkhole. One of those bad men did find them, but Joseph killed him. After that we decided Joseph needed to take some of them away. He moved all but ten out on the prairie with the cattle. We've got a few mares here with foals on the ground, the mules, a couple of riding horses, and the stud. We're gonna have to go round up the rest when we need them."

"Good thinking, Jimmy. I'd hate for those bastards to have our horses."

Hawk glanced around and noticed the cabin was spotless. Jumper always was a very neat person. He liked everything to be in its place and neither required nor wanted too much furniture or too many possessions. Jumper poured coffee from an old battered pot and placed a cup on the small wooden table while Hawk sat down on a stool.

"The outlaws cleared out this morning," Jumper said. "About five days ago, just before Travis disappeared, fifteen of them rode out with their leader. Two came back yesterday. I guess they brought bad news, because all of 'em left this morning, and good riddance."

"Have you been back over to the house?" Hawk asked.

"I watched them leave, but I didn't trust them to be gone for good. I was planning to wait for a few days and then go inside. Hawk, my friend, I thought I recognized the leader and one of his men."

Hawk raised an eyebrow.

"Yes, I believe the leader of the outlaws was that bad apple, Jake Barber. I did not get many chances to see him, but it seemed to me to be him. I thought he was gone from these parts for good when he went up north to join the army, but I am almost sure it was him and his friend Skeeter Jerkins."

"You were right," Hawk said. "They attacked us as we camped beside Lake George. I think we killed him."

"Did you kill Skeeter as well?"

"Don't think so," Hawk said. "We never found either body, but Snake got blown sky-high by a load of explosives. He must be dead."

Hawk and Jumper sat at the table talking and ate cold meat and beans with some hard biscuits Judy Bill had left.

"You never found either body?" Jumper asked around a mouthful of beef.

Hawk shook his head.

"I must tell you, I don't like hearing that, my friend. No, I'm getting a bad feeling about this. A wounded Snake Barber would be worse than a wounded bear. You should have hunted harder to find the body. No body means Snake's not dead."

Hawk nodded. "You could be right, Jumper. I felt the same way at the time. But we had womenfolk to consider. We needed to get out of there fast."

Hawk told Jumper a little about Maddy and her daughter, leaving out what he knew about Maddy and Barber. He found he couldn't tell his old friend that Maddy's baby was also Barber's child. Hawk caught the insightful Indian looking at him strangely.

"Are you gonna to bring this woman here to live?"

"She has no place else to go." Hawk said.

Jumper grinned slyly and cocked his head to one side. "You like her."

Hawk could feel his face burning. He looked at his coffee and cup and smiled sheepishly. "Maybe I do at that."

"That is much good news, old friend. You need a woman in your life. Travis needs a mother. What does she look like? Is she pretty? Got a nice figure?"

Hawk felt his face burning again. Damn if he was gonna talk about Maddy's figure to anyone. But the question brought a mental image into his head he could not erase, the image of Maddy nursing her son. Yeah, she had a really nice figure.

"She's pretty enough. Do you think Travis will accept her? He took his mother's death hard. I always got the feeling Travis blamed me for Katie's death."

"It's hard to say what Travis will do. He's headstrong and rebellious," Jumper said, "and he has so much anger inside, powerful anger. I couldn't stop him from going to the house and watching the outlaws. I knew he played tricks on them. I knew he followed them. But what could I do? He was so mad at being left behind, and he missed you. He needs more guidance than an old Indian can give."

"You did a great job, Jumper. I'm sorry I was gone so long. I know Travis is angry, and he's always been a handful. But I think he'll be fine when we all get back to working on the ranch. I think some hard work will straighten him right out." Hawk yawned. "I plan to start hunting cows as soon as we get settled. In the fall, we'll take us a herd to Tampa."

Jumper smiled. "My friend, I've been waiting a long time to hear you say that."

Hawk had ridden hard. He was tired. He stood up after finishing one last cup of coffee. "I'm going to get some shut-eye. In the morning, we'll ride over and check the place out. Maybe Barber is really dead, and if he's not, maybe he'll leave us alone now."

Jumper shook his head. "You're not thinking the right way, old friend. If Barber is alive, count on him coming back here to take revenge and get what he was here for in the first place."

"You mean the gold?"

"He spent a lot of time checking out the blue spring. Didn't do him no good. How'd he know to look in a spring?"

Hawk told him quickly about being in prison and meeting Barber there.

"That makes much sense. Too bad he was looking in wrong spring, eh, Hawk?" Jumper laughed as he said this.

"Yeah, too bad."

Hawk took care of Beau, unsaddling the horse and feeding him some ground corn before letting him loose in a corral separate from the cracker horses. He didn't need Beau wearing himself out breeding a bunch of mares and getting in fights with the feisty marsh tackies.

Jumper had built the horse corrals deep in a sinkhole in the woods behind the cabin. The Seminole had done a good job of protecting Hawk's land and possessions while he was gone.

Hawk went back into the tiny cabin, walking along the

clever trail cut through dense undergrowth. He carried his saddle and rifle inside and made up a bed on the floor. But it was a while before he could sleep.

In the morning, he and Jumper rode to the D-Wing to see what the outlaws had done to the place.

"That's a lot of horse," Jumper said after clapping eyes on Beau.

"We're tall men, old friend. We need to add a little size to these marsh tackies of ours. I think he'll do the job."

"I bet he's a fast one."

"He is, but a good cracker horse could probably beat him over a short distance. It takes him a while to get going, but once he's got his legs under him, look out. A marsh tacky will have more endurance as well. But Beau can probably smoke anything around here in a mile race."

Hawk was so happy to be home. The familiar path to his house made his heart sing with joy. It had been such a long time. When they got to the homestead, however, his heart sank. The outlaws had torn down fences and the barn lay in ruins. Half of the chicken house was destroyed, chickens gone. The outhouse was on its side, door a few yards away. No pigs, no goats, no cows, not a living thing in sight.

"We took some of the livestock with us," Jumper said. "What we couldn't take, they ate or killed for the fun of killing. All of Travis's animals are dead except for that hawk of his and a few he's found since."

Hawk felt empty as he surveyed the damage. He hated to see senseless death. But everything else could be rebuilt and replaced. "Let's go look inside the house."

He entered the home of his childhood with trepidation.

"I fear the house will be terrible inside," Jumper said, pausing in the breezeway.

He was right. They had to shove with all their might to get into the front door. All the furniture was destroyed, broken into tiny pieces and then stacked against the door. In the kitchen, dishes and crockery lay shattered on the floor. The sink had been torn out and flung through the kitchen window. His mother's pie safe lay in ruins, her baking table and flour bins chopped into firewood. His mother's precious windows, brought all the way from Jacksonville, were all broken.

Feces and puddles of urine were in every corner. But the most overpowering odor was the smell of skunk spray.

"I know animals live cleaner than this," Jumper said.

"They destroyed the house on purpose," Hawk said. "It was their way of showing complete disrespect. At least now we know why they left. After soiling the place, they probably couldn't stand to live here anymore. But why does it stink of skunk? Did they kill one in here? Even this bunch couldn't have been that stupid."

"I do not know why it smells of skunk, my friend, but I do know Travis had a pet skunk, a little sow named Rosie with four wild kits."

Hawk smiled. "Ah! Well, Travis always was a trickster."

Jumper looked around at the devastation. "I'll hunt for an unbroken bucket and draw some water. I can't just stand here and look at this mess without itching to clean it up."

"I'll go see if I can find a shovel. I think we need one."

13 🌿

"CAN'T YOU SEE I'M IN PAIN?" Snake Barber snarled at Skeeter, and then broke out in a fit of coughing. The damp of the cave he'd lain in for two days had settled on his lungs. He knew he wasn't going to die of his injuries because he was going to die of pneumonia instead.

Every cough sent daggers of agony stabbing into his stump. That god-cursed Indian woman, whose name he now knew was Aggie, should have known he would get pneumonia. Every breath he drew hurt as the fluid kept collecting in his chest.

"You need to go to Jacksonville or Pilatka or somewhere and get me some medicine for the pain," Snake told Skeeter for the third time that morning. "I'm dying of pneumonia and you won't help me."

"Aggie says you ain't got pneumonia. She says you got a cold in your lungs and you ain't dying. She says all you need to do is get up and try to walk some with this stick I made for you. Laying down all the time ain't good for you."

"What does that old bitch know about anything? I've

told you I can't get up. Not until I heal more. It's only been a week since that bitch of a butcher cut off my leg."

When he was in one of his stubborn moods, Skeeter's face looked remarkably like that of one of those mules he broke. "You need to stand up some, Snake. I ain't foolin'. She says laying down is causing pus and bad water to collect in your lungs. You need to move around some. Snake, man, she knows what she's talkin' 'bout."

"I know what I need. I need laudanum and I need some dang whiskey. Why don't you ride to Volusia Landing and get me some whiskey and some laudanum. They might have laudanum at the trading post. If they don't, get yourself to Enterprise. I know they got it there. They got a doctor there. I need syrup of poppies, laudanum, or something to kill this pain."

Skeeter sat where Snake could see him on a short bench inside the little chickee Skeeter and the Indian woman had built. That boy of hers, Otter, had helped, but mostly he hunted. The boy had one gift: he could find game where there was none. They ate well, either dining on deer, gator tail, or fish. The old woman had used all her hominy, so there was no sofkee. But she knew how to make bread with flour from the coontie plant, and her fry bread was the best Snake had ever tasted.

"While you're down that way, you can check on my Maddy. Find out where she is for me." Snake shifted on his pallet, trying to get more comfortable. He gingerly touched the stump, rubbing across it gently with one finger. It itched, it burned, and it ached all at the same time.

"I'll go get your whiskey and your medicine, boss. But you need to leave the woman alone. She's poison, boss. I done told you that already. Look what happened to you. And it's all 'cause you had to chase after that woman."

"Don't be talking about Maddy like that, Skeeter. I told you already, she's different. She's special. I'm gonna take her up North and marry her."

Skeeter snorted. "Yeah, you told me all right. But I know what I know and what I know is that she ain't never gonna marry you. You got windmills in yer head if you think she is. I could see plain as the nose on my face she hates you. You was the only one of us that couldn't see. 'Bout made all of us sick to our stomachs, it did."

"You better stop talking about her like that, Skeeter. We been friends for a long time, but if you keep on, well, just don't. You know what I'm like when I lose my temper."

"Yeah, boss, I know."

"I tell you what, Skeeter," Snake said slyly. "I'll get up and walk on that crutch you made, or at least I'll try to, if you'll find out where Maddy went and get me some medicine. I can't take the pain, Skeeter. I need something to dull it a trifle. You got to understand. That swill the Indian woman makes ain't cutting the mustard no more."

Skeeter nodded and pulled the crutch out of the corner. "Fine, boss, you try getting up out of that bed first. And then maybe I'll look for the dang woman."

Snake grunted, but allowed Skeeter to heft him to his one foot. Damn if he could understand why the foot that hurt him the most was the one he'd lost. He knew it wasn't there, but the pain and itching in it drove him near crazy.

The Indian woman came to help when she saw Skeeter struggling to hoist him to a standing position. She grinned shyly at Skeeter, who immediately looked away, his hollow cheeks stained red with embarrassment. Snake was disgusted. So that was the way of things.

Snake reluctantly accepted the Indian woman's help. He just couldn't believe Skeeter would go with an Indian. While Aggie supported him on one side, Skeeter lifted him on the other.

His good foot had lost one toe, burned off, and the rest of the foot still hurt from burns. When he put weight on it, the skin stretched and cracked, even though Aggie had rubbed bear fat into it. He ignored the pain. He just wanted Skeeter to find Maddy. He'd do just about anything to get the man to do this thing for him. Damn if he wouldn't get up and dance a jig if that's what it took.

The crutch Skeeter had made fit under his arm. Skeeter had padded it with moss and covered the moss with scraps of material sewn together by Aggie. He was able to take a few hopping steps before he succumbed to a fit of coughing.

"When boss man stand up, stuff come out of lungs," Aggie said.

Snake glared at her and took a couple more steps. Weakness rushed over him like a wave. "Got to sit down," he muttered.

Skeeter helped him to a log by the camp's fire pit. A fat boar coon roasted in the ashes. Otter sure could hunt— they'd eat well tonight. "You'll head out today and look for Maddy?" Snake asked.

"Damn if you don't got a one-track mind. Yeah, boss. I'll get on my horse and go to Volusia Landing. And on my way, I'll look for yer woman."

"Don't come back without pain medicine. You hear me?"

"I'll go, boss. I'll get the medicine," Skeeter finally said. "Today?"

"Today," Skeeter sighed. "And I might as well take that extra horse I found and bring back some supplies."

❖   ❖   ❖

Ten miles down the trail from Snake, toward Volusia Landing, Maddy and Travis were getting into an argument. Travis wanted to pack up the wagon and follow his pa.

"No, Travis, we won't be leaving," Maddy said calmly. "Your Pa told us to stay here until he came for us, and that's exactly what we will do."

"But it's been five days, Miss Maddy. What if something happened to him?"

Maddy closed her eyes. That was what she was worried about too. In general, she'd had no use for men. Until she met Hawk and now his son Travis, she'd had a low opinion of the male species. From her own experiences, she'd discovered they were lazy and filthy, bathing only when forced, as well as mean-natured and selfish to an extreme.

Her father had thought the world revolved around him, and this opinion had been fostered and nurtured by her mother, who waited on him hand and foot. Her husband had been of the same ilk, and then she'd been exposed to Snake Barber and his men and realized that the meanness she'd seen in her husband was really only a watered-down version of the true evil men were capable of.

But Hawk had shown himself to be a true gentleman, and his son was very sweet-natured. Travis treated her and Sarah with kindness and respect. And the expression on his face when he held Storm was beautiful to see.

She could not imagine what they would do if Hawk did not return. She could not imagine what *she* would do, for she'd come to depend on him. He was strong and capable and very smart, and as Sarah had remarked, Hawk liked her. She was beginning to think she might like him as well.

She'd never longed for the presence of either her father or her husband in their absence, but now she found herself missing Hawk intensely. She missed the long days riding beside him on the wagon seat. She missed the feeling of safety she'd experienced when he was close by, and she missed looking at him. He was very handsome, and she'd spent a lot of time admiring him.

"Your father will be back any day, Travis. He must come back, for we are all here waiting on him and he knows this. Please be patient. Why don't you take Shorty and go hunting? We could use the meat."

"I'll wait just one more day, Miss Maddy, for your sake. But I still think we should pack up and head for home." The tall boy with the ice-blue eyes shuffled his feet and started digging a hole with the toe of his boot. "It's just I ain't very good at waitin', ma'am."

Maddy could see the boy's impatience to be off, and she echoed his sentiments. She wanted to be in a place she could call home, a place where she could relax and let down her guard. She'd been in situations of stress for so long she hardly knew what it would be like to relax.

They would wait as Hawk had instructed, and as sure as the sun came up in the morning, he would come for them. She knew he would. He had to.

"Maybe I'll give Sarah another riding lesson," Travis

said. "Did you know she's a-scared of horses?"

"Yes, she's been terrified of horses ever since her father put her up on one of his hunters and she got thrown. Sarah was only five at the time and he should never have done that to her. But he was not mindful of her fears and her inexperience."

"I'll put her on the bay gelding you got pulling the wagon. He's about dead broke and twenty years old if he's a day."

Maddy sat on a log nursing Storm and watched Travis go find Sarah. Sarah had taken to wearing dresses sometimes in the evenings. Maddy knew her daughter was a young woman to the core. She liked womanly things like perfume and lace and frilly dresses. It was a shame Sarah's hair had been chopped off. She'd had such beautiful hair. But it was growing back, longer every day, and soon she would look just as she had before all this had happened.

Maddy knew where Sarah was. She was sitting in the chickee setting tiny stitches into a dress for Storm. Sarah was the most exquisite seamstress. During the time she'd been locked in the cellar hiding from Barber, she'd spent all the time she could perfecting her stitchery by sewing handkerchiefs and embroidering them with a pattern of wild roses she'd drawn herself. Sarah was an accomplished artist as well. The pile of handkerchiefs Sarah had made out of her father's fine linen shirts was packed away in a trunk on the wagon.

Maddy could see her daughter was not too excited about the prospect of learning to ride. This was the second time Travis had put her on a horse. The first time, he'd ridden with her in front of him on his little marsh horse. Today would be Sarah's first time riding by herself. Maddy had watched her ride in front of Travis and noticed that, despite her fears, the girl would have been happy to ride just about anywhere with the boy.

Sarah had never had any friends, either male or female, close to her own age. This was her daughter's only experience with young men, and it was quite obvious Travis had already made a conquest.

Shorty brought the big bay gelding, Spirit, around for Sarah all saddled and ready. The old horse cocked one foot up and patiently went to sleep while Travis helped Sarah mount. Taking her reins, Travis mounted up on his little bay, while Shorty leaped into the saddle of the red cracker horse. Then the three of them rode out of the clearing, with Travis leading Sarah on the gelding.

Travis looked over his shoulder at Sarah. If she weren't wearing boys' clothes and had some hair, she might be pretty. She was sure scared of horses. Sarah had both hands clamped onto the saddle horn in a death grip.

"Relax some and sit up straight, Sarah, and put your heels down," Travis said over his shoulder.

He watched as Sarah did her best to comply with his instructions.

Travis held the horses to a walk even though he longed to turn Light Foot to the south and ride like the devil for home. This waiting around for Pa stunk. Shorty rode beside him and they talked together like they'd known each other for years. The two of them had become friends in just the little bit of time they'd known each other.

"Why'd you hang around with that gang of outlaws, Shorty?" Travis asked as they slowly walked down the trail.

"It weren't me, it was my brother, John. Well, he weren't my brother really, he just took me up when I was little and my ma died. Pa was away fighting for the Rebs and Brother John lived on the farm next to ours. We was sharecroppers up near Atlanta. Brother John's pa beat him all the time for nothing, and his ma was no good. When my ma died, we run off to join the army. We didn't get far. We ended up with Snake on that Miss Maddy's farm, Twelve Oaks."

"Why did you stay there?" Travis couldn't understand anyone following Snake Barber.

"I didn't know no better and Brother John liked it fine. There was lots of whiskey and plenty to eat. We was hungry."

"Well, I sure hope you know better now," Travis said and looked back at Sarah again. "Are you okay back there?"

She smiled and took one hand off the saddle horn to wave at him. Travis realized she and her ma had the same smile. The three of them rode down a hill to a small clearing beside a creek. Travis was thinking about heading back when he spotted a rider coming down the trail.

"Hey, Shorty, see that rider coming at us from the north?" Travis shaded his eyes with his hand and stared hard in an effort to see the approaching rider more clearly.

Shorty turned in the saddle. "Yeah, I see him."

"Don't he look familiar to you?"

Shorty squinted into the afternoon sun, also shading his eyes with his hand. "Holy shoot, Trav, I know who that is," Shorty said. "We better take cover. It's Skeeter."

The three of them dismounted and led their horses into the thick scrub beside the creek. They watched from the safety of the thick willow and cherry trees as Skeeter came down the trail leading a horse with no saddle.

Skeeter pulled the two horses out of a jog and into a walk. When he got close to the camp, he stopped, got off, and examined the ground.

"He can see our tracks," Shorty said.

"I got the drop on him," Travis said, sighting down the barrel of his rifle. "Should I kill him?"

"Wait and see if he moves on," Shorty said. "He never did nothing wrong by me."

"All right," Travis said. "I won't shoot him if you think I shouldn't."

They watched Skeeter lead the horses to a secluded spot down the trail, tether them to a tree, and then double back, sneaking from one tree to another.

"Let me drop him, Shorty," Travis said. "He's spying on Miss Maddy."

"Give him another minute or two. I'm telling you, Skeeter ain't a bad man. He's rough as can be and been friends with Snake most all his life, but he ain't all bad. I'd hate to see him kilt."

Travis kept Skeeter in his sights as the man crept around the camp spying.

"What's my pa gonna say when I tell him I had the drop on Skeeter and I didn't kill him?"

"Your pa don't kill for the hell of it. I know he'll understand. Skeeter stood up for me against Snake once. I still remember. Saved me a beatin', he did."

Skeeter didn't hang around long. After watching Maddy from the safety of cover, he fetched his horses out of the bushes and rode on down the trail toward Volusia

Landing and the D-Wing Ranch. Travis and Shorty helped Sarah remount, then they all rode back to the camp.

"Miss Maddy," Travis said after they'd put the horses on the picket line. "We saw Snake's man Skeeter Jerkins ride past here. I wanted to shoot him, but Shorty said it would be wrong. Did I do the right thing?"

Travis was torn up inside. He didn't know whether he'd done the right thing or not. He feared he had just made a huge mistake, the kind you regretted your entire life.

Maddy's face registered shock. Her eyes flew open and she tightened her mouth into a thin line. "Did you check everywhere around here to see if there are more of them out there hiding?" she asked.

"No, ma'am. Me and Shorty will do that directly. I just wanted to tell you that he snooped around the campsite. I think he was spying on you, but after a few minutes he climbed back on his horse and rode toward Volusia Landing and home. It didn't look like he had no one else with him. I think he might have seen you."

Maddy put her arm around his shoulders. He immediately felt relief. She wasn't mad at him. "I don't know whether you made a mistake or not, Travis, but I'm glad you didn't kill him. I remember Skeeter. He was never mean to me. He was always outside messing with his horses, braiding leather into whips and bridles, or cleaning his tack. He even fixed the sink in my kitchen for me once. But he's loyal to Snake. They've been friends for almost their whole lives. We better tell your Pa about this as soon as he gets here."

14

"Gidap!" Hawk gathered his reins and slapped leather on the wide rumps of his team of mules. The mules put their backs into it and the big, two-horse buckboard started rolling. He'd decided to take the buckboard to haul Maddy and the baby home in a little more comfort. The buckboard had springs that cushioned the ride. Maddy's old farm wagon would shake the teeth right out of your head.

Beau and a spare mule trotted along behind the wagon. With the fresh mule in the traces of Maddy's wagon instead of the ancient John mule or the equally ancient bay, and two mules to pull the buckboard, they should make good time on the journey home.

Jimmy Jumper rode shotgun, sitting tall and straight with his rifle resting on his lap. Hawk figured it would take at least two days to make it back to the camp where Maddy's baby had been born. It had taken two days to clean his house. Hawk knew he had been gone a lot longer than he'd thought he would. He hoped Travis had obeyed his orders and waited. He knew the boy had ants in his pants.

Between the two of them, he and Jumper had hauled destroyed furniture into the yard and burned a huge pile, then scrubbed every inch of the place with scrub brushes, lye soap, and water. He'd need to make a new table and chairs, or take the trip to Enterprise to purchase furniture. He'd also need to replace the glass in all the windows. He didn't know if he could even buy the glass locally. He might have to order it from Jacksonville and cut it himself to fit.

They'd had to burn all the mattresses, but had saved the bedsteads. Material for new mattresses would have to be bought. And Maddy might want some fabric for curtains, dresses, and baby clothes. It looked like a shopping expedition was in the cards, especially since they also needed supplies, like flour, sugar, lard, corn, salt, leavening, and grits. The outlaws had eaten or ruined everything.

The house was ready to occupy again, but a new barn needed to be constructed, the outhouse door replaced, and the springhouse repaired. The only building left standing was the smokehouse. Building a new barn meant cutting down some stout cedars or cypress poles, hand-milling siding boards, and cutting shingles if they didn't just thatch the roof. If they were lucky, the support poles and the trusses would all be salvageable from the original structure. Hawk was really hoping to get away with using the material that was there. The outlaws hadn't taken it away, just pulled it down.

The horse pasture fences and the corral fences needed mending, while half the chicken coop would have to be rebuilt and the pig pens put back up. Things were a mess. It would take all of them working for many days to set the place in order. And somehow, he had to get it all done in between hunting cattle.

Going out into the prairies and bringing the wild Florida cattle to market was his main source of income. It was also the thing he loved doing most in the world. He was a cow hunter through and through.

Hawk's father had started hunting wild cows and rounding them up soon after settling in Florida. It took a lot of skill, dogs, and whips to accomplish. The cattle hid in the palmettos and scrub oaks. They were a bitch to find, small and elusive. Without dogs, you could ride right by a cow and calf and never see them. His dogs would dive into the brush and bring the cows out. A good cow dog was worth his weight in gold. Gold doubloons, to be specific.

Hawk had been hunting cattle since he was eight years old. He could remember riding out with Pappy for the first time, scared out of his wits, with Jimmy Jumper and the first hand Pappy had ever hired, Dexter McGuire. They'd hunt for the cattle, bring them out of the brush, cut the calves, brand every one they caught, and—when they had enough for a herd—drive them to Tampa to sell. Ships took the scrawny Florida cattle to Cuba and Pap got paid in genuine Spanish doubloons.

"We sure got our work cut out for us fixing up that mess the outlaws left," Jumper said as they rode down the rutted trail toward the campsite.

"I'm glad it's only work and not fighting," Hawk said. "I thought we were going to have to roust the outlaws, just you and me. I came home to scout out the territory and see how many were still living in the house. I don't mind a little fixin' up. It's a sight better than having to attack your own home and maybe burn it down to get the vermin out."

"You were thinkin' of burning the house down?"

"I would have, if it'd meant getting rid of them. A meaner, lower bunch of deserters and layouts I never saw."

"I heard there's bands of them all over the state," Jumper said. "When Joe Tiger came to warn us to get out, he told me there's hundreds of them living on the edge of the Great Swamp. Bunches of deserters and lowlife outlaws have been harassing the Seminoles, robbing the white settlements, stealing cows, and killing folks just about everywhere. He said it all started just about when the war ended. And there ain't no law around to stop them, neither."

"We're gonna have to keep our eyes open and a guard out at the D-Wing from now on," Hawk said. "I think I'll hire on some new hands when we go to Enterprise. Maybe I can find me a couple of good ones."

Jumper grunted his assent as the wagon bounced over a particularly deep rut.

The trip back to the camp where he'd left Maddy and Travis took two full days. The wagon rolled into sight of the familiar clump of pines five days after he had left. It was late evening, and the sun had already set. A wisp of smoke rose above the trees, and Hawk sighed with relief when he saw that universal sign of human habitation. At least someone was still here.

He clucked to the two mules and drove right into the grove of trees. It was almost dark beneath the oaks and pines. Hawk saw the chickee was still standing. He pulled the wagon to a stop just as Maddy came out of the hut. She was holding Storm, and Hawk thought she'd never looked lovelier. When she smiled at him, his heart jumped. He hadn't felt like this about a woman since he was eighteen, when he'd fallen in love with Katie.

"Is that yer woman?" Jumper asked.

"That's Maddy," Hawk said.

"She is a fine woman, Hawk, a fine woman."

"I know, brother, I know."

Hawk didn't see any horses. He wondered where Travis and Shorty were. He climbed stiffly down from the high seat of the buckboard as Maddy ran to greet him. He thought she might have hugged him if she hadn't been holding the baby.

"Hawk, we missed you. What took you so long?" Maddy cradled the infant, rocking Storm in her arms as she smiled up into Hawk's face. "Are the outlaws still in your house?"

"No, they're gone. It took two days to clean up the mess. They destroyed everything they could get their hands on. We'll need new furniture, curtains, and windows, but at least it's clean. Me and Jumper scrubbed it from front to back."

Jumper climbed down from the buckboard and stood expectantly beside him. "Madelaine Wilkes, I'd like you to meet my best friend and partner, Jimmy Jumper," Hawk said.

Jumper pulled his big straw hat off his head and looked at the ground. "Pleased to meet you, ma'am."

Maddy took Jumper's hand and held it. "It's good to meet you as well," she said. "I've heard so much about you and your wife."

"Where are the boys?" Hawk asked. "I expected them to be here. It's almost dark."

"They took Sarah out for another riding lesson," Maddy said. "Travis has been teaching her to ride."

"That was nice of him. Has he been behaving himself?"

"Travis has been wonderful. Are you two hungry? I have supper waiting. Come eat."

Hawk and Jumper each loaded up a plate and sat down. Hawk noticed he was eating catfish stew. The boys must have gone fishing. It smelled great and tasted delicious. They were just tucking into the grub when the boys rode in with Sarah. Hawk looked up and saw Sarah was riding the big bay. She had control of her reins and looked fairly solid in the saddle. What a difference.

Travis waved. "Hey, Pa, look at Sarah. She can ride."

The three dismounted. As Shorty led the horses away, Travis ran to Hawk, his eyes shining. "I waited, Pa. It was hard. I wanted to leave so many times, but Maddy told me to wait, and I did."

Hawk chuckled. "I bet it was hard, son. Did anything happen while I was gone?"

Travis filled a plate and sat beside Hawk. "Pa, that feller Skeeter, the one that's a friend to Snake Barber, he rode by leading a spare horse. I wanted to shoot him, Pa, but Shorty said I shouldn't because Skeeter ain't a bad man. Then I asked Maddy if I done right and she said I did 'cause she didn't think he was a bad man either. Did I do right, Pa? It's about to drive me crazy. I can't help feeling I should have plugged him."

"I'm sure you wanted to, son," Hawk said. "But it's never good to kill in cold blood, no matter what the reason. We may live to regret it, but I'm really glad you let him go. Which way was he heading?"

"Well, he got off his horse right here at the camp and then he started snoopin' around. That's when I wanted to shoot him bad. But he didn't stay long, just snooped around lookin' at Miss Maddy and all, and then he climbed back on his horse and left. He headed south like you come from. I was wondering if maybe you saw him."

"No, we didn't see a soul."

Maddy waited until Hawk was alone. She found him making up his pallet in the back of the buckboard. "If Skeeter is still around, do you think Snake is still alive, Hawk?" Maddy asked, clearly worried. "I'm glad Travis didn't kill him, but it still worries me that he spied on me and this camp. What could he have been looking for? Do you think he knew I was here, or do you think he could have recognized me?"

"I don't know, Maddy. We may never know. The important thing is he rode on. He didn't try to kidnap you and the baby, and you were alone. He left. If he saw you and did recognize you, well, he still didn't do anything and went away. Snake must be dead. Surely if Snake was alive and Skeeter recognized you, he would have tried to grab you."

"You must be right, Hawk. It's still a very worrisome thing, especially thinking he was watching me and I didn't know."

"We'll be leaving first thing for home, Maddy. Try not to worry about Snake or anything. You're safe with me, Jumper, and Travis. We'll take care of you."

"I know you're right, Hawk. Thank you for all you've done for me and Sarah and little Storm. I have no way to repay all your kindnesses. I hope I make you a good housekeeper."

"Don't even think about it, Maddy. You're like family now."

Hawk bedded down in the back of the buckboard with Jumper. He had a hard time falling asleep even though he was tired. It bothered him that Skeeter Jerkins had spied on Maddy and the baby. It bothered him a lot. He figured the man might have stopped to look because he saw smoke from the fire and wanted to see who was camping in the trees. Maybe he'd recognized Maddy and maybe he hadn't.

What really bothered him was, why didn't Jerkins hello the camp and stop to visit? Most folks would do that. It was the way of the traveler and a matter of common courtesy out here where so few people were to be found. When you didn't get to visit with other folks much, few would miss such an opportunity. He hated to think Jerkins had been looking for Maddy. If that was the case, Barber might be alive. But if he he'd only been curious, then recognized her and not wanted her to know he'd been there, maybe Barber was dead and Skeeter was moving on.

Hawk had to comfort himself with the thought that Jerkins had ridden on down the trail. If he'd been strictly looking for Maddy, he would have ridden back the way he'd come. And he was ponying a horse. Maybe it was Snake's horse, which would mean Barber was dead.

These were wild, rough times. Maybe Jerkins had figured the camp was occupied by more than just Maddy. It could have been he'd thought Hawk was still there and didn't want to mess with him. Or maybe he was in one hell of a hurry. The whole affair made Hawk nervous. Like he'd told the boy, he was glad Travis hadn't killed in cold blood. It wasn't something he wanted to encourage in his son. But he couldn't help wishing Jerkins were dead. If the man were safely underground, the matter would weigh on his mind a lot less.

It was a while before he dropped into sleep. When he did, he slept like a rock. In the morning, the boys were up early. Everyone packed, loaded the two wagons, and got ready to leave.

"I want to say a short prayer of thanksgiving for your

safe return and to thank God for Storm," Maddy said as they readied to leave.

Hawk, Jumper, and the boys quickly removed their hats before joining Sarah and Maddy in bowing their heads.

"Dear Lord, thank you for bringing Hawk and Mr. Jumper safely to us. Thanks, Lord, for darling Storm and an easy delivery. Please look after us, Lord, as we set out on the remainder of our long journey. Amen."

Hawk did not understand why he felt so moved when Maddy prayed. He felt comforted, as though she really could speak to God. Heck, what did he know, maybe she could. She certainly believed in the power of prayer. And look what it had done for her. Maybe he was a gift to Maddy from God. And then again, maybe *she* was a gift to *him*.

The trip home took three days because they had to travel slowly and stop often. It was nice to see Sarah riding with the boys mounted on the aged gelding inappropriately named Spirit. Though to be fair, what the bay lacked in energy, he more than made up for in kindness. He took care of Sarah and listened to her inept commands.

Jumper drove the wagon loaded with Maddy's belongings and pulled by the big strong horse mule Hawk had brought from home.

Maddy sat beside Hawk on the cushioned seat of the big buckboard. She held little Storm on her lap some of the time and when he fell asleep, she laid him in his makeshift cradle. He was a peaceful baby, sleeping most of the time and eating with a lusty appetite. Hawk tried not to think about who Storm's father was. Maybe upbringing and love meant more than who your parents were.

Hawk remembered when Travis had found an orphaned

panther kitten. He'd bottle-fed and hand-raised it. For a while, the kitten was gentle. As it grew, though, it became more and more wild. Hawk became afraid the cub would hurt Travis or kill one of the dogs. He'd finally made Travis return the cat to the swamp where he'd found it.

Hawk turned his head and looked at the peacefully sleeping baby. He hoped he wasn't bringing a panther cub into his home.

It was after dinnertime on the third day that they reached the homestead. Hawk's home was high on a shell mound surrounded by grandfather oak trees. The trees shaded the house from the afternoon sun. When Maddy first laid eyes on the house, she wondered why it was built in two sections with an open breezeway in the middle. She'd never seen a house built like that before. She liked the wraparound porches and large windows; they'd keep the house cool. But her first impression of the house was of no matter, as it was Hawk's home and would be theirs—at least for a while. And because of that, she would naturally learn to love it.

Hawk helped her down from the buckboard and handed her Storm. "I can't wait to show you the house," he said, his eyes shining.

Well, it was his home, he should be proud of it. She thought for a moment of Twelve Oaks and the two-story whitewashed house with four stately columns in the front that she'd left behind. The big front parlor had had a stone fireplace and a staircase graced with a polished cherry banister. The newel post had been hand-carved by Mark's father,

Henry Wilkes, a nasty, cold, disagreeable man who had died when he fell through the top of the septic tank and drowned. Maddy, who tried hard never to think uncharitable thoughts, couldn't help but feel Henry Wilkes had come by his just desserts.

Maddy shook her head. Twelve Oaks was gone forever. The memories of the life she had lived there with Mark were all terrible. When he had ridden off to war, she'd enjoyed being in charge of the plantation and enjoyed being her own mistress for the first time in her life. While the war had raged farther north, she'd quietly lived a comfortable and rewarding life with Sarah. Then Snake Barber and his men had ridden in and changed everything.

Now the Yankees had claimed it, and even if she'd found a way to stay, she would undoubtedly have eventually lost it to taxes anyway. She had no money to pay the high taxes invading hoards of Yankees were levying on all Confederate property. She'd heard the news in every town she'd traveled though in Georgia. Not only had the Yankees defeated the South, killing most of the menfolk, but now they were taking the land.

No, she would not think with longing of the life she had left behind nor the grand old house at Twelve Oaks. She and Sarah would embrace this new life and she would thank God for deliverance from her travails.

Putting a smile on her face, she marched onto the porch and into her new home. With no glass in the floor-to-ceiling windows, a cool breeze blew through the house. But with no glass, there was nothing to stop the hoards of invading insects either. Flies buzzed on the ceiling. The smell of lye soap was so strong her eyes watered, and she doubted very much the flies would land on anything but the ceiling. She marveled at their bravery in coming into the house at all.

The structure was made of cypress logs, which were planed and sanded smooth inside, then varnished. The floors were made of thick slabs of cypress, some a foot across. What large trees they must have been.

A kitchen, dining area, parlor, and small bedroom were contained in one side of the house. Maddy walked through the breezeway into the other side and found four more roomy bedrooms with two on either side of the hallway. The bedrooms all contained bedsteads with no mattresses. One had a cupboard and a wardrobe with the door torn off. There were no lamps or candles, but she had several lamps and a box of candles in her belongings, along with enough soft cotton cloth to make the necessary mattress covers.

The bolts of white cotton had been a wedding gift from Rachel. She'd planned to sew all new sheets for Twelve Oaks, but somehow never got around to doing it. When she'd packed to come to Pilatka, of course, she had thought to bring the bolts of cloth. Now they would make new mattress covers for all their beds, as well as new sheets. There was so much work to do.

As she walked around making plans, Sarah joined her. "It's not like Twelve Oaks, is it, Mama?"

"No, it's not at all like Twelve Oaks, and we should be glad. You know, Sarah, I thought we wouldn't be needed here. I thought Mr. Hawk was just bringing us here out of pity or as a charitable deed. But there is so much work to do. This place is crying out for a woman's touch." She hugged Sarah with her free arm. "No, darling, it's not Twelve Oaks, but this will be our home."

Sarah laughed. Shocked, Maddy looked at her daughter.

This was the first time in more than two years she had heard Sarah laugh. The girl wrapped her arms around Maddy. "I know it's our home, Mama, and I'm so glad it's not like Twelve Oaks. I'm going to love it here."

15 ☀

Snake sat on a log with his good leg stuck out in front of him and his ruined leg crossed over it. He ran a hand under the waistband of his pants and scratched his belly. He'd been wearing these same pants for months. They were filthy, and Snake had a sneaking suspicion they were occupied by a host of vermin.

Where was Skeeter? It had been over a week since he'd ridden off for supplies and pain medicine. The only reason Aggie, the Indian woman, stayed was because Skeeter had told her he was coming back. She apparently had developed a fixation on his friend, which as it turned out was a very good thing. He had no desire to starve, and starve he would if she didn't cook. But cooking the game her moronic son brought back to the camp was all she was good for. He'd tried a dozen times to get her to wash his clothes, to no avail. She either pretended she didn't understand him, or just said no. And it was a task he was unable to do himself with only one leg.

Snake had become adept at getting around on his crutch. He found the horrible Aggie was actually right. The more he moved around, the less he coughed and the better his leg healed. He still was tortured by pain in his missing leg and foot. It woke him in the night. The pain in his stump was just bearable, the most pain coming from the severed bones and the pad of skin the woman had sewed over his stump.

The various burns, cuts, and bruises he'd sustained in his fall were gradually healing, but the pain in his missing leg was unbearable at times. He wondered if it was like this for all the men in the Civil War who had suffered amputations like his. Did they too have pain in their missing limbs? Did they wake up in the night screaming in agony and trying to scratch or rub a leg that was no longer there?

Just thinking about it had his missing foot throbbing in agony again. He could do nothing for it. You couldn't rub or massage something that wasn't there. You couldn't scratch itches that didn't exist. You couldn't soak a missing leg in hot water or smear on a soothing salve. Where the hell was Skeeter?

Grabbing his crutch, he hobbled down to the shore of Lake George. Otter was just returning from hunting in the canoe. The stolid Indian youth pulled the boat ashore and jumped out, carrying a string of bream over his shoulder. One thing you could say about Otter— he was dumb as a post, but Snake had to admit you'd never go hungry with him around. The Indian stopped and stared down the road toward Volusia, slowly lifted one thick forefinger, and pointed.

Haltingly turning around with the aid of his crutch, Snake looked in the direction Otter was pointing. Skeeter was riding up the slight hill to the hammock leading his spare horse, which was loaded down with packages. If Snake could have run, he would have.

Skeeter dismounted in the shade of the pines and hugged a beaming Aggie. Her plain brown face was alight with happiness. Skeeter pushed her off, apparently embarrassed by her rare show of affection.

"Did you bring me something for the pain?" Snake asked without preamble.

"Got yer medicine right here, boss. I had to travel all the way to Enterprise to get it. The doctor there would only give me these four bottles. He said it was all he could spare."

Skeeter pulled a brown bottle of milky white liquid out of one of the packs on the spare horse and handed it to Snake. "You're supposed to take ten to twenty-five drops of this stuff, depending on how much pain you're in. That's what the doc told me."

Snake grabbed the bottle and uncorked it. The smell was bad. Ignoring it, he gulped down a big mouthful. Skeeter grabbed the bottle away from him.

"The doc told me you can die if you drink too much of this." Skeeter put the cork back in the bottle and began unpacking bundles and handing them to Aggie.

Snake dropped onto a log. "I don't care if I die. I just want the pain to go away."

Skeeter stopped his unpacking and glared at Snake. "Well, maybe you would care if you knew you had a son."

If he could have, Snake would have leaped to his feet. He grabbed the log beneath him, his fingers digging into the rotten wood. "What did you just say?"

"I said the dang woman done had a child. I didn't get me that good a look, but I thought I heard her call him Storm. She was singing to him and she called him her little man."

Snake felt wild elation fill his chest, immediately followed by a hollow feeling of utter despair. His head began to reel from the laudanum and his stomach lurched. If it was true and Maddy had delivered a son, his son, he would probably never get to see the boy. Snake tore at his hair and lifted his eyes to look at the canopy of tree limbs overhead. What boy would want a crippled, one-legged man for a father?

His momentary descent into self-pity faded, quickly replaced by Snake's inalterable sense of self-importance. Buoyed by the flood of euphoria created by the drug, his thoughts began to run wild.

If he had a son, he would find the boy and raise him. Even if he couldn't have Maddy, he would have this child. The boy was his. Even God couldn't deny him this one gift. Determination filled him, and his sense of purpose was reborn. He would find Hawk's gold, get Maddy back, and take his son as well. He knew he could do it—he was Jake Barber.

Floating on a cloud, pain gone for the first time since he'd been blown to hell, Snake hobbled to the chickee leaning heavily on his crutch. When his stump was healed, he would have Skeeter fashion a wooden leg. He'd seen all kinds in Pointe Lookout. All he needed was a simple wooden peg leg, with a leather holster for his stump and straps to hold it to his leg. He didn't need it to be hinged or jointed or anything complicated. Just a simple peg leg so he could walk again. He knew Skeeter could make one. He was a genius with leather.

❖　　　　　❖　　　　　❖

Hawk stood in the dogtrot and stared at the rubble of his barn. The sun was just coming up over the trees to the east, yet heat was already simmering around him. Bees and butterflies hummed in the honeysuckle Katie had planted against the south side of the house. It was going to be another scorching July morning.

As Hawk stared at the destruction, Jumper came out of the house and joined him.

"It looks like the outlaws hooked a chain to one of the support poles and pulled the whole barn down," Hawk said.

"It's not as bad as I first thought, my brother," Jumper said. "All the poles are still there. Only two are cracked and can't be used. All the siding is still there, it's just in a pile. Even the roof is still there. For all we know, the tools and harnesses and the feed bins are there as well, under the roof."

"You're right, old friend. I'll call Travis and Shorty in and we'll get to work cleaning up the mess and seeing what we got today," Hawk said. "Tomorrow or the next day, we'll take a trip to Enterprise. Maddy is making a list."

"What are your intentions toward her?" Jumper put his hand on Hawk's shoulder. "I believe she would make you a fine wife."

Hawk ducked out from under his hand. "There's a lot to consider. A lot you don't know."

The Seminole half closed his eyes and smiled. "I know what I see, my friend. Yes indeed, I know what I see."

Travis and Shorty were working on fixing the fences in the horse pasture behind the barn. When that was done, they would bring the marsh tacky herd to the homestead.

Hawk and Jumper walked down the hill to the barn to begin the long task of sorting through the lumber and poles and start rebuilding. They used the mules to pull the support poles into a pile and then began piling up shingles for the roof.

It was hot. Hawk took off his homespun shirt and wiped the sweat off his face with a sleeve. Impervious to the temperature, Jumper kept on working. Hawk found himself getting tired. It had been a long time since he'd worked in the heat like this. He'd better get used to it, though. When Maddy called all of them in for dinner, he was glad for the rest.

A table had been improvised from four planks and two sawhorses, along with two hastily built benches. Hawk was stunned at the magnificence of the table setting. Maddy had covered the planks with a white linen tablecloth. China dishes and bowls sat at every place, along with real silverware. There were small wine glasses and a crockery mug at each place. In the center of the table, two candelabra sported four candles each and two silver vases held sprays of yellow wildflowers with brown centers.

Maddy came out of the kitchen smiling and carrying a tureen filled with soup she ladled into each bowl. Sarah, wearing a pretty pink dress with puffed sleeves and a wide satin sash, came into the room behind her carrying a plate of biscuits. Maddy filled each glass half full of red wine.

"I brought this bottle of Bordeaux with me from Georgia and I opened it tonight to celebrate our homecoming," Maddy said.

Hawk stared at Maddy as though he had never seen her before. She wore a blue dress that exactly matched her eyes, covered by a starched white apron. The dress conformed to her figure, displaying curves Hawk had never been able to see before. Her hair was braided and wrapped in a coronet around her head. Around her neck she wore an enormous cameo set in gold. The carved silhouette in the cameo was of a beautiful woman, but not, Hawk thought, as beautiful as Maddy. Travis and Shorty stared. Jumper stared. She looked beautiful.

"Well, aren't you going to sit down?" Maddy asked.

The four of them scrambled for seats as Maddy ladled creamy potato soup into the bowls. It smelled delicious.

"Where did you get the stuff to make this?" Hawk asked Maddy as she took her seat.

"Mr. Jumper supplied the potatoes. He also has a milk cow hidden away at the old cabin. We have cream and milk in the springhouse, which is lovely, Hawk—everything in it stays so cool. And there is butter for the biscuits made with flour Mr. Jumper also supplied from stores he had at his cabin."

"This food is terrific," Travis exclaimed around a large mouthful of biscuit.

"We have another course," Maddy said. "I baked quail Mr. Jumper trapped, and there are turnip greens from the old garden. And a brambleberry pie for dessert."

After they'd consumed the soup and quail and begun working on the dessert, Jumper leaned over and whispered in Hawk's ear. "I hope whatever those considerations you got against marrying Miss Maddy, those ones I don't know nothing about, well, I hope you two work them out real soon. I'd sure hate to see this one get away. If I wasn't already married, I'd grab her up myself."

"Be quiet and eat your grub, you old fool," Hawk said. "You'd let your gut run your life."

"And me, I used to think you was a smart man," Jumper grumbled as he forked a big bite of juicy pie into his mouth.

16 🌾

Maddy sat at the plank table writing her list. Hawk had said they could take the buckboard and go to Enterprise in a few days. She wrote with a quill pen and ink, things she'd brought with her from Twelve Oaks. She wrote her list on a piece of brown paper flattened and saved after unpacking the wine glasses and plates wrapped in it. Storm, still tucked into a box, lay beside her. Everyone else, including Sarah, was outside helping rebuild the barn.

It was late evening. The sun was setting and soon the house would be filled with men . . . her men. That was how she was beginning to feel about them. *Her men and her home.*

The list grew. She wondered how much of this stuff she would be able to find in Enterprise and how much Hawk would allow her to buy. He'd never mentioned a budget. He'd just told her to make a list.

She needed flour, salt, lard, corn, molasses, beans, and bacon. She hoped to find sugar, cinnamon, dried apples, raisins, and pepper. For the baby she needed more diaper pins, and talcum powder. She also needed to procure a quantity of white thread. Sewing all the mattress covers was going to take miles of it. Then she needed wax and cotton string to make candles. If Hawk insisted, she would use tallow, but she preferred beeswax. Tallow smelled. They also needed lamp oil, and she needed pins and a new needle for sewing.

She'd already planted herbs in the garden plot on the side of the house. All afternoon she'd weeded, hoed, and dug. She'd found sweet potatoes, turnips, and rutabagas, along with some shriveled old carrots and some green beans. She'd planted collards, okra, peppers, winter squash and pumpkins, dill, basil, mint, and parsley with seeds she'd brought in the wagon. Jumper had given her some black-eyed peas to plant, but she needed more garden space first. It was too late in the season to plant some things and too early for others. Since it rained nearly every evening, all her seeds should sprout.

The garden was important to her. It meant variety in the meals she cooked and good health for her family. Because it was important, she found the time to work in it.

While she worked, Storm had lain quietly sleeping in his crate. He was the best baby, eager to nurse and easily settled to sleep. Sarah had been a fretful infant. She'd been colicky, gassy, and never wanted to be put down or to sleep. Maddy was able to get a lot more done with Storm.

Before she'd gone out to work in the garden, she'd unpacked clothes and sorted them for washing. The clothesline behind the house was slap full of washed clothes and there was still an enormous pile left to wash. She'd concentrated on diapers and baby clothes. Servants had taken care of washing diapers when Sarah was a baby. It was amazing how quickly the pile of nappies grew.

Besides washing and working in the garden, Maddy had

cooked three meals, cleaned up after them, and checked for supplies in the springhouse and every kitchen cupboard still standing.

She looked up from her list as Hawk came into the house through the breezeway. He called it a dogtrot—and a big leopard hound bounced in behind him. "Come out and sit on the porch with us," he said.

He held out his hand. She smiled and took it. He helped her up and then picked up Storm's crate. The two boys were sitting on benches on the porch with Sarah between them. When Sarah saw Maddy, she leaped to her feet. Maddy looked Sarah over and observed her daughter had gone back to wearing boys' clothes.

"Mama, Travis knows where there's a nest of raccoons. He says he can get me a baby to raise as a pet. We went riding and he showed me a baby deer. It was freckled all over and so cute."

"That's wonderful, Sarah. Are you sure you want a coon for a pet? Is it safe, Hawk?"

"They make great pets, Maddy. Don't worry. The Indians have been making pets out of coons forever." Hawk said, "Sit down over here. You can see the sun setting over the pasture."

The horse pasture fence had been repaired and the marsh tacky mares brought over from the pasture by the old cabin. Maddy could see the mares and Hawk's stud.

"I think I'm gonna cut the marsh tacky stud tomorrow, Jumper," Hawk said. "I checked the almanac and the signs are right. We don't need but one stud on the place."

"You sure you want to geld him, boss? He's four years old. That's pretty old to be cutting," Jumper said as he picked his teeth with a cedar sliver.

Hawk lit his corncob and blew out a fragrant cloud of tobacco. Maddy liked the smell of it. She thought it was unbelievably peaceful here, sitting on the porch like this, talking and enjoying the cool breeze that had blown up.

"I imagine he'll be fine," Hawk said. "I've cut plenty of older horses. We need riding horses for cow hunting, not studs. That last year I hunted cattle, we lost four horses. The more horses we have, the better. We got one of his colts on the ground over at the other pasture. I saw it yesterday and I thought it looked pretty good. If you think we ought to keep a cracker stud, we'll hang on to the colt."

"Whatever you say, Hawk. You know horses," Jumper said.

"We'll work a little on the barn tomorrow and then I want all the riding stock brought up so we can trim their hooves, look 'em over, and tie 'em out. Better get them under saddle again right away. We'll need 'em ready to go. You know it's best to work the buck out of them before we really need 'em."

Hawk turned to Maddy. "Have you got your list ready? It'll be a few days before I can get away, but we'll go in a day or two."

Maddy nodded. "I wasn't sure how much money we could spend so I didn't know how much to put on the list."

"Write down whatever you need. I hope they have all of it in Enterprise. We could go to the trading post at Volusia Landing. It's closer. But they won't have the selection of merchandise available in Enterprise."

"I was wondering. I've been teaching Sarah for years. Does Travis know how to read? I could start teaching him in the mornings when I'm working with Sarah."

"That'd be fine for right now, Maddy. But when we start hunting cows, he'll have to skip the lessons. I need him with me."

She nodded. She knew working the ranch was more important at certain times of the year. "Maybe he'll have more time to learn in the winter."

"When we get back from the cattle drive, he'll have some free time. I know he wants to learn to read. He's been bugging me about books on horse medicine. He says there are some with pictures. I've been meaning to teach him to read. My Ma taught me. Her father was a preacher." Hawk hesitated. "I just never seemed to have the time."

Maddy put her hand on Hawk's arm. "Don't feel bad. It would have been easier for you if your wife had lived and if the war hadn't intruded. It's hard to raise a child alone. I know."

Travis had been listening. "Will you really teach me how to read, Miss Maddy?"

"Of course I will, Travis. I'll add some writing paper and pencils to my list."

Travis looked over his shoulder at Shorty. "What about Shorty? Can he learn too?"

Hawk laughed. "Maddy will have a regular school going. If Shorty wants to learn to read and can still get his work done, I don't see why he shouldn't learn too. What do you think, Maddy?"

"I'll have to get a blackboard and desks," she said, laughing. "But I don't mind teaching both of them—and Sarah needs more lessons too. They can all help each other."

The sun had finished sliding behind the trees. The sky

was turning pink, orange, and purple. Night birds called and Maddy could hear the familiar singing of the cicadas.

Storm woke up and complained. Maddy picked him up and rocked him in her arms. He was hungry. She put a blanket over her breast and nursed him, leaning back against the log wall of the house for support. The baby suckled contentedly.

"I think I will go pick some blackberries tomorrow and make another pie," she said to Sarah. "Do you want to go?"

"No, Mama, Travis is going to give me another riding lesson first thing in the morning."

"Storm is getting too big for that crate," Hawk said to Maddy. "I'll make a real cradle for him as soon as I get time."

"With all the work to do around here, he'll probably be a grown man before you get the time," Maddy said. She meant it as a joke, but he took it seriously.

"Me and Jumper will get to work on it tomorrow or the day after, Maddy, really."

"I know you will, Hawk. You always do what you say you're going to."

The next morning, Maddy woke early. She washed her face in a bowl sitting on one of her trunks, dressed, and went out to the cookhouse. She built up the fire in the wood cookstove and set an enormous ranch-size pot of coffee on to boil. It wasn't a nice big stove with an oven, just a little stove with two holes, more of a wood heater really. Maddy sighed, remembering the big enameled stove she'd had in the kitchen at Twelve Oaks. *Oh, well,* she thought, *you can't have everything.*

She poured a batch of cornbread into an enormous cast-iron skillet, covered it, and set it to cook on the empty hole.

There was no bacon or meat, but they would have cornbread and butter for breakfast. And there was cold milk in the springhouse.

While that cooked, she got the baby up and carried Storm into the cookhouse. It was warm in there, so she bathed him and put him in a fresh diaper. He looked to be throwing out a rash, so she dusted him with some cornstarch.

She heard noise coming from inside the house and knew the rest of the family was waking up. Hawk, tucking his shirt into his pants, came down the steps from the house and into the cookhouse.

The coffee was boiling, so she poured him a cup. "I know we need a bigger stove," he said. "I was meaning to get one, but the war happened."

The cookhouse was roomy, with a big stone cooking hearth complete with spits for roasting meat and hooks for hanging pots. The small stove had obviously been a later addition; the stove pipe funneled smoke out through the fireplace chimney. There were tables, a large sink, and a tall cupboard. When Maddy first saw the cookhouse, crockery had been smashed into pieces on the floor. Luckily cast-iron pots were hard to destroy or they probably would have been broken and smashed too. Apparently the outlaws weren't that good at cooking. Two of the pots had been scorched, with burnt food in the bottom that was so hard Maddy had had to chisel it out.

"I'd love a new stove," she said with a sigh. "Especially one with a hot water reservoir. That would surely be a convenience."

"I tell you what, when I go to Tampa with the cattle in the fall, I'll try to bring back one," Hawk said.

"That would be nice," Maddy said. "Hawk, I hate to add to your chore list, but we really need some meat."

"Travis knows where a large family of wild hogs can be found. He told me earlier this year he and Joseph caught some of the piglets and castrated them. I'll send him to get us one of the smaller ones. They should weigh two hundred by now. That should be plenty of meat. It's not really the right season for butchering hogs, but it'll be fine as long as we get most of it into the smokehouse right away."

"I'd salt some, but we need salt," Maddy said. "I'll get a big pot cleaned out and ready for the rendering. We'll have ourselves a fresh pork shoulder for supper tonight and, of course, blackberry pie."

"That sounds delicious," Hawk said as he took his blue metal mug of coffee and headed down the path to the out-house.

Hawk came out of the outhouse and slammed the door. That had been a disgusting experience. Another inheritance from those filthy outlaws. He'd get Shorty to clean it and then they'd burn it out.

Hawk had looked over Maddy's list of supplies. It was extensive. To pay for all that stuff, he and Jumper would have to go get some of Pappy's gold out of the spring. He set Shorty to cleaning the privy and sent Travis hog hunting, while he and Jumper headed down the path towards the old cabin.

It was early morning. The dew was still heavy on the grass. Hawk spotted a cottontail grazing, pulled out his rifle, and shot it Hawk tied the dead rabbit to his belt with one of the ropes he and Jumper carried.

Halfway to the cabin, they cut off the main trail onto a small path that ran along a creek. The path was dark and ran under tall cypress trees, water oaks, and cedars. The black soil was damp. Ferns grew under the trees along with vines, swamp flowers, and other water-loving vegetation. It flooded down here when it rained, though this time of year the water level was normal. The creek flowing briskly toward the river grew clearer as they walked.

Hawk walked softly, picking his way around rocks and up little hills and down into ditches. Suddenly he stopped. He signaled Jumper to be still. They waited frozen for several minutes, then Hawk shook his head. "I thought I heard something. I must be going crazy. All the fighting with Barber has me looking under every bush."

Jumper nodded.

After climbing a small hill, the two men ran into a big pile of rock. The creek seemed to fountain from beneath the limestone formation. They climbed over the rock using handholds cleverly concealed on its surface. On the other side, a clear spring formed a deep pool. When Hawk looked into the pool, he could see twenty feet down to where the water boiled out of the rocky bottom. Fish of all kinds— bream, mullet, mudfish, and even a gar fish—swam in and out of the shadows.

"Do you think he's still here?" Jumper asked, eyeing the pool suspiciously.

"You know he is," Hawk said as he tied the dead rabbit to the end of one of the ropes. "Are you going in or me?"

"I hate that gator," Jumper said. "I still got the scars on my back from the first time I met up with him."

"He made out a lot worse than you, my friend," Hawk said. "You're the reason he has to stay here. Three-legged gators don't travel well over land."

"I didn't cut off his leg. I just nicked him. It was his own kind that tore off his leg," Jumper said.

"I wonder if that's how he remembers it."

"Well, that's what happened. He does okay with only three legs. He just can't travel far. Look at all the fish. That old boy's got a lot of eatin' to do here before he even thinks about leavin'," Jumper said.

"It ain't for food bull gators roam," Hawk said waggling his eyebrows. "It's for love."

Jumper snorted. "Just get on with it, will ya? I'll watch with the rifle. You go in. But we better find that big bastard first."

"I will," Hawk said. "This'll get him. He eats a lot of fish but doesn't get much meat." Hawk tossed the rabbit into the water. It floated as a gentle trail of blood drifted into the water from the corpse. Hawk jiggled the rope holding the rabbit, making it splash.

"It always gives me a start when he comes out of that cave," Jumper said. "I wish he'd show up. I hate the waiting."

Hawk made the rabbit splash some more.

"Are you sure he's in there?"

"Shush," Hawk whispered. "I thought I heard something." Hawk handed the rope from which the dead rabbit hung to Jumper and stripped off his clothes. He took the end of the second rope they'd brought and hovered over the pool.

Suddenly a huge splash signaled the arrival of the massive gator. Waves lapped the rocks on the edge of the pool as the sixteen-foot alligator swam lazily toward the dead rabbit, his tail moving back and forth slowly, creating more turbulence.

As soon as Hawk saw the gator swimming away from the rock, he slid into the water. Beneath the rock he'd been standing on, just above the water level, was a large cave cut into the limestone with a muddy bottom. It reeked of dead fish and musk. Hawk had been in it many times since he and Jumper had discovered it as boys years ago. Slithering in on his belly, he found what he was looking for at the end of the tunnel.

In the dim light from the entrance, Hawk saw three identical leather-bound trunks lying in the dark and resting safely exactly where Hawk had placed them before heading off on that last cattle drive. Each trunk had brass corners and fittings. He chose the one closest to him. It had a brass ring fitted into one end. Hawk tied the rope to the ring and backed out rapidly. It wouldn't take long for the three-legged monster to scarf down that rabbit. Or if he wasn't all that hungry, take it to the bottom and store it under a log for later.

Hawk scrambled back onto the rock and handed Jumper the rope. Jumper slowly reeled in the trunk while Hawk put his clothes back on. He was shivering. The water temperature of the spring was always the same: cold.

Jumper huffed and puffed as he dragged the trunk hand over hand out of the cave and up onto the rock. "You must have picked out the heaviest one," Jumper said as he heaved the trunk over the lip of the rock.

"You must be getting old," Hawk laughed. "This is the lightest one. It's only half full. We don't need that much money lying around and I don't want to have to put it back right now."

The gator finished stashing his rabbit at the bottom of

the spring and crawled onto a muddy embankment to stare at the two men and warm in a shaft of sunlight.

"He's even bigger than I remember," Jumper said, shuddering. "Damn, I hate gators."

Jumper lowered the trunk down the side of the rock face with the rope and then the two of them clambered down. Safely at the bottom, the two men picked up the trunk, each holding on to a brass handle, and headed back to the house.

Maddy grabbed a big basket out of one of her boxes and put on her oldest dress and a pair of stout boots. Picking blackberries required getting into mud and often getting your dress torn. It was early, and Storm still slept. She wrapped him in a shawl and tied the ends of it diagonally across her body. The baby was cradled in the shawl like he was sleeping in a hammock, and her hands were free to pick berries. She'd seen the slave women doing this countless times, but this was the first time she'd ever had need to try it out. She was amazed at how well it worked.

She took the path away from the house that ran toward the old cabin. She'd seen a lot of blackberries down that way. Walking swiftly with a strong stride, she soon reached the spot where she'd seen the bushes. There were lots of plump berries here because of both the recent rain and the partial shade offered along the path—the ones in full sun often dried up and were sour.

As her basket began to fill, she walked all around the patch, ending up in some pretty deep woods. Just as she was crouching low to get the berries on the bottom of the bushes, she heard a shot.

Terrified, she cradled Storm, who was still deeply asleep, and hid under the bushes. When she peeked out, she sighed with relief. It was Hawk and Jumper. They'd killed a rabbit. She watched as Hawk hung the rabbit on his belt, then the two men continued down the path for a few steps and quickly cut onto a narrow side path she had not noticed before. Where were they going? They had two stout lengths of rope with them and a dead rabbit. What in the world were they going to do?

Climbing to her feet, she slipped down the path behind them, staying far enough back they wouldn't hear her. The trail wove through big cypress trees and old oaks along the path of a small creek. The soil was damp so she tried to be careful of where she stepped. What if they saw her tracks?

Hawk stopped suddenly and she jumped behind a big tree. He looked back down the trail right where she'd been standing only a second before. She couldn't for the life of her understand why she was doing this. Ordinarily, she wasn't a snoop. Maybe she was just naturally curious because they seemed so nervous and secretive. Maybe she should turn around right now and go back to picking her berries.

What right did she have to spy on Hawk and Jumper? For that was what she was doing, spying. Salving her conscience, she decided not to follow them if they kept on walking and went too far. As long as Storm was asleep, she'd tag along, but only for a short ways.

The path began to go uphill. She watched them climb over a big rock. The little creek seemed to spring from under it. She moved a little closer, heard them laughing and then a splash. There was a pond or spring of some kind on the other side of that rock. There was no way for her to work her way around to the other side, and she certainly wasn't climbing the rock. She decided to find a place to hide and wait.

Jiggling to keep the baby quietly sleeping, Maddy stood behind the biggest cypress tree she'd ever seen. From her spot, she could see the rock formation and the path. She'd crossed the creek and waded through swampy water to get to the big tree. It was sitting in the middle of a large hammock. After wading across the lake to that island in the dead of night, a little swampy water was nothing. She'd hiked up her skirts and slopped right through it.

It wasn't long before Hawk and Jumper came back over the rock. They lowered a leather trunk with brass fittings down the side of the rock with ropes and then picked it up, each carrying a handle. As they made their way back down the path, Maddy saw it looked like they were struggling with the weight of the trunk. It obviously contained something heavy.

Aha, Maddy thought. So this was the location of Hawk's mysterious hiding place. The trunk must contain Hawk's father's stash of gold. Snake Barber was a fool if he thought he'd ever find it.

When they were out of sight, she climbed the rock face using the clever handholds carved into the rock. Standing on top, she surveyed a pristine spring. It was deep and blue, surrounded by big trees, rock, ferns, and thick vegetation. The pool teemed with fish and on the other side, resting on a mud bank, was the biggest alligator Maddy had ever seen. So Hawk even had a guard for his money. That was why they had brought the rabbit. Wherever in this pool they had hidden Hawk's gold, it was perfectly safe with that monster on duty.

17 🖌

TRAVIS RODE INTO THE HOMESTEAD later that afternoon dragging a two-hundred-pound pig behind his horse on a travois. On the front of his saddle he carried a piglet.

Maddy ran out to meet him with Sarah. He handed the piglet to Sarah, who struggled to hold on to the squirming animal while Travis climbed off his horse.

"Here, gimme that thing," Travis said to Sarah, who was on the verge of losing control of her burden. "We'll put this pig in the chicken coop until we can get the pig pen repaired. We ain't got no chickens anyway."

"Don't have any chickens," Maddy said, correcting his speech. "You need to learn better speech patterns, Travis, if you're going to learn to read. That reminds me, I need to ask Hawk if we can get any chickens in Enterprise. We need to have eggs."

Shorty walked up and looked Travis over with loathing. "You get to go off hunting and I have to stay here and clean the shitter." Shorty reddened. "I mean the privy, ma'am. Sorry."

Maddy laughed. "Well, now you get to help me clean this hog. Can you boys get it skinned and hung without Hawk's help? He and Mr. Jumper had to go do something."

"Not a problem, ma'am," Shorty said.

"I'll get a rope and hang him in the tree next to the smokehouse. We always hang meat on that tree," Travis said.

"That will be fine," Maddy said. "I have a fire going and a kettle cleaned out just for the fat rendering."

For the next three hours, Maddy toiled in the cook-house, boiling fat and meat and layering it in a wooden cask. Travis hung the side meat and hams in the smokehouse and got an oak fire burning. When Hawk and Jumper returned, Maddy had a fresh shoulder roasting on a spit in the cook-house and a deep-dish blackberry pie cooking in the Dutch oven.

"Looks like good eating tonight," Hawk said. "And we'll be heading to Enterprise in the morning."

The men ate cold biscuits and went off to work on the barn while Maddy and Sarah cut mattress covers and began sewing them. They would be big cotton bags with one end left open. With no feathers, ticking or cotton to stuff in the bags, Maddy knew she would have to find moss, dry it, and clean it. At Twelve Oaks, she'd had a goose-down mattress, but most of the ones her mother had used were stuffed with cotton. It sure would be nice to have some cotton here, but growing cotton took slaves. It would no doubt be some time before cotton was produced in Georgia and Florida again.

That night they all sat on the porch again, talking over the day and making plans for the week to come. Maddy had never enjoyed such comfortable camaraderie. Her parents had been stiff and cold. She was always relegated to her room after supper, while her father sat in the dining room and sipped his favorite libation, port, and her mother went into the parlor to sew or embroider.

When she was older, she was allowed into the parlor to sew with her mother. Her parents had considered sewing to be the foremost skill a woman could learn. She was just lucky her mother had also taught her to read and that she'd been taught to cook by her mammy.

There were no family discussions in her parents' household. Such a thing would have been unheard of. Her father had ruled with an iron hand, and her husband had been the same. After supper, Mark would lock himself in his library and drink. He didn't care to talk about anything with Maddy, and of course Sarah was just a small child. Hawk was so different and life here was less formal and, oh, so much warmer.

Of course, here she had a lot more work to do. There were no servants to do the work, unless you counted Shorty. She smiled as she remembered poor Shorty cleaning the outhouse. He'd been horrified when told of the chore and it had taken him forever to get it accomplished. But when he was finished, Maddy had taken a basket of corn cobs and squares of fabric she'd cut from rags out to place beside the hole, and had been pleasantly surprised to find the outhouse clean as a whistle.

When the sun had set and Storm was fast asleep for the night, Hawk walked her to her room carrying the sleeping infant. "Me and Jumper got started on the cradle you need," he said.

"Thanks, Hawk," Maddy said shyly. They were rarely alone together. His large body next to hers made her feel self-conscious. She pulled her braid over her shoulder and began to smooth it with the tips of her fingers. In her other hand, she carried a candle to light the way.

"We'll be leaving at first light, as it takes most of the day to get to Enterprise," he said as he opened her door for her. He hesitated at the threshold of her room.

"You know, this used to be Travis's room. You sure have fixed it up different."

"Travis gave it to me because he said it was the biggest bedroom and I needed the space because I'm sharing it with Sarah and the baby," Maddy said. "He's got the little room on the other side of the house."

"That was nice of him, to give up his room for you."

"He's a good boy," Maddy said. "He's got a really warm heart."

She and Sarah slept together on pallets laid across the boards forming the bottom of her bed. Everything was clean and neat, her brushes sitting on a crocheted doily on the top of a trunk she used as a nightstand, with her silver jewelry box and an oil lamp next to them. The room smelled of flowers. An open basket of her special potpourri sat on the floor beside the trunk.

She went into her room and lit the lamp. Her nightdress lay neatly folded across her pallet, and Sarah's lay across hers.

Hawk walked into the room like he was walking on eggshells and put Storm's box on the floor beside the bed. He stood awkwardly shifting from one foot to the other. "Well, uh, good night, then," he said.

Maddy handed him the candle, reached up on tiptoes, and kissed him lightly on the cheek. "Good night, Hawk. I'll be ready to leave in the morning whenever you are."

❖   ❖   ❖

Hawk helped Maddy onto the buckboard's padded seat and climbed up after her. Storm slept in his box at her feet. The sun was just clearing the trees and it looked like another scorching day. Tomorrow would be the first of August.

It felt good to be driving Maddy in a wagon again. Hawk gathered up his reins and clucked to the team of mules, slapping their broad backs with the lines. They took off at a smart trot, but Hawk slowed them to a walk. It would be rough going until they got out on the main trail heading for Enterprise.

At noon they stopped for dinner. Maddy climbed down, carrying a big basket with her, and spread a blanket under an oak tree beside the trail, where they sat down to enjoy a picnic. Maddy had cold pork shoulder in the basket, along with cornbread. For dessert, she'd packed bread pudding.

Hawk lay back on the blanket to rest while Maddy packed away the dinner plates. Storm began to fuss and Hawk watched as she picked up the baby, changed him, and nursed him. It was amazing to him how he and Maddy never argued. When he said something to her he knew had made her mad, she pursed her lips and said nothing. It was as though arguing and fighting were beneath her dignity. But she had a temper, he knew that—she just controlled it with an iron will. Someday, he had a feeling, her temper was going to overcome her will.

They arrived in Enterprise before dusk. Hawk drove the wagon through town to the blacksmith's shop, where his old friend Raford Johnston, otherwise known as Rafe, lived behind the shop. They'd been friends since he was a boy, when Rafe had learned to shoe horses from Pappy, later opening his shop in Enterprise. Hawk always stayed with Rafe and his wife, Priscilla, when he came to Enterprise.

The door burst open before he could knock. "If it ain't Caleb Hawkins come back from the dead," Rafe said, pumping Hawk's hand like he was trying to get water out of a dry well. "Come on in. Priscilla will be glad to see your ugly face."

"Rafe, this is my, uh, my housekeeper, Madelaine Wilkes. I brought her here to buy some supplies for the homestead."

Rafe backed up and looked Maddy over. "Your housekeeper?"

"Yes, I hired her to look after the place, take care of Travis . . . you know."

"Oh, yes, you've been needin' someone to help with Travis."

"We're just here for the one night. Can Maddy stay with you folks? I'll bunk in the shop."

"Sure, old friend, Miss Maddy can have the spare room," Rafe said.

"She's brought her infant son with her," Hawk said as they went inside. "Will Priscilla mind?"

"Mind? Hell no, Priscilla just loves babies."

Rafe's wife was putting away the supper dishes. She came out of the kitchen drying her hands on a frilly gingham apron.

"Oh, look, Rafe, a baby," Priscilla cooed.

"See, I told you," Rafe whispered. "Priscilla, this is Hawk's housekeeper and her new baby. She's gonna sleep in the spare room tonight, if that's okay with you, love."

"Of course they can stay. How old is he?" Priscilla pulled Storm's blanket aside so she could see the sleeping child's face. "Oh, he's so beautiful."

"Storm turned a week old yesterday," Maddy said.

"Can I hold him?"

Hawk and Rafe slid out the back door while Maddy and Priscilla marveled over Storm's hands, his toes, and his perfect little features.

"I have a hard time understanding what the womenfolk see in babies," Rafe said as they both lit up corncob pipes and began blowing a cloud.

"Me too," Hawk said. "They leak at both ends and need constant attention. Hey, is the Trail's End Saloon still open? I haven't been inside a bar for three years. Closest I came was driving by one in Pilatka."

"The saloon is still open," Rafe said. "And First Community Christian is throwing a church social later. They're supposed to have dancing. It starts in less than an hour, at seven. Why don't we step over to the bar, have a drink or two, and then drop by the social?"

"Won't Priscilla mind?"

"Nah, she's got your housekeeper and her infant to keep her busy. Uh, by the way, I hope I'm not prying, Hawk, but I just gotta ask. Is that your baby?"

Hawk backed up a step and stared at Rafe. "No. I've only known the woman a month."

"Sorry, old friend. But ever since I saw you two together, the question's been rolling around in my mind. And you know how I am, I had to know."

"It's okay, Rafe, we've known each other since we were kids. I can stand the heat. I met Maddy on the trail home.

She was increasing and needed a place to stay. It just sort of worked out like this, you see?"

"Oh, I see, all right. I see." Rafe chuckled and muttered under his breath. "I see a lot more than you think."

"What did you say?" Hawk tilted his head sideways and stared at his friend. It was as Maddy had foretold. Everyone would think Storm was his and everyone would assume they were a couple. "Let's go get that drink."

Rafe stepped back into the house long enough to share their plans with his wife, and then the two of them walked through the small town enjoying the evening. The Trail's End was less than a mile from the blacksmith's shop. Hawk could taste the whiskey already.

The two of them walked through the swinging doors and up to the bar. The place was filled to capacity with cow hunters, townfolk, and loose women. Hawk leered at a gaudily dressed woman with a large quantity of red hair and an even larger quantity of bosom showing. She sauntered over as Hawk ordered a bottle. When it came, he paid with a doubloon. The bartender gave him back fourteen silver dollars in change.

The woman, dressed in red satin and feathers, introduced herself. She said her name was Lily, and she spoke with a French accent that Hawk doubted was real. Draping her arm over Hawk's shoulder, she brushed her charms generously against his arm. "Hey handsome, how 'bout buying little Lily a drink?"

"Give me another glass, barkeep," Hawk said, then poured three drinks, including one for little Lily. Rafe toasted Hawk's safe return and they both slammed down the whiskey. Hawk coughed as the harsh liquor roared down his gullet. "Damn, this whiskey is younger than Maddy's baby. Hey, bartender, set us up a couple of beers too, will ya?"

The bottle slowly disappeared, the number of empty beer mugs grew, and Lily became more friendly.

"I think it's time we went to the church social," Rafe said. "You look like you've had enough."

"What do you mean?" Hawk demanded. "Are you accusing me of being inebriated?"

"Yes, I am," Rafe laughed. "You're not exactly plowed under yet, but definitely a little bosky."

"Am not," Hawk mumbled. "Oh, all right, if you think I've had enough, then we'll go. Though I don't know who gave you the right to run my life."

"How many times have we been out drinking together, old friend?" Rafe asked.

"Plenty," Hawk mumbled.

"And who always looks out for you?"

"Let's go, then," Hawk said, slamming down the last shot out of the bottle.

Lily clung to Hawk's arm. "But, honey," she cooed into his ear. "You're not gonna go away and leave little Lily here all alone, are you?"

Hawk narrowed his eyes and glanced around the packed saloon. "I think you got plenty of company, little Lily. Find yourself another sucker to pay for your drinks."

Lily drew herself up and pushed the strap of the red dress off her arm with one lace-gloved hand. "You're no fun," she pouted.

Hawk laughed and patted her rump as she flounced away.

"You really shouldn't be messing with the saloon gals, Hawk."

"Why not? I'm a free man."

"Are you?" Rafe asked with one eyebrow raised.

Hawk peered closely at him. "Rafe, you have always been my friend." Hawk worked hard to focus, reached out with an unsteady hand and touched Rafe's nose. "Got a mighty big snoot there, fellow," Hawk said. "What's this on your face for?" He fingered Rafe's bushy yellow mustache.

"I grew it last year. Priscilla likes it."

"Well, I don't," Hawk said. "Makes you look like George friggin' Custer."

"Let's go to the social, Hawk." Rafe tried to lead Hawk out of the bar, but Hawk balked in the doorway. He wasn't thinking too clearly. It seemed, in his fuddled mind, that he was supposed to be somewhere else. But all he knew was he wanted more whiskey. In the back of his mind he knew this was the wrong thing to do. He did bad things when he was drunk. It was why he usually avoided bars altogether. Once he started drinking, it was hard to stop.

"Don't want to go, want another drink."

"I think you've had enough, Hawk, and if I get any drunker, Priscilla will nail my hide to the barn door."

Hawk allowed himself to be led out of the Trail's End. He wanted more whiskey, but Rafe was right. Rafe was always right—had looked after him many times when they were young, Rafe had. But, hey, he hardly ever came to town and he'd been in prison for two and a half years. And he was living with the most beautiful woman in the world and couldn't even touch her. If that didn't entitle him to get rolled up, he didn't know what did. But he allowed Rafe to lead him down the darkened streets.

"Okay," Hawk said. "Let's go dancing. I love to dance. I'm a good dancer."

They walked down the street toward Lake Monroe. The First Community Christian Church was lit up like Christmas. The doors were open to the Fellowship Hall, and candles and oil lamps burned from sconces in the corners and on the walls.

The two men stepped into the room. Everything was blurry for a minute as Hawk struggled to focus. The three-man band consisting of a piano player, a fiddle player, and a guitar player struck up a tune. Their first tune was *Turkey in the Straw*, and a pretty little blonde girl asked Hawk to dance. He accepted.

For a minute he didn't know if his feet would remember how to dance, but he followed the girl's lead and was soon enjoying the square dance. *Turkey in the Straw* was followed by the *Band Polka*. A tall red-headed girl pulled him onto the floor and he was off again capering like a madman.

He thought he might have danced through *The Yellow Rose of Texas* and *Dixie* when he saw the doors of the Fellowship Hall open once again. He was trying to mind his steps when he noticed Maddy had entered the room and was talking to a tall man he'd never seen before with long blonde hair, mutton-chop sideburns, and a striped waistcoat. Where had she come from?

He missed a step and trod on the toes of his partner. Muttering an apology, he whirled the little blonde in the blue flowered dress around so he could see Maddy. She seemed to be having an animated conversation with the yellow-haired fellow Hawk didn't know. Hawk could feel a very strong emotion rising in his chest and he didn't like it at all. What was she doing here anyway, and where was the baby?

When the music stopped, he marched toward her with

a red film covering his eyes. He grabbed her arm. "Who is this man and where is Storm?" His voice was overloud and the words came out slurred.

She snatched her arm out of his grasp. "I came here looking for you. But now that I'm here, I see no reason why I shouldn't enjoy myself. You obviously are. This nice man was just asking me to dance."

The music started and Maddy headed toward the dance floor with her partner. The song was *Jeannie with the Light Brown Hair*.

Hawk grabbed her arm again. "You can't dance with him, dammit."

Maddy shook his hand off her arm and stepped in front of him, standing as tall as she could, and stared him right in the eyes. "And why not, pray tell?"

Hawk backed away. Except for the fact that he didn't like it, he had no idea why she shouldn't dance with the fellow. Well, he did know why, he just didn't want to tell her.

Maddy went out on the dance floor and proceeded to show every woman there what real dancing was all about. Hawk, propping himself against a wall, watched as she whirled gracefully to the music, her partner's arm wrapped lightly around her waist. When the song was over he met her at the edge of the dance floor.

"Let's go, Maddy. Let's get out of here."

Maddy turned to her partner and quietly thanked him for the lovely dance, then turned back to Hawk. "I'll go with you," she said. "But just so I can give you a piece of my mind."

She grabbed his arm and dragged him out of the brightly lit Fellowship Hall. Hawk saw Rafe at the refreshment table making a pig of himself and followed Maddy.

Once outside and in the shadows of the dark street, Maddy turned on him. "How dare you bring me to your friend's home, introduce me as your housekeeper, and leave me there all by myself?" She took a deep breath. "I was never so embarrassed in my life."

"But, Maddy—"

"No, you listen to me, Caleb Hawkins. I'm a single female. You brought me here under your protection and dumped me and Storm on poor Priscilla. I was so mortified I scarcely knew what to say to her. If you don't care anything about me, I can understand that, but you could at least treat me with common civility."

"I thought you two would get along fine," Hawk mumbled.

"We do, but all that poor woman knows is I'm your housekeeper, a mere servant in your home that you left her to take care of and entertain. Is that all I am to you, Hawk? Just a servant?"

"No, Maddy, you know you're much more than that."

"Then why did you leave me there without your support and come down here to become inebriated and to disport yourself with strange women in a dance hall?"

"It's not a dance hall," Hawk protested. "It's a church. And you looked like you were having a fine old time dancing with Mr. Yaller Side-whiskers."

Maddy balled up her fist and socked him in the jaw.

"Ow! That hurt!"

"If loose women and strong drink are what you want, then go ahead, dance and carouse all night. I'm sure I don't care." Maddy spun on her heels and stalked into the night.

"Wait, Maddy, you can't walk back to the blacksmith's

shop in the dark all alone." Hawk, reeling slightly, took off after her. He grabbed her by the shoulder and pulled her into an embrace. She struggled, but he held her close. "This is stupid. Stop struggling, dammit. You just hit me in the mouth with your head. I think I bit my tongue."

Maddy stopped struggling and he lifted her chin. "You know, I ah . . . You know I care about you, Maddy. We all do."

Somehow Hawk could not say what was in his heart. He loved her. He'd loved her from the first time he'd seen her. But pledging his affection to the mother of Snake Barber's son, even if she'd become that mother through no choice of her own, was something he just wasn't ready to do.

"So, you all care about me," she said. "Thank you so very much. I know what's really bothering you, Caleb Hawkins. I'm not stupid. You think I'm ruined, a fallen woman, all because of what Snake Barber did to me. You think I'm damaged goods because I had a bastard child. You think I'm not good enough for you. I'm just a servant and I should know my place. Well, I'll have you know my family can trace its ancestry back to the kings of France. My ancestors ruled over peasants like you. You're not fit to kiss my shoes. And from now on, I'll just be that servant in your home. If that's all you want, then that's what you shall have."

Hawk stood there like a dummy and watched as she pulled away from him and stalked down the street in the dark. He should follow her. He shouldn't let her walk back to the blacksmith's shop by herself.

He grabbed his head. His thoughts were careening around in there in circles. What she said hurt. Her words hurt because they rang of the truth. The thought that she had lain in Snake Barber's bed, whether willingly or unwillingly, galled him. The thought that she had born Barber a son made him want to be sick. And he knew none of it was her fault. She was lovely and wonderful and right—he wasn't good enough for her. Maybe he should run after her and tell her so. But his legs wouldn't move. He stood rooted to the ground, watching her disappear down the dark street.

He turned and looked at the lighted windows of the Trail's End, then turned back and watched Maddy. Her shoulders were back, her head held high. She looked elegant, cool, and totally desirable.

Without looking at her again, he wheeled around and strode back to the Trail's End.

18 🌂

Snake Barber stuck his right foot out in front of him and examined the brand new peg leg Skeeter had made for him. After Skeeter had cut a piece of oak, he'd trimmed it up and carved it by hand, smoothing the wood into a silky sheen with fine sandpaper. Then he'd fastened a leather holster to the top of it with small brass tacks he'd brought back from Enterprise. It buckled over Snake's knee and there was a rabbit-fur pad to cushion his stump.

Snake turned it this way and that, admiring it. After he learned to walk on it, he'd go into a big town and get some silver work done on it, just like on those big fancy Mexican saddles he'd seen. Maybe he'd have some scroll work put on it and his name. He'd have to think about what he wanted, but he wanted it fancy, that much he knew. If he had to wear a peg leg, it might as well be a jam-up peg leg. Now all he had to do was learn to walk on it, and how hard could that be?

Skeeter helped him to his feet and handed him his crutch. "Best I could do, boss."

"You did just like I wanted," Snake said. After he

learned to walk on it, he and Skeeter could get to work rounding up some new recruits and taking his son and Maddy from Hawk. And while he was at it, they could collect all that gold.

He put some weight on the new leg. Skeeter had painstakingly fitted the wooden leg so it would be the same length as his other leg. He took a step, leaning heavily on the crutch and trusting more and more weight to the new leg. It wobbled. He caught his balance and took some more steps. He looked up at Skeeter and grinned. "It's gonna work, Skeeter. Hot damn, I'm gonna be able to walk again."

"Take it easy there, boss, don't be overdoing it. You're still a little weak and you don't want to be aggravating the stump. It ain't all healed up yet."

Snake dropped the crutch and took two halting steps without it. He felt pain shooting from his stump right into his bones. "Hand me my medicine," he said to Aggie, who was watching all of this through her round, black Indian eyes.

She found it in the chickee and handed him the brown bottle. He guzzled the stinking liquid and wiped his mouth on the back of his hand. In minutes, his body was flooded with the familiar euphoria, all pain forgotten.

"You better cut back on that stuff, boss. You're gonna get hooked on it."

"Mind yer own business," Snake said with a sharp edge to his voice. "What do you know about my pain? You got two legs, I don't." With the pain dulled, he was able to take several more steps. The more he walked on his new leg, the easier balancing became.

Later, sitting in the shade, he took a swig of whiskey and another slug off the laudanum bottle. He shook the bottle to see how much was left. He was almost out. Skeeter would need to take another trip to Enterprise.

But when he approached Skeeter about getting him some more drugs, Skeeter flatly refused. "You need to lay off that junk. You're a man, Snake. Take the pain."

"I can take the pain." Snake's voice was rough, his lip drawn back in a snarl. "I just don't want to. And why should I when they make this wonderful elixir of the gods, laudanum?"

Snake took another swig from the whiskey bottle and offered it to Skeeter, but his friend brushed the bottle aside. "Don't think I want to get drunk today, boss. I'm going out in the canoe with Aggie and the boy."

"What do you see in that squat little Indian squaw? I don't understand you, Skeeter. She's nothing but a dirty Seminole."

"You don't need to be talking about her that way, boss. She fixed you up, didn't she?"

"Well, then go out in the canoe with her. I don't give a damn, as long as you go to Enterprise and get me some more laudanum."

Skeeter stood up and looked down at him. There was a frown on his friend's face and a faraway look in his eyes. For the first time in their long friendship, Skeeter appeared to be irritated and fed up with him. So what? It didn't matter. Skeeter worked for him, and he'd remind him of that. "Don't you forget who you work for. I'm the boss here, remember?"

"Well, boss, it looks to me like the table's done turned and yer dependin' on ole Skeeter now and I ain't getting paid a thing."

Snake would be damned if he'd beg the man to get him

what he needed. He watched as Skeeter and Otter pushed the heavy dugout canoe into the water. Aggie and Skeeter climbed in, and Otter took up the stern position to steer while the other two dug in with paddles.

Skeeter was getting awful friendly with those Indians. Snake shook his head. He didn't like the way things were going. He didn't like it at all.

Skeeter didn't come back until long after dark. Snake was drunk and floating on the last of his laudanum. He barely noticed Skeeter when he came into the chickee. He was dreaming he was in Maddy's big feather bed.

"Boss, Aggie made some food for you. Get up." Skeeter shoved Snake's shoulder.

"Don't want nothing to eat. I need more laudanum."

"I'm sorry to have to do this to you, boss, but I've had enough. I'm leaving you plenty of food, but me and Aggie and the boy are gonna go live across the lake. She's got a really nice place on a big spring, with land for grazing. It's a big ole spring, even bigger than that blue spring on the Hawkins ranch. I think I'm gonna raise me some horses."

Snake tried to focus, but failed. In the dim light he could barely make out Skeeter's face. "Go on, leave me. What do you care if I live or die?"

"Stop feelin' sorry fer yerself, boss. You're healed up enough to make it out of here on your own. You just need to get off that stuff you've been drinking."

"What about our plans? Aren't you gonna come with me to get the gold?"

"Take some advice for a change, boss. Ferget about the gold. Ferget about that woman, and go on home to your family. Yer ma'll take you in and care for you. I've got my own life to live, and I need to be gettin' on with it."

"What about all the time we been together? Don't that count for something?" Snake could not believe Skeeter was quitting him, walking out. They'd done everything together for twenty years.

"And what do I have to show fer all the time we been together, boss? I'll tell you what— nothing. I ain't got a cent to show fer it, and in my time of life, if I'm ever gonna have something, I need to get started right now. You go on and keep stealin' and killin', but I'm through with it. I've had me a bellyful. I got me a woman now and a home, and I got me my own plans."

Snake rolled over on one elbow and stared at Skeeter's departing back. He watched as Skeeter and the Indian woman packed her stuff in baskets and one big backpack and loaded the canoe. Skeeter pushed her and Otter into the lake and came back onto the shore. *Oh, good, he wasn't leaving after all*, Snake thought. *He's seen the light and is saying bon voyage to those two.* Snake giggled at his own joke. Bon voyage, like they were off on a steamboat cruise.

It wasn't long, though, before Snake realized Skeeter wasn't going to stay with him, that he really was abandoning Snake to take care of himself. Skeeter walked back to the camp from the lake, got his horse, and saddled it. The moon was so bright it was like daylight and he could see all this clearly.

When Skeeter had the horse ready, he walked over to the chickee. "I'll be seeing you, boss. I'm riding around Lake George to where Aggie's got her place. I left the extra horse and saddle fer ya. It's time you went on home."

"I'm never gonna go live with my family, never again.

You know how much they hate me. They hate us. I can't believe you're leaving me, Skeeter, after all we been through."

"Well, boss, a lot of what we been through, we didn't need to be doing or going through. I'm overing it and you need to do the same. So long, my friend."

Skeeter climbed on his horse, waved once, and rode off into the blue-shadowed night.

And then Snake was alone. "Screw 'em," he muttered. "Screw 'em all." He tipped the bottle of laudanum upside down and drained it of every last drop. Then he stuck his finger in as far as it would reach, swirled it around, and lifted it to his mouth so he could lick off the chalky white residue. Minutes later, he was in a deep sleep.

Snake woke the next morning feeling like he'd been dragged for a mile behind a team of horses. His missing foot ached like the very devil. He reached down, almost certain it must be there, it hurt so bad, but it was still gone.

He rubbed absently at the stump, trying to alleviate the pain. Sitting up on his pallet, he looked into the flickering shadows of the camp. The sun was overhead, filtering through the trees. It must be almost high noon.

"Skeeter!" he called. "Aggie!" Where the hell was everybody? And then he remembered that Skeeter and the Indians were gone. What was he supposed to do now? His leg ached deep in the bones. He picked up the laudanum bottle, but it was empty. There was still a quarter of a bottle of whiskey next to his bed. He uncorked it and drank.

Pulling himself out of bed, he strapped on his new leg. His crutch was nowhere in sight. He finally spotted it next to the fire pit and had to crawl out of the chickee and then another twenty-five feet to get his crutch. Cursing Skeeter all the way, he finally pulled himself upright. To hell with Skeeter. He didn't need the man. He had a horse, he had his new leg, and he could find a new band of outlaws. There were plenty of them—deserters, layouts, robbers, and cattle thieves. They roamed Florida like swarms of bees, feeding off the honey of the land.

Snake checked on the horse Skeeter had left him. It was a big raw-boned gray. He recognized it as Lige Tremblat's mount. Lige had died right here fighting for him and the gold. He remembered.

Snake realized if he was going to ride, he needed to make a change in his right stirrup. He found the saddle, took off the stirrup leather, and sat down to fiddle with it.

Aggie had left him smoked mullet and fry bread. He munched absently, but he wasn't hungry. He wiped his nose with the back of his hand. For some reason it had started running. He shivered, goosebumps rising on his arms. He sure wished he had some laudanum.

Snake fixed the stirrup so it would accommodate his peg leg, and early the next morning, after spending a restless night, he rose, strapped on the peg leg, and saddled up. It was hard getting the saddle on the big gray. He had to balance on his new leg and swing the bulky Texas stock saddle up on the horse with all his might. The first two times, the horse jumped and he fell flat, but he finally got the big horse saddled.

The next obstacle in his path was figuring out how to get on the horse. Good thing he'd lost the right leg and not the left. He managed to scramble into the saddle first try.

He rode hard, pushing the gray. Volusia Landing was six

hours away, and he needed whiskey or he needed laudanum. He needed something, that was for sure. He had bad cramps.

By the time he reached Volusia Landing, he was exhausted and barely hanging on to the horse, his head resting on the gray's neck. But he made it. When he slid off, he had to remember he was wearing the peg leg. He'd never worn it in public before. He felt awkward. He'd tied the crutch to the back of his saddle and it was a relief to lean on it.

He stumped into the Volusia Landing General Store at just about four o'clock. A man—though really he was little more than a boy, eighteen or twenty years old—with a black patch over one eye was leaning against the pickle barrel eating a big dill pickle. Snake nodded to him as he walked by. The kid had a lot of bushy blond curls sprouting from under a Rebel cap, and Snake thought he looked familiar.

The storekeeper stared hard at him as he bought a fifth of the store's cheapest whiskey. He was about to walk out of the store when he realized he needed a hat. His old flat-crowned leather hat had been lost when he'd gotten his leg blown off. Every man had to have a hat to protect his head and to keep from going crazy in the heat of the sun. Casting a quick look around the store, he spotted several big floppy-brim brown felt hats on the top shelf. They were sitting on the highest shelf in a tier of six.

"Storekeep," Snake said, "can you get me one of them hats up there to try on?"

The storekeeper got a long stick with a hook on it and snagged a hat off the shelf, handing it to Snake. He tried it on and the ugly thing fit. He hated the dang hat the moment it sat on his head. He figured it made him look ridiculous, but it would keep the sun and rain off until he could get himself a new leather one. After settling up with the storekeep, he took his bottle and his new hat and plopped down on a bench in front of the store.

"Don't I know you, mister?"

Snake looked up. It was the one-eyed man. "I don't know," Snake said. "You look familiar, but I met hundreds of men. Don't remember none 'round here with only one eye."

"I'm Willy-Pete Turner. I fought at Chattanooga in the summer of sixty-three with General Hill. Mayhap you were there?"

"No, I was in a prison camp in Maryland in sixty-three," Snake said, losing interest. This guy actually fought in the war.

"Then maybe I'm mistaking you for someone else. I was in Tennessee for a long time, but I was born in Georgia, close to Marshallville."

Snake took another swig off the bottle and stared harder at Turner. Marshallville was where Maddy's farm was. Maybe he'd seen this guy there or some relative of his that looked a lot like him. "What was the fighting in Tennessee like? How long were you in for?"

"I wasn't in the regular army all that long. I got hurt pretty bad at Chickamauga. They took me home to Marshallville on a stretcher. I was there in my ma's house for three months. When I got better, I decided I didn't want to go back to the regular army. I still wanted to kill me some Yankees, just not for General Hill."

Snake was thinking. He must have seen this kid in Marshallville, but where? "Whereabouts in Marshallville do you come from?"

"My family lives on a farm just off the main road to Perry."

Maddy had lived out that way. Twelve Oaks was only ten miles from Perry. Suddenly a vivid image appeared in his mind of a young Rebel soldier lying on the ground on a stretcher beside a wagon. The soldier had a lot of his head covered in bandages, but Snake remembered looking at him and noticing a square chin with a cleft in it and a bunch of curly blond hair cascading out of the bandages. He remembered one pale blue eye filled with hate and malice glaring at him.

The mule in the wagon's traces had apparently just keeled over dead. Snake and his boys were leading three extra horses they had just stolen. The horses were thin and poor, but they were horses. One of the three was a big black horse mule. The soldiers had tried to confiscate the mule to pull the wagon. He and the boys had laughed at them and shot the soldier hanging on to the mule's lead.

Snake stared at Willy-Pete out of the corner of his eye. Yeah, now that he looked closer, it probably was the boy on the stretcher. Damn, it wouldn't do for the kid to remember him in that situation.

"I didn't think too much of the way General Hill run his boys or his war, so when I got better, I headed for the mountains and ended up in Monroe County, back in Tennessee. The way Hill and the Confederate Army was tryin' to fight the war head on with the Union was just stupid. Everybody knowed we couldn't beat 'em playin' their game. I hooked up with a bunch of bushwhackers in them mountains. A guy name of Bloody Bill Elliott was teaching men how to kill Union soldiers by hidin' in the woods and ambushin' them. They called it guerilla fighting. I joined up with ole Bloody Bill's gang and stayed with him for over a year. Ever hear of 'em?"

Snake's interest was piqued. "No, what'd they do?"

"We killed Union soldiers and folks what sided with the Union or looked like they was a-going to side with the Union. We took what we wanted and killed who we wanted. Now that was my kind of war, and after the war was over we was still fightin', but Elliott got hisself killed and the band broke up. I'm down here because I heard Josie McGee, a big guerilla fighter from Texas, has moved his operation to Florida. He's getting up another band, and I aim to join up."

Snake offered his new friend the bottle. The bushwhacker took a big swig and passed it back. "My name's Jake Barber, but everybody calls me Snake. Where'd you say you lost that eye?"

"At Chickamauga."

Snake liked this guy, liked what he stood for and liked the idea of finding this Josie McGee and joining up with him. It could be exactly the situation Snake needed to get back on his feet. And Willy-Pete would probably never recognize him or remember where he'd seen him before. The kid had had a bandage covering one eye and most of his head when his boys had ridden by. And he'd been bad hurt. The one thing that bothered Snake was he'd been the one to shoot the soldier. That might have stuck in the kid's mind.

Snake shook his head. Nah, he would have remembered by now if he was a going to remember at all. "You got someplace to stay tonight?" Snake asked.

Willy-Pete took another slug of whiskey out of Snake's bottle. "Nope. I was just gonna bed down in the woods over yonder and light out come morning."

Snake stood up, leaning heavily on his crutch. Willy-

Pete saw the peg leg. "You lose that fighting?"

"Of course," Snake said "Give me a hand up on this nag and we'll make us a camp in that hollow over there."

They did just that, and Willy-Pete made a fire and fried up some bacon and beans. The two of them sat down and ate, sharing the bottle. "Is your real name Willy-Pete?" Snake just had to ask.

"It's William Peterson Turner. I been Willy-Pete for as long as I can remember. I know it's a dumb name, but what you gonna do?"

"Where'd you say this band of bushwhackers is forming up?" Snake asked.

"Somewhere just south of a town called Orlando. I heard McGee's got close to a hundred men. They're mostly rustling cattle, but I heard there's lots of cattle to rustle and it pays good."

"Mind if I ride along?" Snake felt like he'd been destined to meet this guy. He'd be back in business in no time. Two things you could count on when you got a bunch of outlaws together. One, that the bastards were greedy, and two, that before long they'd be fighting amongst themselves. It wouldn't take long to recruit a bunch of malcontents to make a run for Hawk's gold.

"You can come along if you want to," Willy-Pete said. "But when we get there, it's every man for himself."

"Fine with me." Every man for himself exactly described Snake's entire philosophy on life. He stuffed a huge wad of tobacco in his lip and lay back on his pallet. Whiskey and tobacco were poor substitutes for laudanum. First town they hit, he was getting him some.

19 ⚡

THE LONG RIDE HOME FROM Enterprise seemed to go on forever. Maddy had no idea when Hawk had returned to the blacksmith shop. From the look of him, he hadn't had much sleep. His eyes were bloodshot and his clothes wrinkled like he had slept in them. But he didn't complain, not once, not even when he had to stop a couple of times to make a mad rush into the bushes.

The shopping trip she had so looked forward to had been a dismal, desultory affair. Hawk had stood outside the store with his hat pulled low over his eyes, leaning against the side of the building and waiting for her to make her purchases. She didn't even try to find furniture. Her heart just wasn't in it. When she was finished, Hawk had paid and supervised the loading of the buckboard. He didn't even ask what she'd bought.

Last night had really opened her eyes. She'd been dreaming of marrying Hawk and having a home there with him since before she'd delivered Storm. When he'd asked her to come to the D-Wing with him, she'd assumed eventually he would make her an offer of marriage. She knew he was attracted to her and it had somehow seemed so right. She'd let down her guard and let him get under her skin. What a dumb thing to do. You'd think she would know better.

Now she'd discovered he was just like every other man she'd known—selfish and self-centered. And she could add opinionated and bigoted to Hawk's list of qualities. She was so disappointed. She'd never thought he would hold her being raped and used against her. She'd never thought he would think less of her because she had had a child outside of wedlock.

Of course, the center of his unspoken negative feelings was really Snake Barber. It was because it had been Snake. If she had been raped and then had borne a child by some unknown outlaw, it probably wouldn't have bothered him a lick. But Snake Barber was someone he knew and loathed. In her heart, she also knew Hawk would hold his parentage against Storm.

She looked up at him sitting tall on the seat beside her and felt a deep sadness growing in her heart. Eventually, she was going to have to move on. She couldn't stay at the D-Wing much longer. Not after last night. Not with what she now knew and understood. She would do as she'd promised, take care of the house and Travis, and she'd wait for Storm to get older and stronger. Then when the time was right, she'd go back to Pilatka and move into her sister-in-law's boarding house. Maybe they would be back in Pilatka by then. She decided to write them a letter when she got home.

Plans for her future made, she turned on the seat and looked over her purchases. If she was going to stay and be

Hawk's housekeeper, at least for the time being, then she was going to appreciate the things she'd gotten in Enterprise.

She'd actually been able to buy three hens and a rooster. The man who had sold her the hens said they were broody and would hatch out a big clutch and take good care of it. The wooden crate with the chickens in it sat on top of everything else. The birds were alert, watching everything around them.

She'd also bought a bolt of fabric with which to make dresses for her and Sarah, ribbons, and some lace a lady that lived in Enterprise had tatted. She now had fabric for curtains as well. There would be lots of sewing to keep her occupied.

She had managed to locate four big sheets of glass to replace the broken glass in the windows. Hawk would have to cut the glass and fit it into the windows. The glass was packed carefully between the bolts of fabric and sacks of flour and sugar, corn, and grits to cushion it during the trip.

When they finally reached the house, she was exhausted, mentally and physically. Hawk had not said one word to her during the entire ride. He'd stared fixedly at the trail in front of the wagon. They'd eaten their lunch in silence beside a creek and then he'd watered the mules. The strain of riding next to him like that had given her a headache.

Sarah and Travis rushed out to the wagon to greet them when they pulled into the yard. It was such a relief to get off the wagon and hug someone who cared about her.

"What did you buy, Mama?" Sarah asked as she eyed the wagon filled with supplies. The girl was blossoming in this environment. Her eyes were shining and she smiled and laughed more than Maddy could remember her doing in her life.

"We couldn't find any furniture to buy, but I bought supplies for the house and a lot of work for you, darling."

"What do you mean?"

"Sewing."

"Did you buy material for dresses?" Sarah clapped her hands together.

"Yes, and ribbons and lace."

"Oh, Mama, I can't wait to see."

Maddy sighed as she followed Hawk into the house. He was carrying Storm. She wondered if he found this task onerous. Sarah loved it here so much. It would tear her heart out to have to move the child again. But Hawk didn't want them here, not really. She'd come to realize this on the ride home. He'd only offered her a place to live out of a charitable impulse. That was all. There was nothing else to it. She'd stay until she could find her sister, and maybe till the house was fixed up and running smoothly, maybe until spring.

It was like Christmas unpacking all the packages. Maddy couldn't remember enjoying anything so much. Sarah and Travis put away all the supplies, then Travis proudly led her out to place her new flock of chickens in the hen house. While they were away, Travis had rebuilt the pig pens and repaired the hen house. The piglet he had captured was rooting happily, accompanied by two friends.

"Three pigs, Travis? Where did you get them?"

Travis smiled. "I caught 'em out in the woods where I got the hog. There was a whole mess of them."

They set the three hens and the rooster loose in the henhouse and went back inside. Maddy's headache had disappeared the minute she got home. When she got inside the house and saw Hawk was gone, though, her headache came crushing back.

"Where did your father go?" she asked Travis.

"He went off to Jimmy's cabin. They're planning to start hunting cows tomorrow."

Maddy sat down on the bench at her makeshift table. "What is this cow hunting thing he does? I don't understand."

"Several times a year we go out on the palmetto scrub and pull cows out of the brush. We brand the calves right where we find them, cut the bull calves, notch their ears, and let 'em go. We got hundreds of steers and heifers out there on the prairie with our brand and ear notches. We round them up and hold them in pens we've made right out there or we sometimes bring 'em back to the ranch if we're close enough. While we're doing that, we're catching more calves, marking and cutting them, and letting them go. When it's time to take them to market, we catch up all the big steers and drive them to Tampa. It's how we make our living out here." Travis spoke to her like she was an ignorant child. But, indeed, this was all new to her and she was ignorant.

"What do you do with the ones you hold on to?"

"In the late fall of every year, we drive them to Tampa to ship out to Cuba. That's how Pa got all them gold doubloons Barber wants. And my grandpa did it for twenty years before Pa started doing it."

"And there's money in this? How amazing." Maddy couldn't believe the ranchers around here made so much money capturing wild cattle and taking them to market. They didn't have to build any fences or even own any land. She thought of all the hard work that went into farming in Georgia and the small return for the work, and how even that small profit would not have been possible without slaves.

"How long will your pa be gone?" Maddy asked, though she somehow knew what the answer would be.

"We won't be back for a long time. We stay out on the prairie for weeks at a time."

"You have to go too?" Sarah asked.

Travis looked at Sarah and smiled. Maddy realized the boy liked her daughter. Well, Sarah was not a bastard, so maybe Hawk would allow them to marry when Sarah was old enough. She shook her head. Such uncharitable thoughts did her no credit. She would make an effort to only think good of Hawk. He had brought her here and saved her from Snake Barber. He was a good man.

"Me and Shorty have to go. We love it. I can't wait."

"Then who will stay here to help us on the ranch?" Maddy asked.

"Joseph and Judy Bill should be home in a few days, and Jimmy and Judy Bill always stay here while Joseph goes with us. You'll have plenty of help. Pa's gonna have to ride over to Volusia and see if there's any hands looking for work. He was supposed to hire on one or two in Enterprise. I guess he didn't find any he liked. We need at least two more."

"So Jimmy and Judy Bill stay here," Maddy said. That meant she wasn't really needed at all. Hawk already had Judy Bill as a housekeeper. Well, maybe Judy Bill would need her help. Maddy knew she was a good cook and an excellent needle woman. She was good in the garden as well. Surely there would be need of her and Sarah's skills.

With these thoughts in her head, Maddy took a candle and went to bed, though it took her a long time to go to sleep.

20

Hawk hated the long ride back to his ranch from Enterprise. He knew he'd made an ass of himself. He knew getting obliterated and staying out all night had been a bad idea. He knew too that sitting beside Maddy right now and not saying a word was an even worse idea. He just couldn't make himself break the silence. It was as if his lips had been sewn together.

When he'd woken up this morning, he'd been filled with remorse. At first he couldn't seem to find the right words to say so. Now he wasn't sure whether he should say anything or just leave things alone and let what had happened stick. Maybe his silence was for the best.

Besides, he was having a terrible morning. He'd forgotten just how bad a hangover could be. He'd had to stop the wagon three times to bolt for the bushes and his head throbbed like Indians were in there pounding drums. He seemed to feel each step the mules took in his head. And to top everything off, while he couldn't remember a large part of the evening's jollifications, the last thing he did remember was leaving the Trail's End with Lily on his arm. Beyond that was a blank. He wished he could remember whether he'd gone home with her. For some reason it seemed important that he know.

He'd woken up with the sun beating down on him in the back of the buckboard, fully clothed but with his pants on backwards, which was not a good sign. He had no idea how that had happened, but feared he'd gone with Lily.

So between his monstrous headache, feeling guilty, and feeling uncertain about his feelings for Maddy, he rode in silence for the entire journey. His suffering was so intense, time passed in a blur.

Hawk had hoped as they first set out that Maddy would break the ice and speak to him. But she'd remained obstinately silent. After they'd driven halfway home and Maddy hadn't said one word to him, he decided maybe it was for the best that they end it right now before their relationship went any further.

The closer to home he got, the more this decision seemed right. He didn't feel like he was better than her and he certainly didn't think she was damaged goods. In the back of his mind he knew the problem was Snake Barber. If only Storm's father wasn't someone he was acquainted with quite so well. He knew Barber's history and the man was all bad. He didn't hold what had happened to Maddy against her—how could he? In his heart, he knew she had been the sad victim of an unspeakable crime. But he did feel like it was just too much to ask of him to raise Snake Barber's bastard son.

And there was no asking her to get rid of the child. She loved that baby, and he was actually proud of her for it. Some women would have pushed the child aside, seeing the baby as a constant reminder of a degrading experience. Not Maddy. She took excellent, loving care of Storm and always would. Children were forever.

Nope, from now on, he would treat her just as he had planned to when he offered her a place to stay. She was his housekeeper, and as far as he was concerned, she could remain at the D-Wing as long as she needed to or wanted to. He owed her that much.

When they got to the house, he carried Storm in for Maddy, then went looking for Jumper. It was time to get out on the prairie and hunt up some cows. His heart quickened at the thought. He loved working with cattle, loved the danger, the excitement, and the thrill of doing something he knew he was good at. It was hard work that demanded a great deal of skill, and he could do it with ease.

He'd missed the prairies while he was in prison. He couldn't wait to get back out there where the sky was wide open and grass stretched as far as the eye could see. He even planned on moving farther south one day in the not too distant future, somewhere closer to the herds. There were cows around Volusia and Enterprise, but the real herds were all farther south where the land opened up and there was an abundance of grass.

Jumper was in the old cabin cleaning. "Judy Bill should be here soon. My cousin Wildcat Jumper rode by here this morning and said she was on her way."

"I hope she can get along with Maddy," Hawk said. It had already occurred to him that those two strong women in the same house might mean trouble, but at this point all he could do was wait and see.

"Why do you think I'm cleaning?" Jumper said. "When she sees the furniture gone from the house and sees Maddy in it, the fur is gonna fly. I figured I'd make sure the cabin was clean so she can't take her bad temper out on me."

"Poor Jumper, I can see you're in for it."

"Yeah and it's all your fault. You bring that woman here, install her in your house, and then ride off to the prairie to leave me to deal with the mess."

Hawk patted Jumper on the back. "I'd take you with me, old man, but I need you here. I need you to get this place in order and watch out after the women. I got sidetracked and didn't hire any more men in Enterprise. I'll have to take Joseph and Shorty with me as well as Travis."

Jumper eyed him with his head canted to the side and one eyebrow flying. Hawk shuffled his feet. "Sidetracked? How?"

Hawk told Jumper the story. The older man listened quietly, not interrupting. When Hawk was finished, Jumper said, "So that is the secret you'd been holding onto about Maddy's boy. Snake Barber is Storm's father. And you've decided Maddy is not the woman for you and the reason is . . . she had a baby by Snake Barber, but she was not willing? This makes no sense at all, my friend. But it is your life."

Hawk turned on his friend. "You think this was an easy decision for me to make? It's about to kill me. I just want to get away from the whole mess. I'll go out and hunt cattle, do the work I love, and forget about Snake Barber and Madelaine Wilkes. When I come back, my head will be clearer and I'll be able to deal with the problem a lot better."

"Oh, yes, running away always works."

"I'm not running from the problem, Jumper. I'm just

tabling it for a while. Truly, my friend, I don't know my own mind. One minute I'm madly in love with the woman and the next minute all I see is Snake Barber's bastard living in my house forever. I've got nothing against the kid. I just don't want to bring a panther cub into my family."

❖   ❖   ❖

It was late in the night when Maddy was awakened by the sound of many barking dogs. From the commotion, there had to be at least ten of them, and when she stuck her head out the door, she realized it was almost as bright as day. The moon was full and high overhead. Rushing around in the yard and by the barn was a pack of strange dogs. There was also a wagon, as well as a young man riding a horse. She saw an older Indian woman dressed in a brightly colored patchwork shawl get off the wagon. She'd been driving.

The young man stayed to tend to the horses, but the woman headed up the path to the house. It had to be Jimmy's wife, Judy Bill. Maddy lit a candle and went out back to heat some coffee in the cookhouse. There was a loaf of real bread she'd bought in Enterprise, so she cut several slices and arranged them on a plate while the coffee heated. When it was all ready, she carried it into the house. Judy Bill was standing in the middle of the parlor staring around her, obviously aghast.

Maddy held out her hand and smiled. "Hi, Judy Bill, I'm Maddy Wilkes. I have heard so much about you from Travis and your husband. I know you must be glad to be home."

Judy Bill was a tall woman with black hair worn in a very odd style Maddy had never seen before. Her hair was swept up from her forehead and over some kind of frame that made it look like she was wearing a hat with a broad brim. She was very handsome and taller than Maddy. She stared briefly at Maddy's outstretched hand and deliberately ignored it. She had no answering smile for Maddy and no words of hello.

"What has happened to this house and where is all the furniture?" Judy Bill asked Maddy seconds after looking around the house.

"The outlaws broke every piece except the bedsteads," Maddy explained. "And we had to burn all the mattresses. I've started making new ones."

"Oh, Miss Katie would cry to see her furniture destroyed and her house so empty," Judy Bill said.

Maddy felt like she'd been slapped. Miss Katie was Hawk's wife, who'd been dead six years. Judy Bill spoke of her as though she'd only been gone an hour and this was still her house. "I made you some coffee and sliced some bread," Maddy said. "I thought you might be in need of refreshment."

"I only drink tea," Judy Bill said. "A blend of herbs I mix myself."

"Would you like me to heat you some water?" Maddy asked, slipping into icy politeness to cover the hurt this tall woman's intentionally aimed barbs had caused.

"No, thank you, I know my way around the kitchen quite well." Judy Bill took off her beautiful shawl and laid it on a bench. Beneath it she wore a sparkling white blouse and a long patchwork skirt embroidered in black and orange. When she'd smoothed the wrinkles out of her jacket, she walked straight-backed out the back door and down to the cookhouse.

Maddy wanted to follow her but felt she was only in for more insults. Still, if they were to live here together, she'd need to hide her hurt and make the best of the situation. So she went out to the cookhouse.

Judy Bill was bustling about pulling things off shelves and rearranging the placement of the dishes and supplies. She'd built up the fire and had a kettle of water boiling.

"This china with the rose pattern—where did it come from?" Judy Bill asked, holding one of Maddy's fine china plates between two fingers.

"The dishes are mine and currently all we have. The outlaws broke every dish and cup." Maddy wondered how Judy Bill was going to take that announcement and was soon to find out.

"They're much too fine for our way of living," Judy Bill informed Maddy. "I have plainer, more sturdy crockery over in the cabin. I will have Jimmy or Travis bring it over tomorrow. You must pack up all this china and put it away. This is not our way. This is not how we live."

Well, Maddy thought, it's late and I'm tired. From inside, she heard Storm wail. And now the dogs had woken up the baby. It looked like the situation here was going from merely uncomfortable straight into the outhouse.

"My baby is awake," Maddy said. "It's so nice to make your acquaintance."

Judy Bill said nothing, just stared at her as she turned and went back into the house. Maddy could feel her antipathy burning into the back of her robe.

21 ✶

SNAKE AND WILLY-PETE HAD BEEN RIDING
for three days when they hit Orlando. Snake soon discovered, to his great joy, that Orlando was a wild town.

Riders and fancy women crowded the rough streets of
Orlando. Snake and Willy-Pete had to guide their horses
carefully along the rutted track through town. Snake turned
sharply to avoid running into a wagon loaded with trunks,
furniture, and burlap sacks pulled by two oxen. The wagon
lumbered along slowly, blocking the steady stream of riders
and conveyances unable to pass it.

The streets were lined with bars, saloons, gambling parlors, and fancy houses. Every now and then Snake would see
a store. Before his eyes, a fight broke out in the doorway of
the Stud Horse Saloon. Snake stared as one of the men
pulled an old-fashioned pistol out of the front of his pants
and shot the man he was fighting with.

"Let's stop for the night here," Snake said to Willy-
Pete. "This looks like my kind of town."

Willy-Pete frowned and pulled his Confederate cap low

over his eyes. "I ain't got no business with these folks. You can stop here if you want, but I aim to ride on."

"I need to purchase a few supplies," Snake said. He spotted a drugstore down a side street. He really needed the laudanum. His leg kept him up half of every night. "I'll only be a minute."

Willy-Pete waited anxiously on his horse while Snake went into the drugstore. Snake saw him looking up and down the streets like he was afraid of being spotted, making Snake wonder if Willy-Pete was a wanted man.

Once inside the store, Snake became fascinated with the wall-to-wall shelves of different medicines lining the shop. He picked up a box on one of the shelves for "Dr. Bonker's Celebrated Egyptian Oil." He couldn't read a lot of what was printed on the box, so he put it back down. Next to it was a box labeled "Mack Mahon the Rattle Snake Oil King's Luminant for Rheumatism and Catarrh." Who would use rattlesnake oil for anything? The shelves held medicine for every kind of illness he'd ever heard of. There was even a large selection of beauty supplies for women.

But all Snake wanted was his laudanum. He looked out the window to see Willy-Pete shifting around in his saddle trying to keep track of anything coming down the street. Snake decided he'd better hurry or Willy might not wait.

A man wearing a big white apron watched him expectantly from behind a counter piled high with jars and bottles of candy. Snake walked up to him and told him what he needed. It didn't take long to get his four bottles of laudanum and head back out to Willy-Pete.

"What took you so long?" Willy-Pete demanded.

Snake decided Willy-Pete was definitely a wanted man.

He was as nervous as a six-tailed cat in a room full of rocking chairs.

"I had to wait for the clerk to find and wrap up what I wanted," Snake said. As they rode out of town, Snake looked back over his shoulder wistfully. He just knew he would have enjoyed the hell out of Orlando. But at least he had four bottles of the magic stuff in his saddlebags, which should last him quite a while.

He'd been trying to lay off it during the day. If his stump got to aching, he'd nip off the bottle while they were riding, and the alcohol managed to stave off the worst of the pain. With a load of laudanum in him, he hardly noticed his infirmity, unless he had to walk for a long period of time.

He was getting adept at maneuvering around on his peg leg, even managing yesterday a sort of shuffling hop, his speediest gait. He was still awkward. He had bad moments with the pain and disorientation when he first woke up; his nonexistent right foot hurt like the devil in the morning. To make the experience even worse, he usually had a hangover of some kind. Having to maneuver off his bedroll, put on his peg leg, and get up and walk all made starting each day a nightmare.

After hitting Orlando, they rode south through open prairies, swamps, and lowlands. Snake saw hundreds of wild cattle, most with no earmarks or brands. The prairie land opened up into broad vistas of waving grass the like of which Snake had never seen. Cabbage hammocks dotted the prairie like little islands in a grass ocean.

At night, they'd find one of those cabbage hammocks and make camp. When it got dark, packs of wolves prowled the perimeter. Snake kept the campfire burning all night and slept close to it, waking up several times to feed the flames.

Willy-Pete told him they were headed for an old army stronghold, Fort Kissimmee. The fort had been built in 1850 and abandoned in '58. He said McGee and his men had rebuilt it, fortifying it and adding a stockade.

There were no neighbors. Orlando was the closest town and Snake figured it was pretty lawless, judging by the look of things when they'd ridden through. McGee's bushwhackers had the run of the vast prairies, according to Willy-Pete, and could easily guard the road to Tampa where all the herds were taken to be shipped to Cuba. It was an ideal location for a bunch of bushwhacking cattle rustlers out to make their fortunes.

Snake was also thinking it would be the ideal place to ambush Hawk when he pushed his herd through in the fall. When Hawk brought his herd through, would he bring Maddy with him or leave her at home? It didn't matter one way or the other to Snake. He'd hit Hawk's herd, grab Hawk's kid, and ride for the D-Wing. If Maddy was on the drive, he'd grab her too before heading back to Hawk's ranch. But he figured she'd be at home with the new baby. Yeah, she'd be at home just waiting for Daddy to ride in.

"How far is it from here?" Snake was getting sick of the riding, sick of the heat, and heartily sick of the mosquitoes. August was almost over and the weather was at its worst— hot and sultry, with rain almost every evening, huge downpours you could see coming for miles across the open prairie. Black clouds would roll through the open sky like billowing smoke from an oily fire. Great bolts of lightning would shoot from the sky to the ground and sometimes from the ground to the sky.

"We should be able to make it there by this afternoon," Willy-Pete said, taking out a moist brown chaw of tobacco and cramming it in his mouth.

When they got within a mile of the fort, they were accosted by the first sentry. A wild-looking man with a long beard, long hair, a big black duster covering his clothes, and a black large-brimmed hat pulled low over his eyes came out of a clump of palmetto with a double-barrel shotgun pointed right at them.

"Hold up, you two. Just where do you think yer a-going?"

Willy-Pete held his hand up to Snake, indicating he would handle the situation. Snake was more than happy to let him.

"We're looking for McGee. I heard he's still fighting the war, just against a different enemy."

The outlaw laughed, showing his few teeth were black and rotting. "He's fighting a war, all right, but it ain't for no cause. Josie McGee aims to get rich and we'uns fighting beside him aim to get rich too. What makes you think the Captain wants to see you two?" The outlaw's haughty expression oozed scorn.

"Because I fought with Bloody Bill Elliott, that's why," Willy-Pete said. "You ever heard of Bloody Bill?"

"Is that the Bloody Bill who killed all them folks up in Tennessee?"

"That would be him," Willy-Pete said.

"Well, damn. I'm from those parts. Last time I was to home, my pap told me about them bushwhackers up in the mountains that was fighting the war and winning."

"We killed us some Yankees," Willy-Pete said.

"From what I heard you done better than the Rebel army. My name's Orville, Orville Thompson, but most folks just call me Tommy." The outlaw laid his shotgun across the saddle bow, stuck out a grubby paw, and shook hands first with Willy-Pete and then with Snake.

"Ain't most of those men what rode with Elliott wanted?" Tommy asked after the introductions were completed, his eyes resting on Willy-Pete.

"I'm wanted by the Union, if that's what you mean," Willy said.

"I heard they got federal warrants out for them what fought after the war was supposed to be over."

"War ain't never gonna be over for some of us," Willy said. "There's a lot of us that ain't never gonna get over it or forget what was done. There's some things a man just don't forget about."

"I hear ya, brother," Tommy said. The outlaw turned his horse around and pointed west. "Just ride that-a way and I'll signal the next sentry."

Tommy once again stuck out a filthy paw to Willy-Pete. "It's a honor to shake your hand," he said, and then he took out a small hand mirror and began directing flashes of light from the bright sun overhead off its surface.

"I know this kind of folk," Willy-Pete said to Snake. "Just be quiet and let me do the talking."

"I done already figured that out," Snake replied. So, Willy was a wanted man. He'd figured as much. It seemed as though he was a great believer in the Confederacy as well. All that talk of never forgetting what was done. Some people were just naturally stupid and loyal to lost causes. The whole conversation had given Snake the creeps. He knew now if

Willy-Pete ever caught on to who he really was, there'd be hell to pay and Snake would be the one paying.

The next sentry was about half a mile to the west. He was sitting on a spotted horse waiting for them. Without saying a word, he led them toward a big hammock. They crossed a deep creek, swimming the horses in the middle, and began climbing up the side of the hammock. The undergrowth was thick. They would have had a hard time finding the path without their surly guide.

The thick growth ended suddenly, revealing a stockade made of cabbage palm tree trunks. There was ten cleared feet around the stockade. When they rode up, the doors swung open and a small group of men waited inside.

At the center of a group of the scruffiest, nastiest, meanest-looking bunch of outlaws Snake had ever seen was a portly man wearing a leather vest over a bright white shirt. He wore a large straw hat over his gray hair, and Snake was shocked to see the portly man had only one leg. Snake immediately felt right at home.

When he swung off his gray horse, he pulled the crutch off the back of his saddle for the first time without feeling the least bit self-conscious. He always supported himself with the crutch after a long ride. His legs ached and his stump hurt from wearing the fake leg for a long period of time.

Snake let the reins of the gray drag the ground, all of his mounts ground tied. They either learned it right quick, or they hit the road or the road hit them, made no difference to Snake; there were lots of horses. As it turned out, a young boy scooped up the reins of his and Willy's mounts anyway, and Snake and Willy-Pete found themselves standing in front of the portly man Snake assumed was Josie McGee.

"If you made it past Tommy, you must be all right," McGee said. "He's a regular bloodhound when it comes to sniffing out bad 'uns. I'm Captain McGee. Was you by some chance looking for me?"

Willy-Pete introduced himself and Snake, and explained why they were there.

"If you fought with Bloody Bill, you must be a good 'un," McGee said to Willy-Pete. "Where'd you lose your leg?" he asked Snake.

Snake was prepared for this. "I got captured by the Yankees near Richmond in sixty-two. I lost the leg at Pointe Lookout Prison."

McGee took a closer look at Snake's amputated leg. "That looks pretty fresh to me."

"I keep opening it up," Snake explained. "At first it suppurated due to the bad conditions in the prison camp. They had to cut more off, and then there's the fact I just can't seem to stay off it. Got to get up and be on my feet, you know."

McGee nodded. "I remember. I lost mine over a year ago. Same thing happened to me. I kept getting up and aggravating the stump."

Snake eyed McGee's leg. His was cut off above the knee. His wooden leg was a lot longer than Snake's.

McGee invited them into the blockhouse and poured each of them a shot of whiskey from a cut-crystal decanter. The rest of the men disappeared, so Snake sat down sticking his peg leg out in front of him. It felt good to be in a chair and off a horse. The whiskey went down smooth. He and old McGee were going to be great friends. This was going to work out just like he'd planned. Or it would so long as old Willy didn't wake up one morning and suddenly remember where he'd seen Snake before. If that happened, Willy would have to pass on the same way the man with his hand on the reins of that mule had.

22 🖤

"YIPPEE," TRAVIS YELPED AS A YEARLING bull burst from the bushes, followed by three dogs hot on its tail. Travis cracked his whip and hustled Light Foot into a lope, taking off after the yearling. The dogs kept after the bull, nipping its hocks, and when the animal tried to double back to the hammock it'd come from, they went after its nose. Travis made it move on by cracking his whip.

When the bull was safely in the small herd being held together by more dogs, Travis rode over to let his mount catch its breath next to Shorty's red cracker horse. "Think this is enough, or should I get a few more?" Travis asked Shorty. "There's a mama cow and a calf back there in that clump of palmettos I just passed."

Shorty turned his head and looked where Travis was pointing. "Let's take this bunch in. We can come back later."

Travis looked overhead. The sun was low in the sky, casting long shadows. "I don't know, brother. I should probably go get 'em."

"Go on then and I'll wait. But would you hurry up? A

couple of these are pretty nasty. One of the dogs almost got it a minute ago. That spotted cow over there with the red bull calf is a dang mean old bitch."

Travis raced back to the hammock with three of the dogs. The dogs were hot. Their tongues were lolling on the ground, but they were up for the hunt every time, no matter how tired they were or how hot. They loved this work.

High overhead he heard a red-tailed hawk. He looked up and saw Diver sailing on the air currents, hunting. Travis hoped she'd catch a fat rabbit. He'd like to cook one up tonight for dinner. He was getting sick of beans and bacon. But Diver began spiraling down closer and closer. She must have made her kill already, must be fed and ready to go to bed.

Travis took a large leather glove out of his saddlebag and put it on his right arm. He stopped the horse, held his arm up so Diver could see it, and called her. When she came swooping down to land on his glove, Light Foot shied. The hawk was something the little marsh tacky couldn't seem to get used to. He pulled the hawk's hood out of his bag and slid it over her head. She instantly grew quiet, and he followed the dogs back to the hammock where he'd seen the cow. It looked like no rabbit tonight.

When Travis got to the hammock, the three leopard dogs dove into the thickest brush. Travis could hear them in there barking and growling. Pretty soon a skinny little yellow cow popped out of the brush. A minute later, the dogs brought her calf out. The calf was almost as big as the cow. With one crack of his whip, he drove the cow and calf back to the herd, and Shorty got the rest of them moving.

Pa was supposed to be waiting up ahead. He and Joseph

had built a corral out of brush, saplings, and stakes. Inside it, they had over a hundred head milling around, mooing and stirring up a cloud of dust. Tomorrow, they'd do the branding and cutting, then let the cows and small calves go and keep any market-size steers, bulls, and heifers.

When Travis and Shorty got within sight of the corral, Travis went on ahead. "Hey Joseph, I got about twenty—open up."

Joseph opened the makeshift gate, and Travis and Shorty, cracking their whips, pushed the cattle through the gap with the help of all the dogs. "Where's Pa?" Travis asked.

"He's checking on the bunch we have north of here that are ready to go," Joseph said. "He's got another hundred up there. After we sort through this bunch I think we'll have enough to drive to Tampa."

Travis dismounted, took Diver to her perch on the wagon, and put Light Foot on the picket line. He'd hobble the horse so the animal could graze later. It was Shorty's job to get the fire going, and Travis was the cook. They always made him cook. He wished with all his heart that Miss Maddy could have come and cooked for them. He sure missed her biscuits and blackberry pie.

When he got to the campsite, he started pulling things out of the wagon for cooking. He'd soaked beans all day. When Shorty had the fire ready, he set the pot of red beans on to boil. While that was heating, he cut up an onion and chopped some bacon up then he tossed these items into the pot with the beans. He pulled four big sweet potatoes out of a sack in the wagon and put them deep in the fire pit to roast. That done, he went to wash his face and hands in the creek. He felt like he had a month's worth of dirt under his collar.

While he was washing up, Hawk came into the camp. Pa had been as surly as a wounded bear ever since they'd left on this drive. Travis didn't know what ailed him, but he sure wished his pa would get over it. They'd been out here for three months, working every day, and he still wasn't right.

Travis had a feeling his pa's problem was Miss Maddy. In the days before they'd left, Pa and Miss Maddy had made a trip to Enterprise. When they came back Pa went and stayed in the little cabin until they were ready to go on the drive. He and Miss Maddy never talked or sat on the porch together or ate together again. And Pa had turned into a giant pain to be around. Ask any of them.

Hawk rode up and climbed off Beau, tethering him on the picket line. "How many head did you boys pick up today?" Hawk asked immediately.

"We got us nearly thirty today," Joseph said. "I was planning to brand and cut the ones we got in the pen tomorrow. There's so many in there I'm afraid they're gonna bust out."

"So how many we got in the pen here now, over a hundred?" Hawk walked with Joseph toward the wagon.

"At least a hundred, maybe more," Joseph said.

Travis looked at his pa. Hawk looked like hell. He had lost weight, was wearing dirty clothes, and hadn't bothered to cut his hair since they left the D-Wing. His beard was in desperate need of a trimming, and his eyes had a feverish glow. He really didn't look good. His face was covered with a thin sheen of sweat.

"Let's see how many keepers we get out of this bunch and then I'll decide whether we have enough to drive to market," Hawk said.

"We been out here three months almost, Pa," Travis

said. "I was hoping to get home by Christmas. I was looking forward to a big Christmas dinner with Miss Maddy and Sarah."

Hawk whipped his head around and snarled at Travis. "We'll be ready to push cows when I say we're ready and not a moment before."

"Yes, sir," Travis snapped back. Hawk was turning real mean, and Travis didn't like it at all.

The next morning, they got up, swilled down Travis's terrible coffee and some burned fry bread, and went straight to work. Joseph built a hot fire and shoved the D-Wing branding irons deep into the coals. All four of them got big sticks and went into the pen with the cattle. It was dangerous work; the cows were crowded and milling around, and almost all of them had horns and were as wild and crazy as jackrabbits.

They sorted the branded ones from the unbranded first. All the cattle with a non-D-Wing brand went out the gate. Next, they sorted the cattle without brands into a sectioned-off pen. Joseph would cut out a cow or a steer, get a rope on it, and throw it down. Depending on the size of the cow, one or two or even three of them would tie up the cow's feet and hold it down while they branded it. The D-Wing brand was a large capital D with two inverted lazy half Cs under it like the wings of a bird. The branded cow was let go and put back into the main pen.

When they finished the branding, it was past dinner-time. Travis was starving. He fixed them cold bacon sandwiches and then out they went to get more work done.

Now that all the cattle had brands, they sorted out the calves. Hawk wielded the knife as they castrated the bull calves. Joseph would grab a calf and throw him down. If it was a little one, Travis grabbed the hind leg and Shorty would lie on the head and hold the front leg. Hawk would quickly cut the bottom off the bull's sack and yank out the two testicles. If everything went like it was supposed to, the entire operation took less than a minute, but when dealing with wild critters, any number of things could go wrong.

After it was cut, Hawk would notch the calf's ear. The D-Wing used an under bit for heifers and a swallow fork for the steers. All the calves got their ears notched.

Travis was whipped after working the calves, but Hawk wanted to sort. Walking around in the pen with the cows was the most dangerous part of the job. If anything got them real stirred up, they could trample you or you could get a horn in your gut. There were several real crazy sons of bucks in the bunch too.

Travis had already run into a couple of mean older cows that really wanted to get a horn in you. They'd charge out of the bunch and try to hook you, or if you were riding a horse, they would come after the horse. They hooked each other too.

But the sorting went quickly, and Hawk let all but about fifty head loose. The ones he kept in the pen would go to Tampa with the bigger herd Hawk had ready to go.

When they were done, Travis felt like crawling into his bedroll and going right to sleep, but he had to make supper. He was heading for the wagon when Hawk walked up to him and put his hand on his shoulder.

"I know I've been a bear and I'm sorry, Trav," Hawk said to him. "You go clean up down at the creek and I'll fix supper. If you want, you can take Diver out hunting on the prairie."

Imagine that, Pa was being nice. "Thanks, Pa. I'll take her out after I wash the dirt off my face."

"If she catches something good and fat, bring it in and I'll cook it up," Hawk said. "Tomorrow I think we'll join the two bunches and start for Tampa."

Snake jingled the pile of gold doubloons in his poke. Twenty gold doubloons, what a haul. After they had hit two herds and rustled over two hundred head, Snake got an idea. Rustling cattle was hard work. They still had to be driven all the way to Tampa, and it took two to three weeks. And that was if nothing bad happened, and bad things happened constantly.

Once in the middle of the wide-open prairie, a storm hit that made every cow take off running at the same time. The boys from Texas called it a stampede. There were lots of things that caused stampedes as Snake soon found out, things like lightning, gunshots, wolves, or maybe just the wind. It was a nightmare. Snake had found himself in the middle of the herd when the cattle took off running. Being surrounded by a sea of moving horns was very unnerving.

When they had the cows in their possession, the Captain would decide whether the brands had to be altered. In the first bunch, many of the cows had no brands at all. The Captain said not to worry, and they pushed them to Tampa. But in the second herd, over half of them were clearly branded with a double C. They'd had to stop, and one of the men had fashioned an over-brand that turned the double Cs into double Os. It was a hot, nasty, dangerous job and took an entire day. At the end of the day Snake was covered with dirt and cow manure. This cattle business did not suit him.

And then there were rivers to take the herd across, with swamps and predators that scared the cows. Three of them had to be on night watch every night. There were snakes, bugs, and wolves. No, Snake did not like pushing cows—it was way too much like work.

After they'd made the second drive to Tampa, Snake went to Captain McGee with an idea. He suggested that instead of stealing the cows, they trail the herd into Tampa and then hit the drovers when they were on their way home with all that money in their pockets. The Captain, in many ways a man after his own heart, had taken to Snake's plan right way. And it had worked like a charm. Now he had himself a pocketful of gold and was headed to Orlando to bust loose. He needed some more laudanum, a new leather hat, and a new horse or two.

Snake had been doing a lot of thinking lately, a lot of thinking about Caleb Hawkins. It seemed as though all his problems could be traced back to Hawk. If it hadn't been for Hawk, he would be with Maddy right now. How had Hawk met up with her in the first place, and why were they together? How could such a thing have happened?

Add all that to Hawk being the one that made him a one-legged cripple. He could still remember looking at Hawk down the sights of his rifle only seconds before he'd been blown sky high. He'd seen it in Hawk's eyes. Hawk had known Snake was about to be blown up and had planned it that way. Only Hawk had planned for him to die.

Well, he wasn't dead. He was very much alive, and Hawk was soon to discover Snake Barber was not a person to take lightly.

Two new buddies rode beside him. That Willy-Pete character wouldn't leave the stockade to go anywhere near a town because he was afraid of being arrested. He said he'd heard he had federal agents tailing him. That choice piece of information had almost gotten Willy-Pete tossed out of the gang. Captain McGee frowned on federal agents. But there wasn't a lawman on the planet that would attack the Fort Kissimmee stockade, even if they could find it. They'd be nuts to try.

Snake's new friend Butterbean Drinker rode on the left. Bean, as they called him, was a pretty hefty guy and rode the widest horse Snake had ever seen. Butterbean could rope a thousand-pound bull off that horse and hold it rock steady.

Snake figured Bean liked him because deep inside, Bean liked to think of himself as a real outlaw just as bad as Snake. Bean was really just a fat, lazy man, but Snake encouraged him to think he was as mean as they came. But as Snake had noticed, the only thing Bean was mean to was his dinner, which he shoveled into his mouth with a lot of energy. Snake needed men, though, so he played up to the large bush-whacker's equally huge ego.

Riding downwind on his right was a strange guy named Tex. His last name was completely unpronounceable, so he just went by Tex—even though he wasn't from Texas. His parents had immigrated from one of those European countries really far up north and really cold. In America they'd settled in some state up north, like Michigan or thereabouts. They loved the cold, but Tex hadn't, so he'd left home when he was sixteen and joined up with the Captain. Tex didn't have much to say, but he had the fastest draw with a .45 Snake had ever seen.

No one liked Tex. He was weird and had some strange habits that made almost every man in the stockade avoid him. For example, Tex never washed, ever. He was the fastest gun Snake had ever seen and the smelliest man he'd ever met. He slept completely clothed and he only had the one outfit. Furthermore, he would take offense over nothing and then force the man who had insulted him into either drawing or backing down. When you added this quality to his bad smell, it was clear why Tex was the most avoided man in the stockade.

But Tex had qualities Snake liked. He was fast with a gun and horses loved him. So did dogs. When they went into town, dogs would seek him out. Snake felt sure they really just wanted to roll on him and pick up some of that nasty odor. And Snake figured Tex's ruthless ways might come in handy.

The three of them were looking forward to this trip, planning to get as drunk as skunks and find themselves a couple of easy women to spend some quality time with.

As they rode across the prairie, Snake kept an eye out for more herds. They all did. Herds of cows heading down the trail meant gold in their pockets when the herders headed back up the trail from Tampa. McGee paid an extra ten-percent bonus to the guy who spotted a herd.

A cloud of dust on the horizon caught Snake's eye, but he was too far away to see what was causing it. From the size of the cloud, it must be big.

"See that, Tex?" Snake asked as he pointed to the west.

Tex shaded his eyes and looked. "Could be a herd," Tex said.

"I guess I'll ride over and check it out, since I'm the one that spotted it," Snake said.

Snake set his spurs in the gray's flanks and took off toward the plume of dust. When he got closer, he saw it was in fact a herd, and it looked like a big one, maybe over two hundred head.

He didn't want to be seen, so he moved around behind the herd in a large half circle. Coming up from behind, he saw the supply wagon moving slowly, pulled by a team of mules. He reached into his saddlebag and pulled out a small spyglass. Putting it to his eye, he focused in on the man driving the wagon. He looked like an Indian. Snake could have rubbed his hands together. This was gonna be a big haul.

Scanning the herd and looking for riders with the glass, he stopped suddenly. No, it couldn't be. He couldn't be this lucky. And yet, moving in a little closer, he hunted for other riders and spotted his old friend Shorty. Yes indeed, here was Hawk and his herd of cows, and it looked like they were pushing the herd to Tampa.

He turned the glass back on the wagon, hoping to see Maddy. But there was no one in the wagon, just the Indian up front driving and a load of supplies. He snapped the glass shut and put it away. He had some options to consider. Should he just go ahead and take Hawk out here with the cattle, or stick with the plan and wait until Hawk had collected his gold and get him on his way home?

Snake opened the bag again and took the glass out for another look. He couldn't believe his luck, but then he'd already figured he was bound to catch them. One way or another, the herds going to Tampa were under the close scrutiny of Josie McGee's men. He looked through his glass once more and spotted what he was looking for, the kid. He had to be Hawk's son. The boy was riding point, and his presence could change things. Snake needed to think and make some plans.

Spinning the gray, he took off galloping toward the two waiting men. When he rode up, they wanted to know what he'd seen.

"It's a big herd," Snake said. "Looked close to two hundred head."

"Should we ride back and tell the Captain?" Bean asked.

"Let's go on and ride to Orlando and spend a little time," Snake said. "We'll have us some fun tonight and then ride hard for the fort to see what McGee wants us to do."

Snake's mind was working overtime. This was just what he'd been planning for. He'd known Hawk would ride by here sooner or later. He'd been hoping Maddy would be with them, but realized she had to be at home caring for their son.

"Let's ride," he said to the boys, then set spurs into his horse's sides and rode off at a lope toward Orlando. Snake planned to get him a couple of new horses, some laudanum, and a new leather, flat-crowned hat. He absolutely hated this floppy brown thing on his head.

23 🌿

THE BABY CRYING WOKE MADDY UP, so she
climbed out of bed, scooped Storm out of his cradle, and
turned up the wick on the oil lamp beside her bed. Sticking
one finger into his diaper, she discovered the boy was wet.
She changed him quickly and then lay back on her new mattress with him snuggled beside her. It seemed as though
Storm ended up in her bed every night. As she dropped back
into sleep she wondered if he was smart enough to plan it
that way.

Maddy was back out of bed at dawn. She had a ton of
work to do before she left for Volusia Landing. After slipping
into a blue serge skirt and a crisp white blouse, she brushed
out her hair and rebraided it. Then she took her mother's
cameo out of the silver jewelry box and hung it around her
neck. She loved running her fingers over the silky shell carv-
ing. At least three inches long and heavy, it was the only
piece of her mother's jewelry she'd been able to save. When
she was finished dressing, she ran her hand over her hair to
make sure it was neat and went out to the cookhouse to
make some coffee.

Judy Bill was already out there boiling water for her tea. The Indian woman said nothing to her as she made a pot of coffee and set it on to boil. Judy Bill might not drink coffee, but Jumper did.

There was a slight chill in the air this morning. After days of sweltering heat, the temperature had started dropping every night. The milk she had left out the night before was still cold, so she decided to make pancakes if Judy Bill would move over and give her some room.

"I think I'll make some pancakes for breakfast," Maddy said. "Would you like some?"

"I don't eat pancakes," Judy Bill replied.

"Of course you don't. What was I thinking?" No matter how hard Maddy tried to get along with the woman, Judy Bill made it plain she was not wanted in the house.

"Well, Judy Bill, I'm going to make them anyway. Then I'm going to harness the bay gelding and drive to Volusia Landing. Is there anything you need?"

"Who said you could take the wagon and go to Volusia Landing?" Judy Bill asked. "You have work to do here."

"Well, in the first place, it's my wagon and my horse," Maddy returned. "If I want to take it and go to the store, then I will. And I have done all my work except for making the beds this morning and sweeping the house. I will make sure to get that done before I leave."

"You think you're so high and mighty because you came from a big plantation and used to own slaves. Here, we are all the same and must do work to survive."

Maddy calmly made pancake batter while the cast-iron griddle heated. She took a deep breath. "I know we are all the same here, and I do my work. And as I told you a minute ago,

I'm taking the wagon to Volusia Landing. Is there anything you'd like me to get for you?"

"There's nothing you can get for me," Judy Bill snapped. "The only thing you can do for me is leave us here and go back where you came from." Judy Bill gathered her tattered bathrobe around her and stalked majestically out of the cookhouse and up the stairs to the house.

"I'm trying to get out of here," Maddy muttered when she was gone. "I'm doing the best I can."

Two hours later, chores done, Maddy and Sarah drove out of the homestead yard and down the track toward Volusia. As soon as Hawk and the men had left on the roundup, she'd written a letter to her sister-in-law. She had made the trip to Volusia Landing a month ago to see if there was a return letter from Rachel, and there had been nothing. She was praying there would be a letter there for her today.

If Rachel would only come back to Pilatka, then she and Sarah could move up there and get out of this place. With no hope now of ever receiving Hawk's support and love, she had no reason to be here, not to mention that Judy Bill made life miserable for her.

The weird thing was, Judy Bill liked Sarah. She went out of her way to be nice to the girl, sewing Sarah a beautiful patchwork jacket and teaching her how to make the patchwork patterns of the Seminoles. The two of them would sit in the parlor in the evenings and sew while Maddy worked on the mattress covers.

Every bed had a new mattress. Maddy was very proud of that. She'd made curtains for the windows after Jumper had fit the glass into the frames, and when the curtains were done, she'd started braiding rag rugs for the parlor and bedrooms. Sarah was working on cross-stitching a large hanging with a Bible verse on it for the wall.

As soon as Judy Bill had discovered Storm's parentage, she'd refused to even touch the baby. Storm could be screaming in his cradle and Judy Bill wouldn't talk to him or pick him up. But she liked Sarah.

"I need to get some red embroidery floss," Sarah said as they drove down the trail toward the river. "I could use some more light blue and yellow too."

"We'll see if they have some," Maddy said.

"Mama, why are we going to Volusia Landing? We have hardly any money. Why do we need to go?" Sarah asked as she bounced Storm on her lap. Storm was gurgling happily and waving his hands at the shafts of sunlight streaming through the canopy of trees overhead.

"I wrote to your Aunt Rachel, and I am hoping she has written me back," Maddy said. "I told her to mail any reply to the General Store."

"Why did you write to her?" Sarah asked. "We're not going to move up there with her, are we?"

"Well, I thought if she and Uncle Edward had returned, we would go stay with them in the boardinghouse."

Sarah's eyes flew open and her mouth tightened into a thin line. "I won't go with you. I want to stay here with Mr. Hawk and Travis and Miss Judy Bill and Mr. Jimmy. I don't want to move. I can ride horses now and I have my little Bobby Raccoon. Mr. Jimmy said I could have a puppy when the big gyp has her litter. I don't want to go anywhere. This is the first place I've been happy in my life and I love it here. Please don't take me away, Mama, please."

Maddy sighed. She'd had a feeling this was going to

happen. "We'll just have to wait and see, Sarah. In case you hadn't noticed, Judy Bill doesn't think too highly of me or Storm."

Tears were running down Sarah's face. She turned her head away and stared into the dense woods on her side of the trail.

There was a letter waiting when Maddy got to the General Store. Keeping it hidden from Sarah, she put it into the pocket of her skirt. She'd wait until she got back to the homestead to read it. Her heart was torn and she was so confused. She hated to hurt Sarah. The girl's life had been so hard, and Maddy only wanted to make her happy.

They shopped for the little things they could afford. Sarah bought some black cotton fabric, since Judy Bill was going to help her make a skirt just like hers, and several colors of embroidery floss for her cross-stitching. The girl picked out a piece of hard candy to share with Storm on the ride home.

On the way back to the D-Wing, Sarah asked the question Maddy knew was sitting on the tip of her tongue. "Did the letter come from Aunt Rachel?"

"Yes, Sarah, it did."

"What did she say?"

"I'll read it when I get home."

In the quiet of her room, with Storm sleeping in his cradle, she opened the envelope and unfolded two pages filled with Rachel's flowing copperplate.

She said they were indeed back in the boardinghouse and that Pilatka was booming once again. They were working to open the store back up and could use Maddy's help. Rachel wrote that the steamboats were running up and down the St. Johns and made note of the number of people staying at the boarding house.

Maddy put the letter down and sighed. Well, her prayers had been answered. Her mother had been fond of a certain saying that Maddy hadn't understood as a child but that she now knew to be true. "Be careful what you pray for, my daughter," Mama had once told her, "for you just might get your prayers answered."

❖   ❖   ❖

Snake sat at a table in the bunkhouse with his two buddies, Bean and Tex. They were talking quietly among themselves about the herd they'd spotted. "I know the guy running that herd," Snake said. "He's rich. He always carries a bunch of gold with him on every trip."

"Why would he even bother to run cattle if he's so rich?" Bean asked.

"I always wondered that myself," said Snake. "If I had half his money, I'd be living high on the hog. I sure wouldn't be eating the dust of no herd of cattle. I figure he's one of them kind of men that likes working cows. We got a couple here. They're cow-hunting fools."

"I know what you mean," Bean said, glancing over at two of the men sitting at a small table playing poker.

"You damn sure he carries money with him?" Tex asked.

"I seen it with my own eyes. I've knowed him since he was a boy. He got most of his money from his pa. His pa was a cow-hunting fool too."

Snake stuck his peg leg out in front of him and pulled his pant leg up to his knee to admire his newest acquisition.

While he'd been in Orlando, he'd had a jeweler put a silver snake on the side of his peg leg. The snake wrapped around the leg once and the head laid flat, pointing up. Snake had thought he might want the snake's tongue to be sticking out, but decided he didn't like that after all. The snake was fastened on with tiny silver rivets. All in all, it was just what Snake had been wanting to make his leg distinctive.

Tex eyed it. "That's some little doodad you got there."

"I think it makes my leg special," Snake said. "If you got to wear one, it might as well be fancied up a bit."

"It's fancy all right," Bean said, and then changed the subject. "You know the Captain ain't been feelin' up to snuff lately. He's taken to his bed, says his leg is hurtin' him real bad. Don't think he'll be up for this raid you're planning."

"We don't need him to rob two men and two boys," Snake said. "That's all the riders I saw."

"What about the rest of these fellas?" Tex asked.

"Do you think we need them along?" Snake's smile only lifted one corner of his mouth.

"Hell no, we can do it ourselves," Bean said. "There's no need to share the wealth with anybody. I mean, if the Captain don't care to take it on, let's do it alone. We're gonna have to hit 'em tomorrow, when they should be about ten miles from here."

"You better be tellin' the truth about the money, Snake," Tex said.

"Even if there's no money, there's over two hundred head of cattle. We make out either way," Snake said.

"But you're sure there will be money?" Bean fixed his tiny eyes on Snake, who thought he looked remarkably like a pig.

"I'm positive."

Early the next morning, Snake, Bean, and Tex packed their bags and saddled their horses. Snake was leading his brand-new bay cracker horse toward the main entrance just as Willy-Pete walked by. Willy grabbed Snake's arm, and Snake backed off and gave Willy a cold stare.

"Where you headed, Snake?"

"We're just going to ride back into Orlando and have a little more fun," Snake said, sure Willy-Pete would back off when he heard they were going to a town.

"No you're not. I heard Butterbean a-telling Tex about all the money they were gonna be gettin' offa this big job y'all got planned. Now what job would they be a-talkin' about, Snake?"

Damn, Snake thought. He'd have to take Willy-Pete along too. Well, it couldn't hurt, and he might even be a help. They would need an extra hand if they had to push cattle. "You're on to us, Willy-Pete," Snake said. "We spotted a big herd north of here about ten miles, and with the Captain being sick and all, we thought we'd go get it. You're welcome to come if you want to."

"Don't mind if I do," Willy-Pete said. "I'm about sick of being penned up in this stockade. I could use me some action and some extry money."

"Well then, shake a leg," Snake said. "We gotta ride."

Willy-Pete was ready in no time, and the four of them rode out. Many of the bushwhackers were still enjoying their free time in Orlando, so the place was about deserted. Snake adjusted his new flat-crowned leather hat and spurred his horse as they rode across the creek and off into the prairie.

24 🌿

TRAVIS WAS WORRIED ABOUT PA. This morning at breakfast, Pa's hands had shaken when he'd poured himself a cup of coffee, his face had been pale, and he'd refused to eat anything. Pa's behavior had Travis worried, as he'd never seen Hawk behaving like this. Something was definitely wrong.

When he glanced over his shoulder to see where Hawk was, he spotted his father riding along the right side of the herd pushing the cattle, driving them forward with his whip. They were always hard to get started in the morning. It took the dogs and the three of them to get the cows headed down the trail.

From his position on the left flank of the herd, he could see Pa, and while he watched, he thought he saw Hawk sway in the saddle. What could be wrong with him? He seemed to be getting sicker and sicker every day, but he never said anything about not feeling good.

Shorty had ridden on ahead, scouting the trail. Someone had to check out the lay of the land to make sure the trail was clear and the cows could get through. He should be riding in any minute, seeing as how he'd been gone about an hour. And Joseph was in the rear of the herd, driving the wagon.

Travis spurred his horse, riding up and down beside the slowly moving sea of cattle. When he looked over at Hawk again, he was sure he saw his father's shoulders drop. Right away, Travis saw Hawk's horse slow its pace and then Hawk began to fall behind. Something was seriously wrong. With Shorty gone, Joseph driving the wagon, and Hawk dropping back, there was no one but him to mind the dang cows. Travis spun his horse on its hocks and galloped back down the length of the strung-out herd, riding around to where Hawk's horse had actually come to a dead stop in the middle of a dry creek bed.

Leaping off his horse, Travis grabbed Beau's reins. His father was slumped over the horn of his saddle, barely conscious. "Pa, what's wrong?" Travis demanded. "Pa," Travis said again, trying to make his father answer him.

Hawk looked up, his eyes bloodshot and his face dripping with sweat. Travis could see Hawk's clothes were soaked through. When he reached up and touched his father's face, he realized Hawk was burning up with fever. "Malaria," Hawk murmured. "Must be the fever coming back."

Travis remembered his father had told them he'd had malaria while in Pointe Lookout. "Hang on, Pa, Joseph is coming with the wagon."

Joseph must have seen Hawk stop, because he pulled the wagon over into the creek bed and got down from the seat. "What's wrong with Mr. Hawk?" Joseph asked as he walked up beside Travis.

"I think Pa is bad sick, Joseph. Feel his face, he's burning up. He said something about malaria."

Joseph touched Hawk's face. "He's got a bad fever. Didn't he say he had the malaria when he was in prison camp? That sickness comes from bad air in swamps and it never goes away, just keeps coming back over and over again."

"That must be what's wrong with him, then. I'm so worried. Joseph, is Pa gonna die?"

"I don't know, Travis. Let's get him into the back of the wagon."

Travis led Beau, still carrying the slumped-over Hawk, to the wagon while Joseph worked to make room among the supplies. The wagon was packed slap full with enough supplies for two or three weeks, so there was no room in the back for a man. "Just throw the stuff out," Travis said. "We're going to have to stop here anyway. We can't go on with Pa in this shape."

"Take a look around, Travis. This a very bad place to camp. There is no water and no place to get shelter from the weather. We're sitting in the middle of a dry creek bed. If it gets to raining hard, we'll be stuck in water and mud up to our axles. We'll never get the wagon out of here," Joseph said, stacking sacks of flour, sweet potatoes, and grits one on top of the other as he spoke.

Travis looked around. The creek bed Joseph had driven the wagon into ran off toward the herd, with no hammocks close by and no ponds, lakes, or springs in sight. "Where can we go, Joseph? I don't see any good places to make camp for miles."

When Joseph had moved enough stuff to make a place

for Hawk to lie down, he and Travis lifted Hawk, now near-ly unconscious, off the big horse and put him into the wagon. Travis could feel the heat in his father's body burning through his clothes.

"I know a gator hole north of here up by the swamp," Joseph said as he climbed into the wagon's seat. "Get the cows headed there. It can't be but two or three miles."

"But, Joseph, that could take us hours to get to, pushing these cows."

"I'll drive the wagon on ahead and set up camp. Shorty should be back soon to help you. Just head for that big patch of cabbage heads up there." Joseph pointed and Travis could see where he needed to go.

Travis tied his marsh tacky to the back of the wagon. "I'll ride Beau, keep Light Foot here."

Malaria sounded like an awful sickness. Travis could feel worry for his father pushing aside all other considera-tions. His head felt light and he had crazy energy coursing through his body. After he got the cattle settled for the night, he'd have to ride for Orlando and get a doctor, or at least talk to one and find out what he needed to give his pa to make him better.

Racing back to the herd, Travis got the cows moving again. Using his whip and the dogs, he tried to turn them in the direction Joseph was taking the wagon. Joseph had the mules whipped into a smart trot and in minutes was out of sight.

The herd slowly started turning the way Travis wanted the cattle to go. He would have been lost trying to do this without the dogs. As it was, several bunches got away from him. The dogs would bring a few back, but after an hour, at least thirty had split off from the herd and were gone. He couldn't be on both sides of two hundred head of cattle at one time. It was a good thing he was riding Beau. The horse could fly.

Travis kept looking behind him for Shorty. He should be back by now. But his friend was apparently still scouting the trail ahead and nowhere to be found. While he was scanning the horizon, he saw four riders approaching from the south. Travis's guts knotted. He was already upset about Hawk and now he was getting a really bad feeling about this, but what could he do? He was alone with two hundred head of cows in the middle of a vast open prairie. There was nowhere to hide. All he had between him and any bushwhackers were the dogs, his rifle, and Beau.

Snake spotted the herd, but it looked like something was wrong. Instead of heading southwest toward Tampa, a lone rider was trying to turn the herd toward the north.

"I only see one rider," Snake said to Butterbean, who rode on his left.

Bean strained his eyes. "Yeah, Snake, there's only one guy trying to move that entire herd."

"Hold up," Snake said as he pulled the spyglass out of his saddlebag. It only took him a minute to get a good picture of what was going on. Through the glass, he could see the wagon moving north at a smart pace, and he recognized the lone rider as Hawk's kid. The boy was doing a hell of a job getting the cows turned to follow the disappearing wagon.

"Something's gotta be wrong. The kid is trying to turn

all those cows by himself. It looks like he's losing a bunch of 'em too. He must be trying to get them going in the direction of that wagon." Snake pointed at the small dust plume disappearing on the northern horizon. "But I recognize the kid. This is the drive we're looking for."

"Well, if it's only one kid, let's take him," Tex said.

"I'm in," Willy-Pete said.

The four of them took off at a gallop toward the herd and the one rider struggling to control it. They quickly caught up with the cows, but the kid must have seen them. He took off at a gallop on one of the fastest horses Snake had ever seen. In seconds the horse was gone, leaving a trail of dust.

"Follow the kid," Snake shouted.

The four of them took off around the herd, riding like the devil after Hawk's kid. Snake could barely see the boy in front of him. When he had the wagon in view, he saw the kid was already stopped at the wagon and off his horse. The driver got off the wagon and both men took up defensive positions on the ground behind the wagon. Snake only saw the two of them, so where were Shorty and Hawk?

When Snake and his men got closer, he could see that the Indian and the kid had their rifles pointed at them. It was suicide to attack. They were only four, and if they charged, it was likely more than one of them would go down to a bullet.

"Does anyone have something white, like a handkerchief or a shirt?" Snake asked.

"Bean rummaged around in his saddlebag and pulled out an enormous pair of ruffled women's bloomers. They were white. "I'm not even gonna ask," Snake said as he took the bloomers and fixed them to the end of his rifle. "I can't be the one that rides in there waving a white flag—the kid might recognize me. Bean, you do it."

Bean grabbed Snake's rifle with the gently waving bloomers tied to the tip of the barrel and rode slowly forward, waving the makeshift white flag. The rest of them rode behind him. "If they ask you what you want, just tell them you saw the kid having trouble and wondered if there was anything we could do to help. Tell them we were riding into Orlando."

When Hawk's kid and the Indian spotted Bean and the white flag, they stood up behind the wagon but didn't drop their rifles. When the four of them got within twenty feet, Snake stopped Tex and Willy so Bean could ride forward and give his little speech.

Whatever Bean said must have worked because he soon turned around and gestured for them to come forward. Snake pushed the brim of his hat down low over his face and hung back. When he got close enough to the wagon, he saw Hawk lying in the back unconscious. His enemy was helpless before him and Snake could barely contain himself.

Bean had already dismounted and was talking to the Indian. Snake came off his horse and kept it carefully between him and the kid as he quietly circled around behind the Indian and drew his big Navy Colt. The Indian was talking to Tex and Willy-Pete when Snake shoved the barrel of his pistol in the Indian's back.

"Drop those rifles," Snake ordered the Indian and Hawk's kid. "Or I'll plug you right now."

Joseph didn't obey. Instead, he spun on his heels and tried to bring the rifle up to get off a shot. Snake was startled, as he'd expected the Indian to act smart and drop his rifle.

Joseph's rifle struck the barrel of Snake's Colt, but Snake didn't hesitate. He immediately shot him. Joseph fell to the ground and lay still.

Bean and the boys were stunned by the quick action and by Snake's sudden firing of his weapon, so they were slow to react when Hawk's kid took two strides, jumped on his big stud horse, and took off, clinging to the horse's off side like a trick rider. There was no way they could get a shot at the kid.

"Shoot the damn horse," Snake yelled.

Bean and Tex each loosed a shot, but the horse was so fast, he was already out of range. Then Snake noticed Willy-Pete. Willy-Pete's eyes were wide, and he was staring at Snake like he'd never seen him before in his life. Quick as a jackrabbit, Willy-Pete pulled his pistol out of its holster and pointed it at Snake.

"It was you," Willy-Pete snarled. "When I saw you shoot that Indian and you got that dumb-ass, flat-crowned hat on and that mean look on yer face, I remembered where I seen you before. In one second, I knew it was you. You're the son of a bitch that shot Sergeant Anderson. It was you up there in Marshallville. It was you wouldn't give wounded soldiers one of your spare horses to pull our wagon, not even a skinny ole mule."

"What are you talking about, Willy-Pete?" Snake asked coolly.

Snake still had his big Navy Colt in his hand, but it was pointed at the ground, while Willy-Pete's pistol was aiming straight at Snake's heart.

"Don't try nothing, you slimy bastard. I know it was you. It's that dang hat you wear. I mean, it's like I never saw you before. I been a-waitin' for this moment ever since I got better, and damn me, but I been looking fer you everywhere. I knew I'd find your rotten ass in due time."

Snake didn't take his eyes off Willy-Pete's face while he slowly inched his gun higher. He could guess about where it was aiming, so when he figured it had to be pointing at Willy-Pete about crotch level, he fired and leaped to the left, landing on his peg leg. Pain shot into his stump and he went down in a heap.

But his shot had hit Willy-Pete in the lower belly, not the crotch. Willy couldn't even fire his pistol. It dropped out of his opened hands as he grabbed his belly and sank to his knees.

Snake pulled himself back to his feet with the aid of the wagon and stared down at the man he had just shot. "When you want to shoot someone, just shoot," Snake said. "Don't talk."

Snake put his booted foot on Willy's chest and kicked him over backwards. Willy fell over still clutching his belly, his hands now red with blood. "He's dead and he don't even know it yet," Snake said to Butterbean, who was staring at him with a closed expression on his chubby face.

"What'd ya shoot Willy fer, Snake?" Bean asked. "What was he trying to say before you shot him, and what was all that crap about you shooting his sergeant?"

"I have no idea what he was talking about," Snake said as he stuck his colt back into its holster. "Y'all know Willy weren't right in the head."

"Hey, did y'all hear that?" Tex asked. "What's that noise?" Agitated by the sudden violence, Tex rapidly paced back and forth. "It sounds like thunder."

Snake perked up his ears and listened. In the distance,

he could hear a noise that did sound like the rumbling of thunder. He looked up at the sky, but there were no clouds. The sky was as blue as a robin's egg, but the noise kept getting louder.

Suddenly Tex wheeled around and raced for the horses. "Stampede," he called over his shoulder.

Fear flooded through Snake. Not a hundred feet away, just cresting a slight rise, he could see the lead cows of a two hundred-head herd funneling straight into the creek bed and right for them. The ground was beginning to shake under the pounding of eight hundred pounding hooves.

Bean and Snake ran for their horses. Snake was slower, his peg leg a huge impediment. Bean's big horse was spooked by the noise and the ground shaking. When Bean put his foot into the stirrup, the animal reared and Bean fell to the ground. Meanwhile, Snake had reached his cracker horse. The little bay was scared, but stood while Snake clumsily scrambled into the saddle.

The first wave of running cattle hit Bean before he could get to his feet, and he disappeared beneath the hooves of an ocean of crazed cattle. Bean's horse reared again and took off with the herd just as Snake turned the little bay and raced in front of the cattle, trying desperately to get far enough ahead to get out of the creek bed and escape. He saw the massive herd part to pass around the wagon, some climbing the banks of the old creek and heading out onto the prairie. The plunging mules broke out of their traces and raced with the cows, harnesses slapping, along with the little marsh tacky that had been tied to the wagon.

Looking back over his shoulder while the bay horse galloped for his life, Snake saw Hawk's kid and Shorty driving the herd into the dry creek. He heard them firing their rifles over and over, sending the frightened cattle into a complete frenzy. Snake bent low over his horse's neck as the little cracker horse continued to run.

25 ☀

TRAVIS AND SHORTY STOPPED at the wagon. The cattle would run until they got tired or forgot they were scared. The mules and Light Foot were gone, but the wagon had survived. The pile of supplies Joseph had stacked to make room for Hawk was gone and the contents of the sacks and boxes scattered everywhere, but Travis was only concerned about Hawk and Joseph.

When he'd seen Snake shoot Joseph, he'd instinctively turned and jumped on Beau. He'd never been so glad that horse was fast. The big stud had literally outrun the bushwhackers' bullets.

Sending the cattle into a stampede had been Shorty's idea. When Travis had escaped from Snake, he'd ridden like the wind back to the herd. He'd found Shorty there hunting for him and the wagon. After he'd told Shorty what had happened with Snake and about how sick his father was, Shorty had come up with the idea of stampeding the herd right over Snake and his men.

Travis had worried the cattle would destroy the wagon

and kill his Pa, but Shorty said they should go around the wagon since it was pretty big and that even though the plan was risky, it was the only thing he could think of that would be guaranteed to get rid of the bushwhackers. Shorty had thought it was worth a try, and he'd been right.

They'd used the dogs and gunfire to get the cattle moving in the right direction, and then had purposefully worked them into a frenzy.

Travis leaped out of the saddle, immediately looking for Hawk and Joseph. He saw Pa was still in the wagon. Some of the supplies had fallen on top of him and he was thrashing around waving his arms and legs, but Travis could see it was just fever dreams.

"I'll scare up some water," Shorty said. "My ma used to wash me all over with cool water when I had a fever. Mayhap that will help."

Travis shot his friend a look of gratitude. "Thanks, Shorty. I got to see if I can find Joseph's body. I know his ma would want to see him laid to rest with a decent burial."

When Travis walked around to where he'd seen Snake shoot Joseph, he expected to find a gory mess, but Joseph's body was not there, nor was there any sign Joseph had ever been there. He looked under the wagon, and that's where he found the Indian.

"Joseph," Travis called. "Are you alive, old friend? I thought you were dead for sure."

Joseph was huddled up with his head buried in his arms. He groaned, fell onto his back, and then slowly rolled out from under the wagon. His head was covered with blood that still dripped down his face in a steady stream of fat droplets.

Travis helped him out from under the wagon. "Joseph,

you made it!" Travis grabbed the Indian and tried to give him a bear hug. He was never so glad to see anyone in his life. He'd been sure Joseph had been shot dead by Snake Barber.

But Joseph pushed Travis off and grabbed his head, moaning. "My head is aching, Travis. Leave off trying to squeeze me to death."

Travis leaned over the side of the wagon and looked at Shorty, who was gently bathing Hawk's face with cool water he'd taken from the wagon's one surviving water barrel. Shorty had the water in a Dutch oven and was using one of Hawk's shirts to bathe his face. "Shorty, Joseph isn't dead."

Shorty looked up and gave Travis one of his wide grins. "Man am I glad to see that ole Indian. Lookee at all that blood. What happened? Did Snake scalp him?"

"It sure looks like it, but I think Joseph got creased right across the head by Snake's bullet.

"Let me look at that head of yours," Travis demanded. Joseph bent a little and Travis examined the top of the Indian's head. Apparently the bullet had cut a deep furrow through Joseph's black hair. "The bullet gave you a new part, Joseph. Damn, I thought you was dead, my friend. I thought you was shot and then trampled by all them cows."

"What happened? Why did the cows stampede? I barely had time to roll under the wagon after I came to." Joseph gingerly touched the furrow Snake's bullet had plowed through his scalp.

"Why didn't Snake's bullet go right through your heart?" Travis asked. "I thought he had you dead in his sights with that pistol of his."

"I think I slapped his gun with my rifle when I turned around on him. It must have knocked his aim off, but I can barely remember anything at all. Where did Snake come from?"

"Do you remember the four riders?" Travis asked.

"I think I remember something about riders. But everything in my head is all messed up." Joseph wobbled and sat down abruptly on the ground. "I don't feel so good. I think I'm gonna be sick."

Travis supported Joseph while he vomited and then gave him a hand so he could sit back against one of the wheels of the wagon. "You rest here. I've got to go look for the mules and Light Foot. They run off in the stampede. You and Pa need to see a doctor right away."

Joseph looked up. "Is Hawk all right?"

"He's still alive, if that's what you mean, but he ain't all right, not by a long shot. Shorty's in the wagon with him trying to get his fever down. Will you be okay if I leave you here?"

"Go on and get the mules. I'll just sit here and rest against the wheel of the wagon. I'd help if I could, but I'm just too dizzy and my head is killin' me."

Travis climbed back on Beau and headed out to find the mules. His skin crawled every time he passed a clump of palmettos, a bush, or a tree. He just couldn't believe Snake was really dead. The man had more lives than a cat. And if Snake was alive, he'd surely go back for Miss Maddy. Travis hunched his shoulders. It seemed the weight of the entire world had fallen on him with his dad in such sorry shape. Travis looked over his shoulder again, almost wishing he could see Snake Barber riding up behind him because until he saw the man's cold, dead body, Travis wouldn't believe he was dead.

It took him two hours to round up the mules. Mules were smart animals, so Travis had to try and think like a mule to figure out where they'd gone. He figured the mules would hunt for water and food, so he rode to the hammock Joseph had been attempting to reach before they were attacked. There was a big gator hole in the middle of a swampy section at the center of the hammock. He found the mules there grazing, but poor little Light Foot was caught fast in a mud hole and couldn't get out.

There was no way Travis would leave his horse to die, so he took his lariat rope and waded in. Light Foot's head was drooping. Fighting to get out of the mud had worn him out. He barely struggled as Travis ran the loop of the lariat around the horse's barrel and then half swam, half walked his way out of the thick, sucking mud. The horse was lucky; the mud looked liked it turned to quicksand just a few feet away.

Once out of the mud, Travis hooked the rope to the biggest mule's harness. The mules had broken out of their trace chains, but they still had on their collars, bridles, and some of their harness straps. Leading the mule forward, he urged it to put its broad back into pulling Light Foot out of the mud. When Light Foot felt the rope tighten around him and start yanking him forward, he turned onto his side and kicked his way across the top of the black, stinking swamp mud. In minutes, the little marsh tacky was standing up and shaking off the water and filth still clinging to his coat.

Travis linked the mules and Light Foot together. Light Foot's saddle was still on him, but covered with mud. Picking up one of the lead mule's reins, Travis climbed back on Beau and headed to the wagon. Cows were scattered all over the plains eating grass and lying down to chew their cuds in the shade. Each one of them wore the D-Wing brand. Along with the stock, the rest of the D-Wing's working cattle horses were grazing as well. They had been traveling among the cattle when Travis and Shorty had fired up the stampede.

When Travis got back to the wagon, he saw that Shorty had been busy cleaning up the wagon and putting things back in order. He'd taken the trace chains apart and repaired them. He had Hawk lying on a bedroll in the shade of the wagon wearing only his red longhandles. Joseph lay next to Hawk in a deep sleep.

"I see you found the mules," Shorty said. "What in hell happened to yer horse?"

"He fell in a mud hole on that hammock over yonder. I had to haul him out with a mule."

"Yer saddle looks about ruined. You'll have mud under every flap and in every crease of leather and tool mark." Shorty turned to the fire he'd made. "Hey, I got some grub cookin'. I ain't much of a cook, but I got some cold beans heating and some bacon cookin'."

Travis took a dead rabbit off his saddle and tossed it to Shorty. "Diver caught this. I found her flyin' around looking for me and when I whistled to her, she made a kill. Can you clean it?"

"Sure thing, Travis. Rabbit sounds a lot better than beans."

After Travis climbed off Beau and hitched him to the picket line Shorty had strung, he unsaddled his marsh tacky. The girth straps were coated with goop, the saddle was filthy, and the saddle blanket black with mud. "I sure hope I can clean this up," Travis said.

When he was finished cleaning up the horses, he went to check on Joseph. The Indian hadn't said a thing since he got back. When he bent over and tried to wake him up, he saw the Indian must have slipped into unconsciousness. He would not open his eyes.

Travis was ready to scream or maybe cry. He felt as if the weight of the entire world rested on his shoulders. Even Shorty looked to him for direction.

"Let's eat and get the hell out of here," Travis said. "I gotta get these two to a doctor."

Travis fried the rabbit and the two of them ate. Joseph came around long enough to eat a bite of rabbit and drink some water, then he had to lie down again. Once he was down, he seemed to quickly pass into unconsciousness once more.

By the time Travis and Shorty got the two mules hitched up and Hawk and Joseph into the wagon, the sun was just about behind the trees on the western horizon. Travis didn't care. "We'll drive all night if we have to," he told Shorty. "I got to get Pa and Joseph to a doctor. Miss Judy Bill will have my hide if I let anything happen to Joseph. He's her only child."

They drove slowly so as not to disturb their passengers, but the bouncing of the wagon woke Joseph up anyway. He said every bump made his head hurt. The Indian hunkered down with his hands holding his head, and Travis could see he was trying hard not to complain. By the time they got to Orlando, he was out again.

As they drove into town, Travis felt mighty relieved. He'd never had so much responsibility. The crushing weight of having to take care of Hawk and Joseph and to make crucial decisions like leaving the cattle and the horses on the prairie and making the trip into Orlando were taking their toll on his nerves. He was starting to understand why grown men occasionally took to strong drink. Travis felt like getting drunk right now.

After asking directions, they were directed to a two-story building in the center of town. There was a sign on the door for Doctor Jacob Stogumber. Travis handed Shorty the reins, climbed down from the wagon, and rang the bell of the doctor's house. Before long an older man, dressed in a long white nightshirt and slippers answered the door with an oil lamp in hand.

As it turned out, he was Dr. Stogumber. He held the door while Travis and Shorty carried first Hawk and then Joseph into the doctor's office. There were two beds and an examining table in the room, along with cabinets that lined the walls filled with bottles and jars, and a counter with rows of shiny tools, the very sight of which made Travis want to run. Travis and Shorty laid Hawk and Joseph each in a bed and waited expectantly as the doctor put a white apron on over his nightshirt.

The doctor's wife appeared wearing a flannel wrapper with her lace-trimmed night cap over her hair. She began to strip off Hawk's clothes without any comments beyond a few "tut-tuts."

Travis felt like the two-ton weight on his shoulders had been lifted. He was still worried about Hawk and Joseph, but at least someone else was looking after them, someone who actually knew what he was doing.

The doctor was busy taking Hawk's pulse and feeling his forehead. He lifted Hawk's eyelids and looked at his eyes, then went to a sideboard with a big cabinet over it and began mixing medicine. When he had a big draft of some elixir in a cup, he turned to Travis. "I believe you're right and your father is suffering from a relapse of malaria," he said. "It's a particularly debilitating disease and your father's attack is fairly acute. He should come around in a few days after I administer several doses of quinine and bleed him for the fever."

"What about Joseph?" Travis asked.

The doctor made a sour face. "I'm not in the habit of taking Seminole Indians as patients. From the look of his injuries, he had a severe concussion to the brain and will either recover or not. There's very little I can do except recommend rest."

"But he won't wake up," Travis said, completely exasperated. "And he's not just any old Indian, he's a member of our family."

The doctor made another face, pursing his lips and shaking his head. He wore a pair of tiny wire-rimmed glasses perched on the end of his pointed nose. He removed the glasses and stared at Travis through very watery blue eyes. "It's my understanding that all Indians are savages. But since you vouch for him, he may stay here until he awakens, if he does so. And then he must leave. My other patients will not tolerate the company of a dangerous red man."

Travis put his hand on the doctor's shoulder. "You mean he might not ever wake up?"

"If his brain is indeed swollen, and he is very badly concussed, he might fall into a deep coma and die. There is also the wound to consider—it could suppurate and cause an infection of the brain. Only time will tell."

"But what should I do?" Travis asked as the feeling of being very young and inexperienced filled his chest once again.

"Go find a place to sleep for the night and come back in the morning. My capable wife and I will care for your father and clean up the Indian's wound."

"He's not 'the Indian,' " Travis snapped. "His name is Joseph. Come on, Shorty, let's get a room. This has been the longest day of my life."

26

MADDY THOUGHT SHE HEARD DOGS barking. She woke up and looked around the bedroom. Sarah lay sleeping beside her, and Storm was in his cradle. The only dogs on the property were Jumper's old gyp and her puppies, and they were under the barn.

Her sleep disturbed, she tossed and turned trying to get comfortable. Suddenly, she heard the dog barking again, followed by a gunshot and a yelp. Grabbing her wrapper, she woke up Sarah.

"There's someone out there, Sarah," she whispered inches from her daughter's ear. "I think whoever it is just shot Jumper's old mama dog."

Sarah bolted to her feet, but Maddy laid a restraining hand on her arm. "Put on your boys' clothes and get ready. You might have to run."

"No, mama, I won't leave you."

"Yes, you will, and you'll ride to Volusia Landing and get help if need be," Maddy said as she got dressed.

Sarah tried to protest again, but Maddy gave her a

quelling look. "Get dressed very quietly."

Maddy listened, her heart in her throat. She heard Jumper get up and go out onto the front porch. "Who's out there?" Jumper yelled into the darkness.

A shot rang out, and Maddy's heart plummeted to her feet when she heard Jumper grunt and fall to the floor of the porch.

"*I'm* out here, old man, and I've come for my woman," a familiar voice spoke from very close to the porch. Rage and hysteria warred within Maddy for control of her emotions. It was Snake. He was supposed to be dead.

Maddy ran to the rag rug on the floor, yanked it aside, and pulled up Travis's secret trapdoor. She shoved Sarah toward it and made her climb through. "Go to Volusia Landing. If you can't find anyone who will help, just stay there. I'll send for you when everything here is safe."

"No, Mama, I can't leave you, and I'm scared to saddle a horse and ride in the dark. I can't do it. Please don't make me." Sarah's frightened eyes pleaded with her from her position under the house.

"Sarah, I'm not asking you, I'm telling you. You must do this for me and for Storm. I can't save your brother and myself while I'm worrying about you. I need to have at least one of you out of harm's way. Be very quiet, saddle up Spirit, and lead him into the woods before you get on him. Snake's out there, Sarah. Don't let him catch you."

Tears running down her cheeks, Sarah said, "I'll do my best."

When the trap was closed, Maddy sat back breathing hard. Snake was alive and on her doorstep. This was the worst thing that could happen, the very worst. She gathered

Storm in her arms. All the boxes of her possessions were piled in a corner of the room. Recklessly throwing them aside, she pulled open the crate with her cutlery and rummaged around until she had her filleting knife. It was razor sharp and just what she was looking for. She tucked it carefully into the pocket of her skirt.

She had always played the meek and subservient woman with Snake, doing his bidding without complaint to keep Sarah from being discovered. Well, this time Snake Barber was going to meet the real Madelaine Wilkes.

Racing through the house, she saw that the front door was open and that Jumper was lying in a pool of blood on the porch, with Judy Bill kneeling over him weeping loudly. Her quick glance did not reveal Snake, but she knew he was out there. She wondered how many men he had with him. Snake never traveled alone. He relied on his bully boys to back him up.

Maddy tore through the house and down the back steps into the cookhouse. Encouraged by the ease with which she had escaped the house, she ran into the shadows of the cleanly swept backyard and started to make her way around the house. If she could just get to the path leading to the old cabin, she would be able to hide from Snake. He would never find her there.

Maddy felt terrible leaving Jumper and Judy Bill to fend for themselves, but she had to escape Snake and keep him from getting his hands on Storm. Protecting her child was uppermost in her mind, as it had always been. She'd sacrifice just about anything for the sake of her children.

But Storm, usually such a sweet, happy baby, decided to wail just as Maddy was coming around the corner of the house and cutting across the open front yard, making for the path to the cabin. She tried to hush the baby, covering his face with the blanket. Maybe Snake had not heard him over Judy Bill's keening cries.

Hiking up her skirts with her free hand, she prepared to run.

"Don't move, Maddy," came a low voice, and she froze.

"Turn around slowly and keep yer hands where I can see them."

"I'm holding onto a baby—where else would I keep my hands?" Maddy said as she straightened and turned around.

Snake stood next to the porch with a big pistol trained on her and Storm. Looking down the barrel of a big pistol was certainly a terrifying experience. Maddy's heart was in her throat and her legs felt weak.

"Now don't be foolish. You always were such a good girl. Be a good girl now and ain't nothing bad will happen to you. Hand me the boy. I want to see my son."

"No, Jake, let me hold Storm. You can look at him all you want, but let me hold him." She didn't want to let go of her baby, not for a moment. As long as Storm was in her arms, she felt he was safe.

Snake stepped closer and she pulled the blanket away from Storm's face. For a minute, Snake's harsh features softened. As he looked upon his child, Maddy thought she could see a tear gleaming in the corner of Snake Barber's glinting dark eyes.

"He looks like me," Snake said. "He has my chin and dark hair." His voice seemed to be filled with awe and wonder. But what new father wouldn't feel those emotions when gazing at their legacy? *Children are the best of what we leave behind.*

But Snake could only hold on to a good emotion for so long. His eyes narrowed and he snatched Storm from Maddy in one swift move. Her child screamed as Snake held him at arm's length to look him over. "He's got all his parts, eh, Maddy? You're a good broodmare, old girl. Bred me up a proper son, didn't you? Now, you seen Hawk anywhere around here?"

"He's out working cattle, Jake," Maddy said, her voice quivering as she shook like a leaf with fear for her baby.

Snake tucked Storm under his arm like a sack of flour. The baby's head was in front and his feet stuck out the back behind Snake's arm. "I know he was out there a couple of days ago, 'cause I saw him, and he didn't look too pert. I was only wondering if he showed up here before me. I just been stampeded by his entire herd, a stampede started by that hellion kid of his. I almost died out there. Have you ever faced two hundred head of cattle comin' straight at ya?"

"You saw Hawk? Why do you say he wasn't looking too pert? Was he sick, or did you do something to hurt him?" Maddy went cold inside; something bad had happened to Hawk.

"I didn't do nothing to him. He was laying in the bed of the wagon pale as a ghost. I hope he went and died. Everything bad that's happened to me can be laid at his door, the sorry son of a bitch."

As Snake talked he jerked the baby terribly, and Storm started to scream. "Let me have him back, Snake. He's probably wet or hungry."

"Not until you tell me if Hawk or that kid of his is here."

"Neither he nor Travis has been home, I swear to you,

Snake. None of them came back. As far as I know, he, Travis, and Shorty and Joseph are all out there working cows. Now please, give me back my baby."

"Oh no, my girl, we're gonna go talk to Mrs. Indian over there and find out where all that Hawkins gold is hid."

"She doesn't know anything," Maddy cried as she followed behind Snake. Snake stalked to the porch and took the steps with an odd halting walk, toting the screaming child under his arm. When Maddy looked closer, she realized there was no leg under Snake's brown pants. Where there should have been a foot at the bottom of his right leg, there was a wooden peg. He must have lost it when Hawk blew him up.

"That isn't how you hold a baby, Jake. Please let me take him."

Snake ignored her. Judy Bill was still kneeling over Jumper. Jumper had been hit in the side, and blood still oozed steadily from the bullet hole. Unable to take Storm from Snake, Maddy knelt next to Jumper. "Judy Bill, go get rags and my scissors from the sewing basket," she said.

Judy Bill nodded without saying a word and went into the house. Maddy tore off Jumper's shirt. He groaned and opened his eyes. "Don't worry, Jumper," Maddy said with tears flowing down her face. "You'll be just fine."

After probing the wound with a finger, she half turned Jumper over and looked at the exit wound. The bullet had torn an even bigger hole going out the back, but at least it wasn't inside Jimmy. "Get me some hot water too," she yelled to Judy Bill.

"This is quite an affecting scene," Snake said. "And I'll even let you tend to the old Indian, if he tells me where the gold is hidden."

Maddy sighed, having just about made up her mind as to the course of action she intended to take. With so few options, she felt there was only one thing she could do. It was only money, after all, and Jumper's life was worth more than that.

Jumper groaned and looked up at Snake. "I'll never tell you nothing, white man," Jumper said.

"Hush." Maddy put her fingers over Jumper's lips, then said, "I know where the gold's hidden, Jake. I'll take you to it. Just let me take care of Jumper first."

Through his pain, Jumper looked at Maddy with a puzzled expression. "I saw you and Hawk going to the spring," Maddy told him. "I followed you."

Jumper struggled as though he would get up. "You can't," he gasped. "It's Hawk's money."

"I know it is, Jumper, but Hawk would want me to save you. I know he'd think you were more important than all of his money."

The old Indian groaned and fell back onto the porch.

When Judy Bill came back with the hot water and rags, Maddy began cleaning Jumper's wound. "Get me the bottle of wine on the sideboard in the kitchen," Maddy said.

Judy Bill rushed off again and returned immediately with the bottle. Maddy pulled the cork out with her teeth and poured wine into Jumper's wound. He gasped and ground his teeth.

"Now give me the needle threaded with white cotton," Maddy said. "I've been using it for weeks, so I know it has to be there and already threaded."

Judy Bill pulled a paper of needles out of the basket and handed Maddy one threaded with the cotton. "This is going to hurt, Jumper," she said. "But I have to sew it up to stop the bleeding."

"You really know where Hawk's gold is, Maddy?" Snake asked. He had sat down on the porch steps with Storm on his lap. The child seemed to fascinate him. He examined Storm's fingers and toes and touched his silky brown hair. "He looks like me, doesn't he, Indian woman?"

Judy Bill nodded her head up and down in answer to Snake's question. Her face was white, her eyes huge.

She's in shock, Maddy thought as she stitched the entry wound. When it was closed and the bleeding stopped, she turned Jumper over and poured wine into that hole. The exit wound was larger and more ragged, so it took Maddy longer to stitch it up; Jumper passed out halfway through the procedure.

When she was finished, Maddy stood up and looked at Judy Bill. The Indian woman had aged ten years in the past ten minutes. She stared at her husband as if he weren't there. Maddy gently shook her shoulder. "Help me carry Jumper into Travis's room," she said.

The two of them hoisted Jumper to his feet and half carried, half dragged him to the small bedroom in the main part of the house. When he was on the bed, Judy Bill seemed to snap out of her daze. She began to plump the pillows under Jumper's head and then covered him with a bright patchwork quilt.

"That's enough stallin', girl. Now shake a leg and take me to the money." Snake was back to toting Storm under his arm.

Maddy moved in close to Snake and pulled her baby loose. She'd had enough of watching Snake abuse him that way. When she had him safely in her arms, she cradled Storm against her. The baby looked up into her face with what Maddy felt was gratitude. Storm knew very well who had hold of him.

"As long as I can hold Storm, I'll take you. If you snatch him away from me again, the deal is off." Maddy was feeling stronger. She had a plan. It was a desperate plan, but she was out of options. Snake had to go along with what she asked if he wanted her to take him to the money, even though she had no idea where in that spring the money was actually hidden. That was the tiny little catch in her plan. But she finally had a few cards in her hand, and she intended to play them.

Carrying Storm, she marched out of the house, back straight, head held high. Snake was right behind her. "What happened to your leg?" she asked as she walked down the steps. Snake had to slow down and take each step very carefully.

"You know what happened. Your man Hawk blew me all over the place. I almost died, that's what happened." Snake followed close behind her, pulling out his pistol as he walked. "I got this big ole .44 aimed right at you. If you mess around with me, I'll shoot you and take that baby. He's mine anyway."

"I am taking you to Hawk's gold," Maddy said. "And Hawk is not my man—he's not anything to me, because he doesn't want anything to do with Storm. He doesn't care to raise your child."

Snake laughed, a harsh, cruel sound. "Thinks the boy will be too hot to handle, just like his daddy, eh?"

"Who knows what he thinks," Maddy muttered. "I certainly don't." Maddy headed down the trail toward the old cabin. The blackberries were still thick. She remembered making Hawk blackberry pie and wondered if she would ever see him again.

"You said Hawk looked bad when you saw him. What do you think was wrong with him?

"Yeah, he looked right puny laying there in the back of the wagon half dead. He was unconscious, from the look of him, and raving in some fever dream. I thought I had him dead to rights and was gonna put him out of his misery after I shot the Indian, but then that damn kid of Hawk's tried to kill me with a stampede. I barely got out of there alive. But I figured with Hawk poorly, his kid kinda tied up and the Indian dead, it might be some time before either of them could get back here to the good old homestead. And it looks like I had it figured right. What sane man leaves a woman like you home with only two old Indians to protect her, anyway?"

Maddy ignored his question. It was probably rhetorical anyway. "What do you think was wrong with Hawk?" she asked again, hoping he'd be more specific.

"Hell if I know. He was laying in the back of the wagon talking to hisself, waving his arms all over the place and sweating like a pig. Looked to me like he got the fever back."

Hawk's malaria must have returned. She'd heard the disease never really left the body and came back in times of weakness or stress.

Maddy took the turn that led down the path to the spring. It was cool under the trees and the temperature change felt good. She was hot and sweaty with fear and the unusually warm day. Overhead, the sun blazed down on the trees, but only a few rays made it through the canopy to this sanctuary of shade.

Storm gurgled and grabbed her braid, then tried to suck on it. Poor little man was probably starving and scared out of his wits. He watched her and everything around him out of alert brown eyes. He seemed to understand he and his mother were in trouble because he clung to her and, aside from a little babbling, was unusually quiet. He rarely cried even on a normal day.

"You know I ain't leaving here without you, Maddy," Snake said as they crossed the stream again.

Just to be mean, because she realized she wasn't losing Snake anytime soon, she was zigzagging back and forth across the little creek. It was hard for Snake with his peg leg to get over the rocks and through the muddy spots. But when she glanced over her shoulder to see if he had dropped behind, she saw that even though he was struggling, his gun never wavered and he was managing to keep up.

"I'm not going anywhere with you, Jake," Maddy said as she crossed the creek yet again, jumping from one side to the other easily. "I don't want you; I never did. You were holding me hostage in that house and I had nowhere else to go and no one to run to. Don't you remember threatening to turn me over to your men if I wasn't nice to you? Well, I was nice to you, and see what it got me." She indicated Storm by holding him out in front of her. "But he's mine and I'll never let you have him—nor me again."

"It don't matter what you want or what you intend to do—you're my woman, the mother of my child, and I'm here to claim you and my son. You're leaving with me. We'll be rich, Maddy. When we get Hawk's gold, we can go anywhere and live anywhere. I can buy you a beautiful house in the city. We can live like rich folks, and I'll buy you fancy clothes and jewels. The brat will be able to go to school. Don't you want that?"

"No, Jake, I don't want to live anywhere with you. I don't love you and I'm not ever going to love you."

Snake caught up to her and grabbed her around the waist. He tried to press kisses to her neck, but she pulled away and walked faster.

"You could learn to love me, couldn't you?" Snake's voice had taken on a plaintive note. Maddy knew his moods. Next would come the ranting and railing and then violence. But Maddy's face was hard as stone. She wasn't giving in to the fear of his moods and his unpredictability.

"We're almost there," she said. Let him think what he wanted. If her plan worked, she wouldn't have to worry about Snake and his moods ever again.

When she got to the base of the big rock formation, she stopped. How was Snake going to get up that with only one leg?

Travis woke up before dawn the next morning. He rolled over in bed and groaned, hoping for a better day than the one before. "Shorty, wake up, we got to get going. If Snake is alive, he's sure to go to the homestead if he thinks Pa is sick and Joseph dead. And he's bound to know we're pretty tied up dealing with them."

Shorty pulled the covers over his head. "No, Travis, don't make me get up. I just went to bed. What time is it?"

"It's time to get up, Shorty." Travis yanked the bedclothes off Shorty and tossed them onto the floor. Shorty was fully clothed, except for his boots and his hat. The boots, with spurs still attached, sat at the foot of the bed, while the hat was on the rack by the room's front door.

After only a few minutes they were both out the door. "Let's get some breakfast in the hotel dining room and then go check on Pa," Travis said. "We can't head out until the sun comes up anyway."

They ate bacon, eggs, and grits, and drank coffee. "After that swill you been feedin' us every morning, this coffee tastes beautiful," Shorty said.

"Are you slanderin' my coffee?" Travis laughed. "I hate cookin'. I don't know why Pa always makes me do it."

"Probably 'cause nobody else wants to neither."

"If you're done, let's go," Travis said.

They paid for breakfast and walked over to the doctor's office. Lamps were lit inside, so they opened the door and walked in. They had to step through the doctor's little parlor—set up with chairs for his patients to sit in while they waited—and into the treatment room. Travis and Shorty took off their hats as they walked into the quiet room.

Pa's eyes were open, but he was lying flat in the bed. Joseph was sitting in a chair pulling on his boots.

"Hey, Joseph, you look a lot better." Travis said.

"What happened to me? I woke up here and I can't remember a thing."

Shorty sat beside Joseph and explained what all had happened the day before, while Travis went to sit next to his father's bed. Hawk looked up at Travis, his eyes still fever-bright but clear.

"What happened, Travis? Me and Joseph can't remember a thing about how we got here."

"Pa, it was the worst day of my life," Travis said. "And Pa, I done a terrible thing. I stampeded the cows and horses. They're all over the prairie."

"Was it Snake?" Hawk asked. "Did he attack the camp? I can remember a gunshot. I thought I was dreamin' it, but I guess Joseph got shot. And then I dreamed I was in the middle of a stampede. I guess it wasn't a dream after all."

"No, you wasn't dreamin', Pa. I was afraid the cows were gonna go right through the wagon, parked like it was in the middle of that dry creek, but they went around. And I thought Snake had killed Joseph. He had three armed bushwhackers with him, and the only thing me and Shorty could think of to do to get them away from you and the wagon was to stampede the cows, and it worked. It was a good thing Joseph stopped the wagon in that dry creek. The way we ran the cattle, they had to run straight down the creek bed."

"You did good, son. I'm proud of you."

"When I got back to the wagon," Travis said, "I found Joseph was still alive, and I had to find the mules and drive you two here. It was an awful day, Pa."

Hawk lifted his hand off the quilted coverlet and put it on top of Travis's hand. "It sounds like you done a good job. We'll round up the cows again, don't worry none about that, and we'll find all the horses. You're a real man, Travis. And now I got to ask you to do something else for me. I need you to ride for home. I'm bettin' if Snake's still alive, he went to find Maddy."

Travis stood up. "That's what I was figuring too. I'll believe Snake Barber is dead when I see his body. Me and Shorty better be on our way. Snake's gotta be a day ahead of me."

Hawk tried to rise up out of the bed at the mention of Snake. "He'll head straight to the D-Wing for Maddy and the baby!"

Travis carefully pushed his father back down. "I'm heading straight there. Don't worry. Jumper's with her, and me and Shorty can take care of it. We're gettin' pretty good at fixin' tough siutations."

"Well, I sure can't get up and go just yet, so I gotta depend on you again, son." Hawk looked right into Travis's eyes. "One other thing, and this is very important to me, Trav. I need you to tell Maddy I love her and I'm coming for her as soon as I can."

"I'll tell her, Pa, if she'll listen to me," Travis said.

"You can even tell her I was a fool if you want to."

"I'll tell her. We'll be back for you as soon as we can, Pa. You get better, now, and do what that doctor says. He might not like Indians much, but he seems to know what he's doing."

Travis turned and beckoned to Shorty. "We got to ride, Shorty. Pa thinks Snake will head for the house."

Shorty stood up, spurs jingling. "Then let's ride."

"I'm coming too," Joseph said, grabbing his hat off the bed he had just vacated. "You ain't leavin' me here with this old white doctor. He wants to kill Joseph. Doctor thinks all Indians are bad red savages. He told me so."

The three walked out of the doctor's office and headed for the livery stable. "We got a job to do, boys," Travis said. "Let's go get Snake Barber."

27 ☀

It took Snake awhile to get the hang of climbing the rock with his peg leg. He took Storm away from Maddy and made her climb the rock first. He stood on the ground holding Storm and watching her climb with his pistol aimed at her back. When she was halfway to the top, he handed her the baby and started following her. It was smart, but he didn't know it. Once at the top, there was nowhere for her to go.

While he was climbing, Maddy saw he had a silver snake set into his peg leg that coiled around the entire leg. The snake was complete with scales and eyes, and just looking at it gave Maddy the creeps.

While Snake was managing the rock face, she was able to pull the fillet knife out of her pocket and slide it under Storm's blanket. She hated the idea of using Storm to mask her subterfuge, but had no other choice. She could not face Snake unarmed. Especially not when he heard she really had no idea where in the spring the money was located. Snake was going to come apart when she told him, and she'd need the knife to protect herself and Storm. He might try to throw the baby into the spring or push her in, and Maddy knew all about the big gator waiting somewhere in that spring.

When Snake had climbed to the top of the rock, he turned around and gazed at the picturesque little spring. "So this was the blue spring Hawk was talking about. My men and I combed that big old spring close to the river and never found nothing. No wonder; we was looking in the wrong spring. We never would have found this little hidey-hole. We didn't even know it existed. Clever, clever Hawk, giving me a clue that led me straight to the wrong place." While he spoke, he waved his pistol around to punctuate his comments.

Maddy stood back and let him walk out to the end of the rock and look around, watching the pistol in his hand all the time. When he was standing close to the edge looking into the water with the pistol pointed at the ground, she pulled out the fillet knife and held her breath. It was now or never.

Holding Storm with one arm, she stepped close to Snake and stabbed the razor-sharp knife up to the hilt into his right side, and then she shoved him. He turned and looked at her with a stunned expression on his face and wobbled, but did not fall into the water as she'd planned. The gun in his hand wavered, and he tried to lift it to point it at her.

"Maddy," he croaked. "How could you hurt me? I love you."

Maddy couldn't take her eyes off the wavering gun. "You don't love me, Jake," she said, watching the gun shaking in his right hand. "You just want to add me to your pile of possessions. You don't know what love is. Love is kindness and giving and understanding. All you do is take."

Then she realized that while she'd only ever thought of him as possessive and selfish, maybe he did love her in his own way, if he was capable of loving anything. "I'm sorry," she said, and then she pushed him harder.

Snake wavered on the brink, his peg leg slipping and sliding as he tried to regain his footing on the slippery rock. His eyes grew round with surprise and horror. Of course he was surprised. All those months she'd lived under his power, she'd never even made the slightest rebellious move, never threatened him or acted anything other than exactly like a cowed, docile slave. But Sarah had been there. She'd always had to think of what was best for Sarah.

Now she had to think about what was best for Sarah and Storm, and this time the best thing for both of them was for Snake to die. She pushed him again and he fell backward. He tried to twist his body around to look at the water and landed with a huge splash in the clear blue spring.

Thrashing and trying to swim, he was hampered by the weight of his clothes and his peg leg and by trying to hold the pistol out of the water. Snake floundered in the deep pool with blood leaking out of the wound in his side.

Maddy waited, looking over the edge of the rock, watching. Where was the big alligator? Had it left the pool and traveled to bigger and better hunting grounds, or was it a big bull gator that had gone looking for a mate? Where was the monster when she needed it?

Snake had recovered from the fall and was awkwardly swimming with one hand in the direction of the shore and a mud beach, still trying to keep the pistol dry, when Maddy heard another splash. Something had come out of the rock directly under her feet. When she looked down, she saw the gator's big head and shuddered. No matter how much she disliked Snake Barber, thinking about what was surely going to take place within moments was horrible.

She wanted to look away, but was transfixed. And she needed the finality of knowing Snake was really dead. The last time they'd thought he was dead, Snake had proved them wrong.

She saw the gator slide into the water and quickly submerge. Snake obviously heard the gator hit the water and felt the disturbance in the pool. He stopped swimming and started treading water, looking around wildly, turning his head this way and that, the whites showing in his eyes. He must have known or at least had an inkling. He looked up one last time at Maddy, his eyes pleading. She did not look away.

"Help me," he cried to her, his eyes wild with fear. Then the monster came up from below and grabbed him. Snake screamed and fired his pistol wildly. But the huge gator easily gripped Snake in his jaws and pulled him, struggling, under the water. Maddy tried not to watch but could not help herself. It was so horrible, but she had to know Snake was truly finished.

The big gator rolled over and over with Snake in his jaws on the water's surface, then began a lazy dive into the crystal-blue depths, taking Snake with him. A stream of bubbles drifted from the dark cave below and exploded on the surface, and then Maddy couldn't see them anymore.

She found a rock to sit on and collapsed. Was it truly over? Had she really just coldly planned a man's death and carried it out to perfection? Storm cried, and she opened her blouse and began feeding him. This normal act in the midst of horror comforted her. When Storm was full, she calmly buttoned her blouse and climbed down the rock. It was all over. She and her family were safe from Snake Barber forever.

❖   ❖   ❖

Travis held Beau to a trot so Shorty and Joseph could keep up. He wanted to let the horse run, he was so worried about Maddy and Sarah. When they hit the wooded trail to the homestead, he saw fresh hoof marks.

"Stop, Shorty. I'm gonna check these tracks out," Travis said. He got off Beau and began following them on foot. It looked like the horse was going around in circles, passing into the woods and then coming back to the trail.

"Look, Trav, a horse," Joseph called.

Travis looked up and saw Spirit. The big bay was walking, aimlessly grazing, with his reins dragging the ground. A small bundle lay draped over Spirit's neck, clutching a fistful of mane. Travis dropped Beau's reins and ran.

When he reached Spirit, the horse looked up, startled. But the big bay would never spook or doing anything to dislodge his small passenger. The horse stopped and let Travis catch up the reins. "Sarah, wake up." Travis shook the girl.

She was apparently deeply asleep. When she finally sat up and opened her eyes, she said, "Travis, is that you?"

As soon as she realized who he was, she flew off the horse and into his arms, hugging his neck to the point of strangling him.

"Whoa there, little filly, you're chokin' me. Why are you out here all by yourself? Where's your mother? What's happening at home?" Travis peeled her arms from around his neck and held her out where he could look her over. "Are you all right?"

"Oh, I'm fine now that you're here," she sobbed. "Snake Barber came to our house and shot Jimmy, and Mama made me run and hide. She wanted me to saddle Spirit and get help, but I didn't want to leave, so I kept walking around and around in the woods and then I got lost and then I fell asleep."

"Whoa, back up. Did you say Snake shot Jumper?" Travis asked.

Both Joseph and Shorty had dismounted and were standing close, listening.

"Yes, he shot Mr. Jimmy, and also Gypsy out in the barn. Mr. Jimmy fell down on the porch and he was bleeding. Mama made me climb out the trapdoor in the floor. I had to find Spirit's saddle and bridle and get them on him myself. And poor Gypsy was just lying there dead with all the puppies around her. It was so horrible, and then I had to climb onto the fence and jump onto Spirit because he's so tall and I didn't have anyone to help me up. I was so scared, Travis. I tried to find the trail to Volusia Landing, but it was so dark and I got lost and Spirit didn't really want to go. I had to kick him and kick him. He's such a slug." She hugged Travis hard. "I'm so glad you're here. Where is Mr. Hawk?"

"Pa's sick, but never mind that, we need to ride for home. If Snake's still there, he's gonna regret all the killing he's done. I'll see to that. Mount up, boys."

Travis didn't have to tell Joseph and Shorty; they were already halfway into the saddle. Travis took Sarah up on Beau with him, collected Spirit's reins, and handed them to Shorty. "Let's ride boys. We need to get there fast."

Shorty waved him on. "Go on ahead, Trav. I'll bring this old slug and get there as soon as I can."

Joseph was already galloping as fast as he could push his horse for home.

When Travis and Joseph came within sight of the homestead, Travis held up his hand to Joseph. "We better leave the horses out here."

They could see Snake's horse tethered to the hitching post in front of the barn. Travis got off Beau and helped Sarah down. When he glanced along the path toward the old cabin, he got the surprise of his life. Trudging determinedly up the trail, skirts held in one hand and Storm in the other, was Maddy. Her head was high and Travis instantly saw dark red bloodstains on the front of her shirt and skirt. What could have happened?

Sarah saw her too, and went tearing off to meet her mother and grab her in one of those hugs like Travis had just had which about strangled him. Travis and Shorty went to meet her, while Joseph walked toward the house. "Wait, Joseph," Travis called. He turned to Maddy. "Where's Snake?"

"He's dead," she said in a monotone. "I've killed him."

"Go on ahead and find out about Jumper," Travis said to Joseph.

Travis put his arm around Maddy on one side, and Sarah wrapped her arm around Maddy's waist on the other side. "Tell us what happened," Travis said gently.

Maddy looked up into his face. Her eyes were big and shining with tears and her chin quivered, but she was calm.

"I planned it all out, Travis, because I knew he had to die. If I hadn't killed him, he would have stolen all Hawk's money and taken me and Storm away with him. He was never going to leave us alone. I had no choice—I had to kill him."

"You don't have to tell me, ma'am," Travis said. "I know Snake needed killing. He just about killed Joseph and he did kill one of his own men. Shot him down in cold blood. Me and Shorty see'd the whole thing."

They reached the front porch and climbed the steps. "I need to see how Jumper's doing," Maddy said. "Snake shot him and he's badly hurt."

Judy Bill met them at the door. The tall Indian woman immediately greeted Maddy and took Maddy's hands into hers. "I can't thank you enough for what you did for Jumper. Where is that terrible man, Snake Barber? I hope he's dead and he rots in hell."

"It's likely that he will—rot, anyway," Maddy said. "He's at the bottom of that spring out there in the woods. I stuck my filleting knife in his side and shoved him into the water. Then a giant gator grabbed him and dragged him to the bottom."

"I was very wrong about you, Miss Maddy, and I apologize for saying you were not wanted here," Judy Bill said, her head down and tears in her great dark eyes. "You are a strong and a brave woman, and you have saved my man's life."

"I did my best, Judy Bill, but I don't think Jumper is out of the woods yet. It will take a lot of nursing to get him back on his feet. That wound he has is really dangerous." Maddy moved into the house, followed by Sarah. "Can I see Jumper now?"

Judy Bill took Maddy's hand and led her into Travis's bedroom. Jumper, pale but awake, opened his eyes when they entered.

"He's dead, Jumper," Judy Bill said. "Miss Maddy whooped him. She fee-layed him and pushed him into the spring."

"Did the gator get him?" Jumper asked in a raspy voice.

Maddy knelt beside Jumper's bed. "That old gator dragged him clear to the bottom. We'll never see him again."

"Took him and crammed him under that log down there to tenderize," Jumper said. "He'll eat him later."

"Don't try to talk, Jumper," Maddy said, standing up. "You just concentrate on getting better."

Jumper nodded and closed his eyes.

Joseph stood at the foot of his father's bed with tears running down his face. When they left the room, he took Maddy's elbow. "He ain't gonna die, is he?"

"I hope not, Joseph. As long as we keep him quiet and he doesn't get a bad infection, he should make it. But it's going to be touch and go for a while."

Storm began fussing. "I think I'm going to take Storm into my room and lie down on the bed to rest," Maddy said. "I'm feeling very tired."

"Miss Maddy," Travis said. "Before you go to your room, I need to give you a message from my Pa."

Maddy's features stiffened. "What could he possibly have to say to me?"

Travis was embarrassed. Why had his father given him this chore? Why couldn't Pa just wait and tell Maddy how he felt himself? But a promise was a promise, especially one you made to a sick person. "Well, Pa ain't feelin' too good hisself. He's got the malaria again, and me and Shorty had to tote him off to the doctor in Orlando. He told me when I was leavin' him to give you a message."

"Well?" Maddy said.

"He wanted you to know, uh, well he said to tell you he loved you and all and he's been a dumb-ass. Well, he's been a fool, I mean, sorry."

"No, Travis you had it right the first time. Your father is a dumbass. I'm glad he's finally realized that, and I thank you for delivering his message."

Travis watched her go out the door and across the breezeway. "She's such a great woman," he said.

"Yes, Travis, she truly is," Judy Bill said.

28 𝕸

Maddy gave the coverlet in room number ten a final twitch and stood back to admire her handiwork. Cleaning rooms wasn't much fun, but at least here she was needed and welcome. Picking up the pail of soapy water, a feather duster, cleaning rags, and lemon oil, she walked out into the second-floor hallway of Ned's Boarding House and Emporium and closed the door to room ten behind her.

Checking the watch she wore pinned to her blouse, she saw it was nearly time for dinner. The guests were served a breakfast at seven, their dinner promptly at twelve, and a light supper at six. When the house was full, there was sometimes an English tea at four P.M. as well. There were currently six guests at the boarding house: a gentleman from Jacksonville selling shoes, a small family enjoying a holiday from the cold up north, and a rich gentleman in his mid forties come to Pilatka to open a new steamboat company that would take supplies up and down the St. Johns all the way to its headwaters in Lake Monroe.

This gentleman's name was Henry Ampleforth, and he

had been plainly making advances to Maddy over the past week. But Ampleforth wasn't her only suitor. There was also Captain Ronald Quimby from the fort at St. Augustine and Zeke Stone, the local corn chandler. Rachel liked to tease her about her suitors, but for some reason, Maddy had no sense of humor where they were concerned.

She treated all of them politely, but firmly refused all of their offers of picnics on the river or riding expeditions or even quiet suppers in the dining room.

She just wasn't ready to meet men. Her heart still ached for the one she couldn't have, the one she had left behind in Volusia. When she closed her eyes at night, her visions were haunted by dark eyes, lean cheeks, and strong arms.

After placing the cleaning supplies in the closet at the end of the hall, Maddy made her way to the top floor and the room she shared with Sarah. Sarah was terribly unhappy, and for the first time Maddy could remember, Sarah was not being obedient or well behaved.

Her daughter was currently sulking in her room while watching Storm so Maddy could get her work done. When Maddy walked into their rooms, Sarah was sitting at a small marquetry writing desk penning a letter. It was the fifth one she'd written to Travis, who could not read, since they had arrived in Pilatka. And she walked each one to the post office and mailed them all herself, paying for the stamps with money she earned working in the Emporium.

Three times a week, Sarah cleaned the shelves, dusted, and helped Edward Carver put out more stock.

Maddy sighed. She wasn't happy either. She missed Jumper and her chickens and pigs and the house, and she missed Hawk. Every night she'd lie awake and wonder whether she'd acted hastily when she'd packed up her two children and moved to Pilatka the day after she'd killed Snake Barber.

"Does Storm need changing before we go down to dinner?" Maddy asked.

"No, Mama, I just changed him right before you walked in. Can I run this down to the post office before we eat?"

"Wait until after, please. I have to go down to the kitchen and see if that new cook got the recipe right for my cream of chicken soup. I told her to use only the white wine, but I fear she will use the red. She is a wonderful cook, but has never made soup in the French style. She can make fried chicken that will make you cry it tastes so good, but cream of chicken soup, no."

"Cooks as good as you don't grow on trees, Mama. Maybe someday I'll be able to cook like you."

"I had no idea you wished to learn," Maddy said. "This is the first time I have ever heard you say you'd like to cook. What brought this on?"

"Oh, I was just thinking how much Travis liked your biscuits and blackberry pie."

The two of them walked down the wide staircase, Maddy carrying Storm. She nodded politely to Mrs. Newley, the head housekeeper, as they passed her tiny office, where she sat pouring over the accounts. At the entrance to the dining room, Maddy glanced inside briefly and then handed Storm to Sarah.

Her daughter looked particularly lovely today, dressed in white cotton with pink flowers and a long-sleeved pink jacket. Her flaxen hair had grown long enough to pull into a small chignon at her neck.

"I see Mr. Ampleforth is waiting for you," Sarah said pertly. "He's very stuffy, and fat as a Christmas goose, don't you think?"

"I have no opinion of Mr. Ampleforth," Maddy replied. "And how many times have I told you not to speak of other people behind their backs?"

"Sorry," Sarah intoned.

"I'll be back shortly," Maddy told her. "Just keep Storm happy until I return. I believe Rachel wants us to help hang Christmas decorations after dinner."

Maddy walked through the big house and out the back door. The cookhouse was situated fifteen feet behind the boarding house on a hill. It had big windows that opened to let in the river breeze in the summer. But it was late November and cold enough for a body to be glad of the warmth provided by the big stove. The cook, a massive black woman named Lulei, was stirring a big pot filled with creamy soup.

"Oh, Miss Maddy, I sure am glad you came to help ole Lulei wi' dis soup. I done forgot already. Is it de white or de red wine I be putting in der?"

Maddy grabbed an open bottle of French white wine sitting on one of the wooden preparation tables. As she poured a generous amount into the pot, she heard a commotion coming from the front of the boarding house. What could be going on? It sounded like several riders and a wagon had parked out in the street, and she could hear dogs barking.

Maddy finished helping Lulei, wrapped her old paisley shawl tighter around her, and picked up her skirts. When she came around the corner of the house, walking on the porch, she saw Travis and Hawk strapping down a huge yellow enamel wood cookstove in the back of the buckboard. Two horses were tied to the back of the wagon, and three of Hawk's cow dogs were barking wildly at one of Mrs. Galloway's cats sitting high in a tree behind the fence to her yard.

She froze, her heart beating wildly. What was he doing here? Had he just come to Pilatka to get that gorgeous stove, a stove any woman in her right mind would go absolutely insane over? Or was he here for her?

She walked on around the porch to the front doors. Mr. Ampleforth was standing on the threshold, his meal apparently interrupted, as he still had a large linen napkin tucked into the front of his shirt.

"What's all this ruckus about?" Ampleforth demanded. "The noise has severely disturbed my dining experience." He spotted Maddy and bowed stiffly. She was sure she heard the distinct creaking of a corset.

"Mrs. Wilkes, what is all the noise? I'm quite sure my digestion will be destroyed. And who is this wild-looking gentleman?" He indicated Hawk, who indeed looked quite wild wearing chaps, spurs, and his large-brimmed hat. Maddy thought he also looked wonderful. She could not take her eyes off him as he clanked onto the porch.

"I'm Mrs. Wilkes' fiancé," Hawk said, and promptly swept Maddy into a crushing embrace and kissed her.

Ampleforth's protuberant eyes bulged. "Well, I never," he said.

Hawk glanced up. "No, I imagine you haven't," he said to Ampleforth, and went back to kissing Maddy.

Maddy struggled, briefly, and then succumbed to his passionate kiss with equal fervor. "Oh, Hawk," she murmured. "I've missed you so much."

"Why'd you do it, Maddy? Why'd you leave us?" Hawk whispered into her ear as he pressed more kisses to her hair and her neck.

"Stop," she finally said. "Look at the crowd we've drawn."

Most of the dinner guests, the cook, Mrs. Newley, and several other housemaids were gawking, plus Mrs. Galloway from across the street and even a few strangers. Sarah came rushing out of the boarding house carrying Storm and screamed "Travis!"

Maddy managed to grab the baby out of her arms before he was thrown aside as Sarah ran into the street and hugged Travis. Then Sarah saw Shorty, pushed Travis aside, and hugged him.

Smoothing her hair with one hand, then her skirts, Maddy tried to regain some of her lost composure. What had she been thinking, allowing her emotions to run wild like that?

Standing with Storm on one hip, she looked up into Hawk's face. He had lost weight. The attack of fever must have been severe. He had a little gray hair coming in over his ears too, but she thought it gave him a distinguished air.

"What did you mean by telling Mr. Ampleforth that I was your fiancé, when you know it is untrue?" she scolded, still trying to get a grip on her dignity. She'd succumbed to his kisses like a street trollop.

Hawk dropped to one knee in front of the gaping crowd. "Madelaine Wilkes, I love you with all my heart. Will you please marry me?"

Out of his fringed leather coat pocket he pulled a small

jewelers' box and, after opening it, pulled out a gold ring. "I had this made out of one of the doubloons just for you," he said.

Maddy could feel the blood rushing into her cheeks. Tears slowly began dripping down her face. This was all too much for her. She'd been so miserable just minutes before, and now she was so happy. "What about Storm?"

"I promise to love him as if he were my own child," Hawk said. "He's like my own anyway, since I helped deliver him."

"What about panther cubs and all that you were so worried about?" Madelaine was holding on to her pride to the last second.

"What panther cub?" Hawk asked innocently.

"Get up, Hawk, you're making a spectacle of yourself. Of course I will marry you, as long as you mean to bestow that beautiful stove on me. Where on earth did you get it?"

Hawk leaped to his feet, grabbed her around the waist, and swept her and Storm into a wild embrace. "Yes, the stove is for you. We've all been starving to death with no Maddy to cook for us. Hurry, love, and get into the buckboard. I have the preacher waiting."

"Pretty sure of yourself, weren't you?" She said as they walked out to the buckboard arm in arm.

"You know how determined I can be."

High overhead, a red-tailed hawk cried. It circled for a minute, then descended to land on Travis's arm.

❖   ❖   ❖

Eight months later Maddy, Hawk, and Travis stood in front of the big limestone rock formation guarding Hawk's secret spring. Hawk pushed Maddy up the rock face, helping her grab the handholds and climb to the top. Travis easily leaped from stone to stone, making the ascent in seconds.

Maddy was seven months pregnant with Hawk's child. His heart was full of love for her. Life with Maddy was filled with warmth and love, and together they thanked God every day for His gift of their love.

The three of them looked down into the spring. As soon as the new baby was born, Hawk was taking them all out to their new home on the prairie south of Orlando. The outlaws had been burned out of Fort Kissimmee, and Orlando was still a lawless town, but Hawk felt the future of cow hunting lay in the big open prairies of south Florida.

Hawk had taken much of the gold and purchased a huge parcel of land from the government. During the spring of this year, he and Travis, Shorty, and Joseph had worked hard building a home for all of them on the new D-Wing.

Maddy had wanted to come out to the secret spring one last time before they moved and before she was too big with child to climb the rock. The three of them stood staring into the deep crystalline pool. On the far mud bank, the old three-legged gator basked in the warm sun.

"Good-bye, Snake Barber," Maddy said. "I hope you finally found some peace."

"I think he has, Maddy," Hawk said. "This is a good place to end your days. It's beautiful and serene."

"What's beautiful and serene about spending eternity in the gullet of that gigantic gator?" Maddy asked.

"Maybe Snake didn't get eaten, Miss Maddy," Travis

said. "Maybe he was too tough or too bitter. Gators like the sweet meat."

Suddenly, something drifted to the top of the water in the gentle current caused by the spring's boil.

"What's that?" Travis said.

Maddy leaned over to stare at the object floating around and around in the boil's current.

Hawk thought it was a stick at first. Then he saw the bright flash of silver on the stick and the trailing ends of a leather strap.

"It's Snake's leg," Maddy said.

The peg leg swirled slowly around in the current trailing scraps of leather harness, while the silver snake still coiling around and across it glinted in the flickering sunlight.

Janet Post has been a reporter and photographer for several north Florida newspapers, garnering multiple Florida Press Awards for agricultural and sports stories. Now she lives on a Suwannee County ranch with her husband, who makes his living shoeing horses and cowboying. She has learned how to leg a bull calf, run the hot shot (cattle prod), and operate a squeeze chute. Around their place everything is counted by the head. They have thirty head of cattle, two head of horses, four head of dogs, ten head of chickens, two head of cats, and eight head of grandchildren.

Here are some other books from Pineapple Press on related topics. For a complete catalog, visit our website at www.pineapplepress.com. Or write to Pineapple Press, P.O. Box 3889, Sarasota, Florida 34230-3889, or call (800) 746-3275.

CRACKER WESTERNS

Bridger's Run by Jon Wilson. Tom Bridger has come to Florida in 1885 to find his long-lost uncle and a hidden treasure. (hb & pb)

Ghosts of the Green Swamp by Lee Gramling. Features that rough-and-ready but soft-hearted Florida cowboy, Tate Barkley, introduced in Riders of the Suwannee. (hb & pb)

Guns of the Palmetto Plains by Rick Tonyan. Tree Hooker dodges Union soldiers and Florida outlaws to drive cattle to feed the starving Confederacy. (pb)

Riders of the Suwannee by Lee Gramling. Tate Barkley returns to 1870s' Florida to save a young widow's homestead from outlaws. (pb)

Thunder on the St. Johns by Lee Gramling. Riverboat gambler Chance Ramsay combats a slew of greedy outlaws seeking to destroy the dreams of honest homesteaders. (hb & pb)

Trail from St. Augustine by Lee Gramling. A trapper, an ex-sailor, and a servant girl cross the Florida wilderness in search of buried treasure and a new life. (pb)

Wiregrass Country by Herb and Muncy Chapman. In 1835, the Dover family battles Indians and cattle rustlers to preserve their way of life on Three Springs Ranch. (pb)

Ninety-Mile Prairie by Lee Gramling. Cowhand Peek Tillman sets out to rescue a beautiful woman and her archaeologist husband from a band of greedy outlaws. (hb & pb)

OTHER FICTION

A Land Remembered by Patrick D. Smith. This well-loved, best-selling novel tells the story of three generations of MacIveys, a Florida family battling the hardships of the frontier, and how they rise from a dirt-poor Cracker life to the wealth and standing of real estate tycoons. (hb, pb)